Many Happy Returns
of the 27th
with love from
Vida

U. M. C

THE LOST AMBASSADOR

THE NOVELS OF

E. PHILLIPS OPPENHEIM

I RAISED MY GLASS, LOOKING HER FULL IN THE FACE, AND DRANK.

Page 30

The Lost Ambassador

Or, The Search for the Missing Delora

By E. PHILLIPS OPPENHEIM

Author of "The Illustrious Prince," "The Missioner,"
"Jeanne of the Marshes," "A Prince
of Sinners," etc.

WITH FOUR ILLUSTRATIONS IN COLORS
BY HOWARD CHANDLER CHRISTY

A L. BURT COMPANY

PUBLISHERS   NEW YORK

Published, September, 1910

CONTENTS

THE LOST AMBASSADOR

CHAPTER I

A RENCONTRE

THERE was no particular reason why, after having left the Opera House, I should have retraced my steps and taken my place once more amongst the throng of people who stood about in the *entresol*, exchanging greetings and waiting for their carriages. A backward glance as I had been about to turn into the Place de l'Opera had arrested my somewhat hurried departure. The night was young, and where else was such a sight to be seen? Besides, was it not amongst some such throng as this that the end of my search might come?

I took up my place just inside, close to one of the pillars, and, with an unlit cigarette still in my mouth, watched the flying *chausseurs*, the medley of vehicles outside, the soft flow of women in their white opera cloaks and jewels, who with their escorts came streaming down the stairs and out of the great building, to enter the waiting carriages and motor-cars drawn up in the privileged space within the enclosure, or stretching right down into the Boulevard. I stood there, watching them drive off one by one. I was borne a little nearer to the door by the rush of people, and I was able, in most cases, to hear the directions of the men as they followed their womankind into the waiting vehicles. In nearly every case their destination was one of the famous restaurants. Music begets hunger in most capitals, and the cafés of Paris are never so full as after a great night at the Opera. To-night there had been a wonderful performance. The flow of people down the stairs seemed interminable. Young women and old, — sleepy-looking beauties of the Southern type, whose dark eyes seemed half closed with a languor partly passionate, partly of pride; women of the truer French type, — brilliant, smiling, vivacious, mostly pale, seldom good-looking, always attractive. A few Germans, a fair sprinkling of Englishwomen, and a larger proportion still of Americans, whose women were the best dressed of the whole company. I was not sorry that I had returned. It was worth watching, this endless stream of varying types.

Towards the end there came out two people who were becoming almost familiar figures to me. The man was one of those whose nationality was not so easily surmised. He was tall and thin, with iron-gray hair, complexion so sallow as to be almost yellow, black moustache and imperial, handsome in his way, distinguished, indescribable. By his side was a girl who had the air of wearing her first long skirt, whose hair was arranged in somewhat juvenile fashion, and whose dark eyes were still glowing with the joy of the music. Her figure, though very slim, was delightful, and she walked as though her feet touched the clouds. Her laugh, which I heard distinctly as she brushed by me only a few feet away, was like music. Of all the people who had passed me, or whom I had come across during my fortnight's stay in Paris, there was no one half so attractive. The girl was absolutely charming; the man, remarkable not only in himself, but for a certain air of repressed emotion, which, while it robbed his features of the dignity of repose, was still, in a way, fascinating. They entered a waiting motor-car splendidly appointed, and I heard the man tell the tall, liveried footman to drive to the Ritz. I leaned forward a little eagerly as they went. I watched the car glide off and disappear, watched it until it was out of sight, and afterwards, even, watched the spot where it had vanished. Then, with a little sigh, I turned back once more into the great hall. There seemed to be no one left now of any interest. The women had become ordinary, the men impossible. With a little sigh I too aimlessly descended the steps, and stood for a moment uncertain which way to turn.

"Monsieur is looking for a light?" a quiet voice said in my ear.

I turned, and found myself confronted by a Frenchman, who had also just issued from the building and was himself lighting a cigarette. He was clean-shaven and pale, so pale that his complexion was almost olive. He had soft, curious-looking eyes. He was of medium height, dark, correctly dressed according to the fashion of his country, although his tie was black and his studs of unusual size. Something about his face struck me from the first as familiar, but for the moment I could not recall having seen him before.

"Thank you very much," I answered, accepting the match which he offered.

The night was clear, and breathlessly still. The full yellow moon was shining in an absolutely cloudless sky. The match — an English wax one, by the way — burned without a flicker. I lit my cigarette, and turning around found my companion still standing by my side.

"Monsieur does not do me the honor to recollect me," he remarked, with a faint smile.

I looked at him steadfastly.

"I am sorry," I said. "Your face is perfectly familiar

to me, and yet — No, by Jove, I have it!" I broke off, with a little laugh. "It's Louis, isn't it, from the Milan?"

"Monsieur's memory has soon returned," he answered, smiling. "I have been chief *maître d'hôtel* in the café there for some years. The last time I had the honor of serving monsieur there was only a few weeks ago."

I remembered him perfectly now. I remembered, even, the occasion of my last visit to the café. Louis, with upraised hat, seemed as though he would have passed on, but, curiously enough, I felt a desire to continue the conversation. I had not as yet admitted the fact even to myself; but I was bored, weary of my search, weary to death of my own company and the company of my own acquaintances. I was reluctant to let this little man go.

"You visit Paris often?" I asked.

"But naturally, monsieur," Louis answered, accepting my unspoken invitation by keeping pace with me as we strolled towards the Boulevard. "Once every six weeks I come over here. I go to the Ritz, Paillard's, the Café de Paris, — to the others also. It is an affair of business, of course. One must learn how the Frenchman eats and what he eats, that one may teach the art."

"But you are a Frenchman yourself, Louis," I remarked.

"But, monsieur," he answered, "I live in London. *Voilà tout.* One cannot write menus there for long, and succeed. One needs inspiration."

"And you find it here?" I asked.

Louis shrugged his shoulders.

"Paris, monsieur," he answered, "is my home. It is always a pleasure to me to see smiling faces, to see men and women who walk as though every footstep were taking them nearer to happiness. Have you never noticed, monsieur," he continued, "the difference? They do not plod here as do your English people. There is a buoyancy in their footsteps, a mirth in their laughter, an expectancy in the way they look around, as though adventures were everywhere. I cannot understand it, but one feels it directly one sets foot in Paris."

I nodded — a little bitterly, perhaps.

"It is temperament," I answered. "We may envy, but we cannot acquire it."

"It seems strange to see monsieur alone here," Louis remarked. "In London, it is always so different. Monsieur has so many acquaintances."

I was silent for a moment.

"I am here in search of some one," I told Louis. "It is n't a very pleasant mission, and the memory of it is always with me."

"A search!" Louis repeated thoughtfully. "Paris is a large place, monsieur."

"On the contrary," I answered, "it is small enough if a man will but play the game. A man, who knows his Paris, must be in one of half-a-dozen places some time during the day."

"It is true," Louis admitted. "Yet monsieur has not been successful."

"It has been because some one has warned the man of whom I am in search!" I declared.

"There are worse places," he remarked, "in which one might be forced to spend one's time."

"In theory, excellent, Louis," I said. "In practice, I am afraid I cannot agree with you. So far," I declared, gloomily, "my pilgrimage has been an utter failure. I cannot meet, I cannot hear of, the man who I know was flaunting it before the world three weeks ago."

Louis shrugged his shoulders.

"Monsieur can do no more than seek," he remarked. "For the rest, one may leave many burdens behind in the train at the Gare du Nord."

I shook my head.

"One cannot acquire gayety by only watching other people who are gay," I declared. "Paris is not for those who have anxieties, Louis. If ever I were suffering from melancholia, for instance, I should choose some other place for a visit."

Louis laughed softly.

"Ah! Monsieur," he answered, "you could not choose better. There is no place so gay as this, no place so full of distractions."

I shrugged my shoulders.

"It is your native city," I reminded him.

"That goes for nothing," Louis answered. "Where I live, there always I make my native city. I have lived in Vienna and Berlin, Budapest and Palermo, Florence and London. It is not an affair of the place. Yet of all these, if one seeks it, there is most distraction to be found here. Monsieur does not agree with me," he added, glancing into my face. "There is one thing more which I would tell him. Perhaps it is the explanation. Paris, the very home of happiness and gayety, is also the loneliest and the saddest city in the world for those who go alone."

"There is truth in what you say, Louis," I admitted.

"The very fact," he continued slowly, "that all the world amuses itself, all the world is gay here, makes the solitude of the unfortunate who has no companion a thing more *triste*, more keenly to be felt. Monsieur is alone?"

"I am alone," I admitted, "except for the companions of chance whom one meets everywhere."

We had been walking for some time slowly side by side, and we came now to a standstill. Louis held up his hand and called a taximeter.

"Monsieur goes somewhere to sup, without a doubt," he remarked.

I remained upon the pavement.

"Really, I don't know," I answered undecidedly. "There is a great deal of truth in what you have been saying. A man alone here, especially at night, seems to be looked upon as a sort of pariah. Women laugh at him, men pity him. It is only the Englishman, they think, who would do so foolish a thing."

Louis hesitated. There was a peculiar smile at the corners of his lips which I did not quite understand.

"If monsieur would honor me," he said apologetically, "I am going to-night to visit one or perhaps two of the smallest restaurants up in the Montmartre. They are by way of being fashionable now, and they tell me that there is an *Homard Speciale* with a new sauce which must be tasted at the Abbaye."

All the apology in Louis' tone was wasted. It troubled me not in the least that my companion should be a *maître d'hôtel*. I did not hesitate for a second.

"I 'll come with pleasure, Louis," I said, "on condition that I am host. It is very good of you to take pity upon me. We will take this taximeter, shall we?"

Louis bowed. Once more I fancied that there was something in his face which I did not altogether understand.

"It is an honor, monsieur," he said. "We will start, then, with the Abbaye."

CHAPTER II

A CAFÉ IN PARIS

THE Paris taximeters are good, and our progress was rapid. We passed through the crowded streets, where the women spread themselves out like beautiful butterflies, where the electric lights were deadened by the brilliance of the moon, where men, bent double over the handles of their bicycles, shot hither and thither with great paper lanterns alight in front of them. We passed into the quieter streets, though even here the wayfarers whom we met were obviously bent on pleasure, up the hill, till at last we pulled up at one of the best-known restaurants in the locality. Here Louis was welcomed as a prince. The manager, with many exclamations and gesticulations, shook hands with him like a long-lost brother. The *maîtres d'hôtel* all came crowding up for a word of greeting. A table in the best part of the room, which was marked *reservé*, was immediately made ready. Champagne, already in its pail of ice, was by our side almost before we had taken our places.

I had been here a few nights before, alone, and had found the place uninspiring enough. To-night, except that Louis told me the names of many of the people, and that the supper was the best meal which I had eaten in Paris, I was very little more amused. The nigger, the Spanish dancing-girl with her rolling eyes, the English music-hall singer with her unmistakable Lancashire accent, went through the same performance. The gowns of the women were wonderful, — more wonderful still their hats, their gold purses, the costly trifles which they carried. A woman by our side sat looking into a tiny pocket-mirror of gold studded with emeralds, powdering her face the while with a powder-puff to match, in the centre of which were more emeralds, large and beautifully cut. Louis noticed my scrutiny.

"The wealth of France," he whispered in my ear, "is spent upon its women. What the Englishman spends at his club or on his sports the Frenchman spends upon his womankind. Even the *bourgeoisie*, who hold their money with clenched fists like that," he gesticulated, striking the table, "for their women they spend, spend freely. They do all this, and the great thing which they ask in return is that they are amused. After all, monsieur," he continued, "they are logical. What a man wants most in life, in the intervals between his work, is amusement. It is amusement that keeps him young, keeps him in health. It is his womankind who provide that amusement."

"And if one does not happen to be married to a French-woman?"

Louis nodded sympathetically.

"Monsieur is feeling like that," he said, as he sipped his wine thoughtfully. "Yes, it is very plain! Yet monsieur is not always sad. I have seen him often at my restaurant, the guest or the host of many pleasant parties. There is a change since those days, a change indeed. I noticed it when I ventured to address monsieur on the steps of the Opera House."

I remained gloomily silent. It was one thing to avail myself of the society of a very popular little *maître d'hôtel*, holiday making in his own capital, and quite another to take him even a few steps into my confidence. So I said nothing, but my eyes, which travelled around the room, were weary.

"After all," Louis continued, helping himself to a cigarette, "what is there in a place like this to amuse? We are not Americans or tourists. The Montmartre is finished. The novelists and the story-tellers have killed it. The women come here because they love to show their jewelry, to flirt with the men. The men come because their womankind desire it, and because it is their habit. But for the rest there is nothing. The true Parisian may come here, perhaps, once or twice a year, — no more. For the man of the world — such as you and I, monsieur, — these places do not exist."

I glanced at my companion a little curiously. There was something in his manner distinctly puzzling. With his lips he was smiling approval at the little *danseuse* who was pirouetting near our table, but it seemed to me that his mind was busy with other thoughts. Suddenly he turned his head toward mine.

"Monsieur must remember," he said quietly, "that a place like this is as the froth on our champagne. It is all show. It exists and it passes away. This very restaurant may be unknown in a year's time, — a beer palace for the Germans, a den of absinthe and fiery brandy for the *cochers*. It is for the tourists, for the happy ladies of the world, that such a place exists. For those who need other things — other things exist."

"Go on, Louis," I said quietly. "You have something in your mind. What is it?"

He shrugged his shoulders.

"I think," he said slowly, "that I could take monsieur somewhere where he would be more entertained. There is nothing to do there, nothing to see, little music. But it is a place, — it has an atmosphere. It is different. I cannot explain. Monsieur would understand if he were there."

"Then, for Heaven's sake, let us pay our bill and go!" I exclaimed. "We have both had enough of this, at any rate."

Louis did not immediately reply. I turned around — we were sitting side by side — wondering at his lack of response. What I saw startled me. The man's whole expression had changed. His mouth had come together with a new firmness. A frown which I had never seen before had darkened his forehead. His eyes had become little points of light. I realized then, perhaps for the first time, their peculiar color, — a sort of green tinged with gray. He presented the appearance of a man of intelligence and acumen who is thinking deeply over some matter of vital importance.

"Well, what is it, Louis?" I asked. "Are you repenting of your offer already? Don't you want to take me to this other place?"

"It is not that, monsieur," Louis answered softly, "only I was wondering if I had been a little rash."

"Rash?" I repeated.

Louis nodded his head slowly, but he paused for several moments before speaking.

"I was only wondering," said he, "whether, after all, it would amuse you. There is nothing to be seen, not so much as here. Afterwards, perhaps, you might regret — you might think that I had done wrong in not telling you certain things about the place which must remain secret."

"We will risk that," I answered, rising. "Let me come with you and I will judge for myself."

Louis followed my example, but I fancied that I still detected a slight unwillingness in his movements. My request for the bill had been met with a smile and a polite shake of the head. Louis whispered in my ear that we were the guests of the management, — that it would not be correct to offer the money for our entertainment. So I was forced to content myself with tipping the head-waiter and the *vestiaire*, the *chausseur* who opened the door, and the tall *commissionnaire* who welcomed us upon the pavement and whistled for a *petite voiture*.

"Where to, messieurs?" the man asked, as the carriage drew up.

Even then Louis hesitated. He was sitting on the side of the carriage nearest to the pavement, and he rose to his feet as the question was asked. It seemed to me that he almost whispered the address into the ear of the coachman. At any rate, I heard nothing of it. The man nodded, and turned eastward.

"*Bon soir*, messieurs!" the *commissionnaire* called out, with his hat in his hand.

"*Bon soir!*" I answered, with my eyes fixed upon the flaring lights of the Boulevard, towards which we had turned.

CHAPTER III

DELORA

I FOUND Louis, during that short drive, most unaccountably silent. Several times I made casual remarks. Once or twice I tried to learn from him what sort of a place this was to which we were bound. He answered me only in monosyllables. I was conscious all the time of a certain subtle but unmistakable change in his manner. Up to the moment of his suggesting this expedition he had remained the suave, perfectly mannered superior servant, accepted into equality for a time by one of his clients, and very careful not to presume in any way upon his position. It is not snobbish to say this, because it was the truth. Louis was chief *maître d'hôtel* at one of the best restaurants in London. I was an ex-officer in a cavalry regiment, brother of the Earl of Welmington, with a moderate income, and a more than moderate idea of how to spend it. Louis was servant and I was master. It had pleased me to make a companion of him for a short time, and his manner had been a perfect acknowledgment of our relative positions. And now it seemed to me that there was a change. Louis had become more like a man, less like a waiter. There was a strength in his face which I had not previously observed, a darkening anxiety which puzzled me. He treated my few remarks with scant courtesy. He was obviously thinking about something else. It seemed as though, for some inexplicable reason, he had already repented of his suggestion.

"Look here, Louis," I said, "you seem a little bothered about taking me to this place. Perhaps they do not care about strangers there. I am not at all keen, really, and I am afraid I am not fit company for anybody. Better drop me here and go on by yourself. I can amuse myself all right at some of these little out-of-the-way places until I feel inclined to go home."

Louis turned and looked at me. For a moment I thought that he was going to accept my offer. He opened his mouth but said nothing. He looked away into the darkness once more, and then back into my face. By this time I knew that he had made up his mind. He was more like himself again.

"Monsieur Rotherby," he said, "if I have hesitated at all, it was for your sake. You are a gentleman of great position. Afterwards you might feel sorry to think that you had been in such a place, or in such company."

I patted him on the shoulder reassuringly.

"My dear Louis," said I, "you need have no such fears about me. I am a little of an adventurer, a little of a Bohemian. There is no one else who has a claim upon my life, and I do as I please. Can't you tell me a little more about this mysterious café?"

"There is so little to tell," Louis said. "Of one thing I can assure you, — you will be disappointed. There is no music, no dancing. The interest is only in the people who go there, and their lives. It may be," he continued thoughtfully, "that you will not find them much different from all the others."

"But there is a difference, Louis?" I asked.

"Wait," he answered. "You shall see."

The cab pulled up in front of a very ordinary-looking café in a side street leading from one of the boulevards.

Louis dismissed the man and looked for a moment or two up and down the pavement. His caution appeared to be quite needless, for the thoroughfare was none too well lit, and it was almost empty. Then he entered the café, motioning me to follow him.

"Don't look around too much," he whispered. "There are many people here who do not care to be spied upon."

My first glance into the place was disappointing. I was beginning to lose faith in Louis. After all, it seemed to me that the end of our adventure would be ordinary enough, that I should find myself in one of those places which the touting guides of the Boulevard speak of in bated breath, which one needs to be very young indeed to find interesting even for a moment. The ground floor of the café through which we passed was like a thousand others in different parts of Paris. The floor was sanded, the people were of the lower orders, — rough-looking men drinking beer or sipping cordials; women from whom one instinctively looked away, and whose shrill laughter was devoid of a single note of music. It was all very flat, very uninteresting. But Louis led the way through a swing door to a staircase, and then, pushing his way through some curtains, along a short passage to another door, against which he softly knocked with his knuckles. It was opened at once, and a *commissionnaire* stood gazing stolidly out at us, a *commissionnaire* in the usual sort of uniform, but one of the most powerful-looking men whom I had ever seen in my life.

"There are no tables, monsieur, in the restaurant," he said at once. "There is no place at all."

Louis looked at him steadily for a moment. It seemed to me that, although I was unable to discern anything of the sort, some sign must have passed between them. At any rate, without any protest or speech of any sort from Louis the *commissionnaire* saluted and stood back.

"But your friend, monsieur?" he asked.

"It will be arranged," Louis answered, in a low tone. "We shall speak to Monsieur Carvin."

We were in a dark sort of *entresol*, and at that moment a further door was opened, and one caught the gleam of lights and the babel of voices. A man came out of the room and walked rapidly toward us. He was of middle height, and dressed in ordinary morning clothes, wearing a black tie with a diamond pin. His lips were thick. He had a slight tawny moustache, and a cast in one eye. He held out both his hands to Louis.

"Dear Louis," he exclaimed, "it is good to see you!"

Louis drew him to one side, and they talked for a few moments in a rapid undertone. More than once the manager of the restaurant, for such I imagined him to be, glanced towards me, and I was fairly certain that I formed the subject of their conversation. When it was finished Louis beckoned, and we all three turned towards the door together, Louis in the centre.

"This," he said to me, "is Monsieur Carvin, the manager of the Café des Deux Épingles. He has been explaining to me how difficult it is to find even a corner in his restaurant, but there will be a small table for us."

Monsieur Carvin bowed.

"For any friend of Louis," he said, "one would do much. But indeed, monsieur, people seem to find my little restaurant interesting, and it is, alas, so very small."

We entered the room almost as he spoke. It was larger than I had expected to find it, and the style of its decorations and general appearance were absolutely different from the café below. The coloring was a little sombre

for a French restaurant, and the illuminations a little less
vivid. The walls, however, were panelled with what
seemed to be a sort of dark mahogany, and on the ceiling
was painted a great allegorical picture, the nature of which
I could not at first surmise. The guests, of whom the
room was almost full, were all well-dressed and apparently of the smart world. The tourist element was lacking.
There were a few men there in morning clothes, but these
were dressed with the rigid exactness of the Frenchman,
who often, from choice, affects this style of toilet. From
the first I felt that the place possessed an atmosphere.
I could not describe it, but, quite apart from Louis' few
words concerning it, I knew that it had a clientèle of its
own, and that within its four walls were gathered together people who were in some way different from the
butterfly crowd who haunt the night cafés in Paris. Monsieur Carvin himself led us to a small table against the
wall, and not far inside the room. The *vestiaire* relieved
us of our coats and hats. A suave *maître d'hôtel* bent
over us with suggestions for supper, and an attendant
sommelier waited by his side. Monsieur Carvin waved
them away.

"The gentlemen have probably supped," he remarked.
"A bottle of the Pommery, Goût Anglais, and some bis-
cuits. Is that right, Louis?"

We both hastened to express our approval. Monsieur
Carvin was called by some one at the other end of the
room and hurried away. Louis turned to me. There
was a curious expression in his eyes.

"You are disappointed?" he asked. "You see nothing
here different? It is all the same to you."

"Not in the least," I answered. "For one thing, it
seems strange to find a restaurant de luxe up here, when

below there is only a café of the worst. Are they of the same management?"

"Up here," he said, "come the masters, and down there the servants. Look around at these people, monsieur. Look around carefully. Tell me whether you do not see something different here from the other places."

I followed Louis' advice. I looked around at the people with an interest which grew rather than abated, and for which I could not at first account. Soon, however, I began to realize that although this was, at first appearance, merely a crowd of fashionably dressed men and women, yet they differed from the ordinary restaurant crowd in that there was something a little out of the common in the faces of nearly every one of them. The loiterers through life seemed absent. These people were relaxing freely enough, — laughing, talking, and making love, — but behind it all there seemed a note of seriousness, an intentness in their faces which seemed to speak of a career, of things to be done in the future, or something accomplished in the past. The woman who sat at the opposite table to me — tall, with yellow hair, and face as pale as alabaster — was a striking personality anywhere. Her blue eyes were deep-set, and she seemed to have made no effort to conceal the dark rings underneath, which only increased their luminosity. A magnificent string of turquoises hung from her bare neck, a curious star shone in her hair. Her dress was of the newest mode. Her voice, languid but elegant, had in it that hidden quality which makes it one of a woman's most attractive gifts. By her side was a great black-moustached giant, a pale-faced man, with little puffs of flesh underneath his eyes, whose dress was a little too perfect and his jewelry a little too obvious.

"Tell me," I asked, "who is that man?"

Louis leaned towards me, and his voice sunk to the merest whisper.

"That, monsieur," said he, "is one of the most important persons in the room. He is the man whom they call the uncrowned king. He was a saddler once by profession. Look at him now."

"How has he made his money?" I asked.

Louis smiled — a queer little contraction of his thin lips.

"It is not wise," he said, "to ask that question of any whom you meet here. Henri Bartot was one of the wildest youths in Paris. It was he who started the first band of thieves, from which developed the present horde of *apaches*."

"And now?" I asked.

"He is their unrecognized, unspoken-of leader," Louis whispered. "The man who offends him to-night would be lucky to find himself alive to-morrow."

I looked across the room curiously. There was not a single redeeming feature in the man's face except, perhaps, the suggestion of brute, passionate force which still lingered about his thick, straight lips and heavy jaw. The woman by his side seemed incomprehensible. I saw now that she had eyes of turquoise blue and a complexion almost waxenlike. She lifted her arms, and I saw that they, too, were covered with bracelets of light-blue stones. Louis, following my eyes, touched me on the arm.

"Don't look at her," he said warningly. "She belongs to him — Bartot. It is not safe to flirt with her even at this distance."

I laughed softly and sipped my wine.

"Louis," I said, "it is time you got back to London. You are living here in too imaginative an atmosphere."

"I speak the truth, monsieur," he answered grimly. "She, too, — she is not safe. She finds pleasure in making fools of men. The suffering which comes to them appeals to her vanity. There was a young Englishman once, he sent a note to her — not here, but at the Café de Paris — at luncheon time one morning. He was to have left Paris the next day. He did not leave. He has never been heard of since!"

There was no doubt that Louis himself, at any rate, believed what he was saying. I looked away from the young lady a little reluctantly. As though she understood Louis' warning, her lips parted for a moment in a faint, contemptuous smile. She leaned over and touched the man Bartot on the shoulder and whispered something in his ear. When I next looked in their direction I found his eyes fixed upon mine in a steady, malignant stare.

"Monsieur will remember," Louis whispered in my ear softly, "that I am responsible for his coming here."

"Of course," I answered reassuringly. "I have not the slightest wish to run up against any of these people. I will not look at them any more. She knew what she was doing, though, Louis, when she hung blue stones about her with eyes like that, eh?"

"She is beautiful," Louis admitted. "There are very many who admire her. But after all, what is the use? One has little pleasure of the things which one may not touch."

We were silent for several minutes. Suddenly my fingers gripped Louis' arm. Had I been blind all this time that they had escaped my notice? Then I saw that they were sitting at an extra table which had been hastily arranged, and I knew that they could have only just arrived.

"Tell me, Louis," I demanded eagerly, "who are those two at the small round table on the left, — the two who seem to have just come in, — a man and a girl?"

Louis turned his head, and I saw his lips come together — saw the quick change in his face from indifference to seriousness. For some reason or other my interest in these two seemed to be a matter of some import to him.

"Why does monsieur ask?" he said.

"The idlest curiosity," I assured him. "I know nothing about them except that they are distinctive, and one cannot fail, of course, to admire the young lady."

"You have seen them often?" Louis asked, in a low tone.

"I told you, Louis," I answered, "that my mission in Paris is of the nature of a search. For ten days I have haunted all the places where one goes, — the Race Course, the Bois, the Armenonville and Pré Catelan, the Rue de la Paix, the theatres. I have seen them nearly every day. To-night they were at the Opera."

"You know nothing of them beyond that?" Louis persisted.

"Nothing whatever," I declared. "I am not a boulevarder, Louis," I continued slowly, "and in England, you know, it is not the custom to stare at women as these Frenchmen seem to do with impunity. But I must confess that I have watched that girl."

"You find her attractive," murmured Louis.

"I find her delightful," I assented, "only she seems scarcely old enough to be about in such places as these."

"The man," Louis said slowly, "is a Brazilian. His name is Delora."

"Does he live in Paris?" I asked.

"By no means," Louis answered. "He is a very rich

coffee-planter, and has immense estates somewhere in his own country. He comes over here every year to sell his produce on the London market. I believe that he is on his way there now."

"And the girl?" I asked.

"She is his niece," Louis answered. "She has been brought up in France at a convent somewhere in the south, I believe. I think I heard that this time she was to return to Brazil with her uncle."

"I wonder," I asked, "if she is going to London with him?"

"Probably," Louis answered, "and if monsieur continues to patronize me," he continued, "he will certainly see more of them, for Monsieur Delora is a client who is always faithful to me."

Notwithstanding its somewhat subdued air, there was all the time going on around us a cheerful murmur of conversation, the popping of corks, the laughter of women, the hurrying to and fro of waiters, — all the pleasant disturbance of an ordinary restaurant at the most festive hour of the night. But there came, just at this moment, a curious interruption, an interruption curious not only on its own account, but on account of the effect which it produced. From somewhere in the centre of the room there commenced ringing, softly at first, and afterwards with a greater volume, a gong, something like the siren of a motor-car, but much softer and more musical. Instantly a dead silence seemed to fall upon the place. Conversation was broken off, laughter was checked, even the waiters stood still in their places. The eyes of every one seemed turned towards the door. One or two of the men rose, and in the faces of these was manifest a sudden expression in which was present more or less of absolute terror. Bartot for a moment shrank back in his chair as though he had been struck, only to recover himself the next second; and the lady with the turquoises bent over and whispered in his ear. One person only left his place, — a young man who had been sitting at a table at the other end of the room with one of the gayest parties. At the very first note of alarm he had sprung to his feet. A few seconds later, with swift, silent movements and face as pale as a ghost, he had vanished into the little service room from which the waiters issued and returned. With his disappearance the curious spell which seemed to have fallen upon these other people passed away. The waiters resumed their tasks. The room was once more hilariously gay. Upon the threshold a newcomer was standing, a tall man in correct morning dress, with a short gray beard and a tiny red ribbon in his button-hole. He stood there smiling slightly — an unobtrusive entrance, such as might have befitted any habitué of the place. Yet all the time his eyes were travelling restlessly up and down the room. As he stood there, one could fancy there was not a face into which he did not look during those few minutes.

CHAPTER IV

DANGEROUS PLAY

I LEANED towards Louis, but he anticipated my question. His hand had caught my wrist and was pinning it down to the table.

"Wait!" he muttered — "wait! You perceive that we are drinking wine of the vintage of '98. I will tell you of my trip to the vineyards. Do not look at that man as though his appearance was anything remarkable. You are not an habitué here, and he will take notice of you."

As one who speaks upon the subject most interesting to him, Louis, with the gestures and swift, nervous diction of his race, talked to me of the vineyards and the cellars of the famous champagne house whose wine we were drinking. I did my best to listen intelligently, but every moment I found my eyes straying towards this new arrival, now deep in apparently pleasant conversation with Monsieur Carvin.

The newcomer had the air of one who has looked in to smile around at his acquaintances and pass on. He accepted a cigarette from Carvin, but he did not sit down, and I saw him smile a polite refusal as a small table was pointed out to him. He strolled a little into the place and he bowed pleasantly to several with whom he seemed to be acquainted, amongst whom was the man Bartot. He waved his hand to others further down the room. His circle of acquaintances, indeed, seemed unlimited. Then, with a long hand-shake and some parting jest, he took leave of Monsieur Carvin and disappeared. Somehow or other one seemed to feel the breath of relief which went shivering through the room as he departed. Louis answered then my unspoken question.

"That," he said, "is a very great man. His name is Monsieur Myers."

"The head of the police!" I exclaimed.

Louis nodded.

"The most famous," he said, "whom France has ever possessed. Monsieur Myers is absolutely marvellous," he declared. "The man has genius, — genius as well as executive ability. It is a terrible war that goes on between him and the *haute école* of crime in this country."

"Tell me, Louis," I asked, "is Monsieur Myers' visit here to-night professional?"

"Monsieur has observation," Louis answered. "Why not?"

"You mean," I asked, "that there are criminals — people under suspicion —"

"I mean," Louis interrupted, "that in this room, at the present moment, are some of the most famous criminals in the world."

A question half framed died away upon my lips. Louis, however, divined it.

"You were about to ask," he said, "how I obtained my entry here. Monsieur, one had better not ask. It is one thing to be a thief. It is quite another to see something of the wonderful life which those live who are at war with society."

I looked around the room once more. Again I realized the difference between this gathering of well-dressed men and women and any similar gathering which I had seen in Paris. The faces of all somehow lacked that tiredness of expression which seems to be the heritage of those who drink the cup of pleasure without spice, simply because the hand of Fate presses it to their lips. These people had found something else. Were they not, after all, a little to be envied? They must know what it was to feel the throb of life, to test the true flavor of its luxuries when there was no certainty of the morrow. I felt the fascination, felt it almost in my blood, as I looked around.

"You could not specify, I suppose?" I said to Louis.

"How could monsieur ask it?" he replied, a little reproachfully. "You will be one of the only people who do not belong who have been admitted here, and you will notice," he continued, "that I have asked for no pledge — I rely simply upon the honor of monsieur."

I nodded.

"There is crime and crime, Louis," said I. "I have never been able to believe myself that it is the same thing to rob the widow and the millionaire. I know that I must not ask you any questions," I continued, "but the girl with Delora, — the man whom you call Delora, — she, at least, is innocent of any knowledge of these things?"

Louis smiled.

"Monsieur is susceptible," he remarked. "I cannot answer that question. Mademoiselle is a stranger. She is but a child."

"And Monsieur Delora himself?" I asked. "He comes here when he chooses? He is not merely a sightseer?"

"No," Louis repeated, "he is not merely a sightseer!"

"A privileged person," I remarked.

"He is a wonderful man," Louis answered calmly. "He has travelled all over the world. He knows a little of every capital, of every side of life, — perhaps," he added, "of the underneath side."

"His niece is very beautiful," I remarked, looking at her thoughtfully. "It seems almost a shame, does it not, to bring her into such a place as this?"

Louis smiled.

"If she were going to stay in Paris — yes!" he said. "If she is really going to Brazil, it matters little what she does. A Parisian, of course, would never bring his woman-kind here."

"She is very beautiful," I remarked. "Yes, I agree with you, Louis. It is no place for girls of her age."

Louis smiled.

"Monsieur may make her acquaintance some day," he remarked. "Monsieur Delora is on his way to England."

"She is a safer person to admire," I remarked, "than the lady opposite?"

"Much," Louis answered emphatically. "Monsieur has already," he whispered, "been a little indiscreet. The lady of the turquoises has spoken once or twice to Bartot and looked this way. I feel sure that it was of you she spoke. See how she continually looks over the top of her fan at this table. Monsieur would do well to take no notice."

I laughed. I was thirty years old, and the love of adventure was always in my blood. For the first time for many days the weariness seemed to have passed away. My heart was beating. I was ready for any enterprise.

"Do not be afraid, Louis," I said. "I shall come to no harm. If mademoiselle looks at me, it is not gallant to look away."

Louis' face was puckered up with anxiety. He saw, too, what I had seen. Bartot had walked to the other end of the room to speak to some friends. The girl had taken a gold and jewelled pencil from the mass of costly trifles which lay with her purse upon the table, and was writing on a piece of paper which the waiter had brought. I could see her delicately manicured fingers, the blue veins at the back of her hands, as she wrote, slowly and apparently without hesitation. Both Louis and myself watched the writing of that note as though Fate itself were guiding the pencil.

"It is for you," Louis whispered in my ear. "Take no notice. It would be madness even to look at her."

"Louis!" I exclaimed protestingly.

"I mean what I say, monsieur," Louis declared, leaning toward me, and speaking in a low, earnest whisper. "The café below, the streets throughout this region, are peopled by his creatures. In an hour he could lead an army which would defy the whole of the gendarmes in Paris. This quarter of the city is his absolutely to do with what he wills. Do you believe that you would have a chance if he thought that she had looked twice at you, — she — Susette — the only woman who has ever led him? I tell you that he is mad with love and jealousy for her. The whole world knows of it."

"My dear Louis," I said, "you know me only in London, where I come and sit in your restaurant and eat and drink there. To you I am simply like all those others who come to you day by day, — idlers and pleasure seekers. Let me assure you, Louis, that there are other things in my life. Just now I should welcome anything in the world which meant adventure, which could teach me to forget."

"But monsieur need not seek the suicide," Louis said. "There are hundreds of adventures to be had without that."

I shrugged my shoulders.

"If mademoiselle should send me the note," I said, "surely it would not be gallant of me to refuse to accept it."

"There are other ways of seeking adventures," Louis said, "than by ending one's days in the Seine."

The girl by this time had finished her note and rolled it up. She looked behind her to the other end of the room, where only Bartot's broad back was visible. Then she raised her eyes to mine, — turquoise blue as the color of her gown, — and very faintly but very deliberately she smiled. I was not in the least in love with her. The affair to me was simply interesting because it promised a moment's distraction. But, nevertheless, as she smiled I felt my heart beat faster, and I reached a little eagerly forward as though for the note. She called a waiter to her side. I watched her whisper to him; I watched his expression — anxious and perturbed at first, doubtful, even, after her reassuring words. He looked down the room to where Bartot was standing. It seemed to me, even then, that he ventured to protest, but mademoiselle frowned and spoke to him sharply. He caught up a wine list and came to our table. Once more, before he spoke, he looked behind to where Bartot's back was still turned.

"For monsieur," he whispered, setting the wine list upon the table, and under it the note.

I nodded, and he hastened away. At that moment Bartot turned and came down the room. As he approached he looked at me once more, as though, for some reason or other, he was more than ordinarily interested in my presence. It may have been my fancy, but I thought, also, that he looked at the wine card stretched out before me.

"Be careful!" Louis whispered. "Be careful! And, for God's sake, destroy that note!"

I laughed, and as Bartot was compelled to turn his back

to me to regain his seat, this time at the table with his companion, I raised my glass, looking her full in the face, and drank. Then I slipped the note from underneath the wine card into my pocket. She made the slightest of signs, but I understood. I was not to read it until I was alone.

"Go outside," Louis whispered to me. "Read your letter and get rid of it."

I obeyed him. A watchful waiter pulled the table away, and I walked out into the anteroom. Here, with a freshly lit cigarette in my mouth, I unclenched my fingers, and looked at the few words written very faintly, in long, delicate characters, across the torn sheet of paper:

Monsieur is in bad company. It would be well for him to lunch to-morrow at the Café de Paris, and to ask for Léon.

That was all. I tore it into small pieces and returned to my seat, altogether puzzled. It seemed to me that Louis watched me with an incomprehensible anxiety as I resumed my place by his side.

"If monsieur is ready," he suggested, "perhaps we had better go."

I rose to my feet reluctantly.

"As you will, Louis," I said.

But the time for our departure had not yet come!

CHAPTER V

SATISFACTION

DURING the whole of the time people had been coming and going from the restaurant, not, perhaps, in a continual stream, but still at fairly regular intervals. It seemed to me, who had watched them all with interest, that scarcely a person had entered who was not worthy of observation. I saw faces, it is true, which I had seen before at the fashionable haunts of Paris, upon the polo ground, at Longchamps, or in the Bois, yet somehow it seemed to me that they came to this place as different beings. There was a tense look in their faces, a look almost of apprehension, as they entered and passed out, — as of people who have found their way a little further into life than their associates. Louis was right. There was something different about the place, something at which I could only dimly guess, which at that time I did not understand. Only I realized that I watched always with a little thrill of interest whenever the hurrying forward of Monsieur Carvin indicated the arrival of a new visitor.

We had already risen to go, and the *vestiaire* was on his way towards us, bearing my hat and coat, when Monsieur Carvin, who had hurried out a moment before, reappeared, ushering in a new arrival. The events that followed have always seemed a little confused to me. My first thought was that this was indeed a nightmare into which I had wandered. The slight unreality which had hung like a cloud over the whole of the evening, the strangeness of my

being there with such a companion, the curious atmosphere
of the place, which so far had completely puzzled me, —
these things may all have served to heighten the illusion.
Yet it seemed to me then that, dreaming or waking, this
thing with which I was confronted was the last impossi-
bility. I suppose that I must have stared at him like some
wild creature, for the conversation around us suddenly
stopped. Standing upon the threshold, looking around
him with the happy air of an habitué, I saw this man to
whom I owed my presence in Paris, this man concerning
whom I had sworn that if ever I should meet him face to
face my hand should be upon his throat. I remember
nothing of my progress, but I know that I stood before him
before he was conscious even of my presence. I addressed
him by name. I believe that even my voice was not
upraised.

"Tapilow!" I said.

He turned sharply towards me. I saw him suddenly
stiffen, and I saw his right hand dart as though by instinct
to his trousers pocket. But I was too quick for him. The
blood was surging into my ears. Nothing in the whole
room was visible to me but that pale, handsome face with
the thin lips and dark, full eyes. I saw those eyes contract
as though my hand upon his throat were indeed the touch
of Death. I shook him until his collar broke away and his
shirt-front flew open, shook him until from his limp body
there seemed no longer any shadow of resistance. Then I
flung him a little away from me, watching all the time,
though, to see that his hand did not move towards that
pocket.

"Tapilow," I cried, "defend yourself, you coward!
Do you want me to strangle you where you stand?"

He came for me then with the frenzy of a man who is

in a desperate strait. He was as strong as I, and he had the advantage in height. For a moment I was borne back. He struck me heavily upon the face, and I made no attempt to defend myself. I waited my time. When it came, I dealt him such a blow that he reeled away, and before he could recover I took him by the back of his neck and flung him from me across the table which our struggle had already half upset. He lay there, a shapeless mass, surrounded by broken glass, streaming wine, a little heap of flowers from the overturned vase. Then the hubbub of the room was suddenly stilled. A dozen hands were laid upon me.

"For God's sake, monsieur!" I heard Louis cry.

Monsieur Carvin led me away. I looked back once more at the prostrate figure and then followed him.

"This is not my fault," I said calmly. "He knew quite well that it was bound to happen. I told him that wherever we next met, whether it was in a street or a drawing-room, or any place whatsoever upon the face of the earth, I would deal out his punishment with my own hands, even though it should spell death. Perhaps," I continued, "you would like to send for the police. You can have my card, if you like."

"We do not send for the police here," Monsieur Carvin said hoarsely. "Louis will take you away at once. Where do you stay?"

"At the Ritz," I answered.

"Keep quiet to-morrow!" he exclaimed. "Louis will come to you. This way."

I shrugged my shoulders. At that moment it mattered little to me whether I paid the penalty for what had happened or not. I even looked back for a last time into the restaurant. I saw the strained, eager faces of the people bent forward to watch me. Some of the men had left their seats and come out into the body of the hall to get a better view. The man Delora was among them. The girl was leaning forward in her place, with her fingers upon the table, and her dark eyes riveted with horrible intensity upon the fallen figure. I saw mademoiselle — the turquoise-covered friend of Bartot. She, too, was leaning forward, but her eyes ignored the man upon the floor, and were seeking to meet mine. There was something unreal about the whole scene, something which I was never able afterwards to focus absolutely in my mind as a whole, although disjointed parts of it were always present in my thoughts. But I know that as I looked back she rose a little to her feet and leaned over the table, and heedless of Bartot, who was now by her side, she waved her hand almost as though in approbation. I was within a few feet of her, upon the threshold of the door, and I heard her words, spoken, perhaps, to her companion, —

"It is so that men should deal with their enemies!"

A moment later, Louis and I were driving through the streets toward my hotel. It was already light, and we passed a great train of market wagons coming in from the country. Along the Boulevard, into which we turned, was sprinkled a curious medley of wastrels of the night, and men and women on their way to work. It had been raining a little time before, but as we turned to descend the hill a weak sunshine flickered out from behind the clouds.

"It is later than I thought," I remarked calmly.

"It is half-past five o'clock," answered Louis.

He accompanied me all the way to the hotel. He asked for no explanation, nor did I volunteer any. As we drove into the Place Vendôme, however, he leaned towards me.

"Monsieur is aware," he said, "that he has run a great risk to-night?"

"Very likely," I answered, "but, Louis, there are some things which one is forced to do, whatever the risk may be. This was one of them."

"You have courage," Louis whispered. "Let me tell you this. There were men there to-night, men on every side of you, to whom courage is as the breath of life. They have seen a man whom nobody loved treated as he probably deserved. Let me tell you that there is no place in the world where you could have struck so safely as to-night. Remain in the hotel to-morrow until you hear from some of us. I may not promise too much, but I think — I believe — that we can save you."

At that moment Louis' words meant little to me. I was still under the spell of those few wonderful moments, still mad with the joy of having taken the vengeance for which every nerve in my body had craved. It was not until afterwards that their practical import came home to me.

CHAPTER VI

AN INFORMAL TRIBUNAL

I was awakened about midday by the *valet de chambre*, who informed me that a gentleman was waiting below to see me — a gentleman who had given the name of Monsieur Louis. I ordered him to prepare my bath and bring my coffee. When Louis was shown upstairs I was seated on the edge of my bed in my dressing-gown, smoking my first cigarette.

Louis had the appearance of a man who had not slept. As for myself, I had never opened my eyes from the moment when my head had touched the pillow. I had no nerves, and I had done nothing which I regretted. I fancy, therefore, that my general appearance and reception of him somewhat astonished my early visitor. He seemed, indeed, to take my nonchalance almost as an affront, and he proceeded at once to try and disturb it.

"Monsieur was expecting, perhaps, another sort of visitor?" he asked.

I shook my head.

"I really had n't thought about it," I said. "After what you told me last night I have been feeling quite comfortable."

"Do you know that it is doubtful whether Monsieur Tapilow will live?" Louis asked.

"It was the just payment of a just debt," I answered.

"The law," he objected, "does not permit such adjustments."

"The law," I answered, "can do what it pleases with me."

Louis regarded me steadily for a moment or two, and I fancied that there was something of that admiration in his gaze which a cautious man sometimes feels for the foolhardy.

"Monsieur has slept well?" he asked.

"Excellently," I answered.

He glanced at the watch which he had taken from his waistcoat pocket.

"In twenty minutes," he announced, "we must be at the Café Normandy."

I raised my eyebrows.

"Indeed!" I said dryly. "I don't exactly follow you."

Louis shrugged his shoulders.

"Monsieur," he said, "it is no time, this, for the choice of words. There is a man who lies very near to death up there in the Café des Deux Épingles, and it must be decided within the next few hours what is to be done with him."

"I am not sure that I understand, Louis," I said, lighting a cigarette.

"You will understand at the Café Normandy in half an hour's time," Louis answered. "In the meanwhile, have you a servant? If not, summon the *valet de chambre*. You must dress quickly. It is important, this."

"I will dress in ten minutes," I replied, "but I must shave before I go out. That will take me another ten. In the meantime, perhaps you will kindly tell me what it all means?"

"What it all means!" Louis repeated, with upraised hands. "Is it not clear? Have you forgotten what happened only a few hours ago? It rests with one or two people as to whether you shall be given up to the police for what you did last night, — does monsieur understand that ? — the police !"

"To tell you the truth, Louis," I answered, "I never dreamed of escaping from them. It did not seem possible."

"In which case ?" Louis asked slowly.

I pointed to the revolver upon my mantelpiece.

"We all," I remarked, "make the mistake of over-estimating the actual importance of life."

Louis shivered a little. I noticed both then and afterwards that he was never comfortable in the presence of firearms.

"A last resource, of course," I said, "but one should always be prepared !"

"In this city," Louis said, "it is not as in London. In London there are no corners which are not swept bare by your police. In London, by this time you would have been sitting in a prison cell."

"That," I remarked, "is doubtless true. So much the more fortunate for me that I should have met Monsieur Tapilow in Paris and not in London. But will you tell me, Louis, why you want me to go with you to the Café Normandy, and how you think it will help me ?"

"It would take too long," Louis answered. "We will talk in the carriage, perhaps. You must not delay now — not one moment."

I humored him by hastening my preparations, and we left the place together a few minutes later. There were many things which I desired to ask him with regard to the events of last night and the place to which he had taken me, but as though by mutual consent neither of us spoke of these things. When we were already, however, about half way towards the famous restaurant which was our destination I could not keep silence any longer.

"Louis," I said, "tell me about this little excursion of ours. Who are these men whom we are going to meet?"

He turned towards me. The last few hours seemed to have brought us into a greater intimacy. He addressed me by name, and his manner, although it was still respectful enough, was somehow altered.

"Captain Rotherby," he said, "you do not seem to appreciate the position in which you stand. You are young, and life is hot in your veins, and yet to-day, as you sit there, your liberty is forfeit, — perhaps even, if Tapilow should die, your life! Have you ever heard any stories, I wonder," he added, leaning a little toward me, "about French prisons?"

"Are you trying to frighten me, Louis?" I asked.

"No!" he answered, "but I want you to realize that you are in a very serious position."

"I know that," I answered. "Don't think, Louis," I continued, "that what I did last night was the result of a rash impulse. I had sworn since a certain day in the autumn of last year that the first time I came face to face with that man, whether it was in the daytime or the night-time, in a friend's house or on the street, I would punish him. Well, I have kept my word. I had to. I have had my fill of vengeance. He can go through the rest of his life, so far as I am concerned, unharmed. But what I did, I was bound to do, and I am ready to face the consequences, if necessary."

Louis nodded sympathetically.

"Monsieur," said he, "you have but to talk like that to convince the men whom you will meet in a few moments that you had a real grievance against Tapilow, and all may yet be well."

"Who are these men?" I asked. "Is it a police court to which you are taking me?"

"Monsieur," Louis answered, "there are things which I cannot any longer conceal from you. I myself, believe me, am merely an outsider. I am, as you know, a hard-working man with a responsible position and a family to support. But here in Paris I come on to the fringe of a circle of life with which I have no direct connection, and yet whose happenings sometimes touch upon the lives of my friends and intimates. It is a circle of life into which is drawn much that is splendid, much that is brilliant; but, monsieur, it is life outside the law, life which does as it thinks fit, which lives its own way, and recognizes no laws save its own interests."

I nodded.

"Go on, Louis, please," I said. "Tell me, for example, who these men are whom I am going to meet."

"They are men," Louis answered, "who have great influence in that world of which I spoke. The law cannot touch them, or if it could it would not. They wield a power greater than the power which drives the wheels of government in this country. If they hear your story, and they think well, you will go free, even though the man Tapilow should die."

"You believe this, Louis?" I asked curiously.

"I am sure of it," he answered.

It was not for me to dispute what he said. I merely shrugged my shoulders. Yet, as a matter of fact, I was expecting every moment to find the hand of a gendarme upon my shoulder. I expected it as the carriage stopped before the restaurant and we crossed the pavement. I expected it even when two men who were sitting in the anteroom of the restaurant rose up to meet us. Louis, standing between, performed an introduction.

"Monsieur Decresson and Monsieur Grisson," he said, stretching out his hand, "permit me to make you acquainted with Monsieur le Capitaine Rotherby, a retired officer in the English army, and brother of the Earl of Welmington."

The two men bowed politely and held out their hands. They were both typical well-dressed, good-looking Frenchmen, apparently of the upper class. Monsieur Decresson had a narrow black beard, a military moustache, a high forehead, pale complexion, and thoughtful eyes. Monsieur Grisson was shorter, with lighter-colored hair, something of a fop in his attire, and certainly more genial in his manner.

"It is a pleasure," they both declared, "to have the honor of meeting Monsieur le Capitaine."

The usual inanities followed. Then Monsieur Decresson pointed with his hand into the restaurant.

"If monsieur will do us the honor to join us," he said, "we will take luncheon. Afterwards," he continued, "we can talk over our coffee and liqueurs. It would be well for us to become better acquainted."

I saw no reason to object. I was, in fact, exceedingly hungry. We lunched at a corner table in the famous restaurant, and I am bound to admit that we lunched exceedingly well. During the progress of the meal our conversation was absolutely general. All the events of the previous night were carefully ignored. When at last, however, we sat over our coffee and liqueurs, Monsieur Decresson, after a moment's pause, turned his melancholy gray eyes on me.

"Capitaine Rotherby," he said, "my friend and I represent a little group of people who have some interest in the place where we met last night. We are deputed to ask you to explain, if you can, your conduct, — your attack, which it seemed to us was absolutely unprovoked, upon an habitué of the place and an associate of our own."

"There is only one explanation which I can make," I answered slowly. "I went there, as Louis will tell you, absolutely a stranger, and absolutely by chance. Chance decreed that I should meet face to face the one man in the world against whom I bear a grudge, the one man whom I had sworn to punish whenever and wherever I might meet him."

Monsieur Decresson bowed.

"There are situations," he admitted, "which can only be dealt with in that manner. Do not think me personal or inquisitive, I beg of you, but — I ask in your own interests — what had you against this man Tapilow?"

"Monsieur Decresson," I said, "I will answer you frankly. The man whom I punished last night, I punished because I have proved him to be guilty of conduct unbecoming to a gentleman. I punished him because he broke the one social law which in my country, at any rate, may not be transgressed with impunity."

"What you are saying now," Monsieur Grisson interrupted, "amounts to an accusation. Tapilow is known to us. These things must be spoken of seriously. You speak upon your honor as an English soldier and a gentleman?"

"Messieurs," I answered, turning to both of them, "it is agreed. I speak to you as I would speak to the judge before whom I should stand if I had murdered this man, and I tell you both, upon my honor, that the treatment which he received from me he merited. He borrowed my money and my brother's money. He accepted the hospitality of my brother's house, the friendship of his friends. In return, he robbed him of the woman whom he loved."

"The quarrel," Monsieur Decresson said softly, "seems, then, to have been another's."

"Messieurs," I answered, "my brother is an invalid for life. The quarrel, therefore, was mine."

Decresson and his companion exchanged glances. I leaned back in my chair. The three of them talked together earnestly for several minutes in an undertone. Then Louis, with a little sigh of relief, rose to his feet and came over to my side.

"It is finished," he declared. "Monsieur Decresson and Monsieur Grisson are of one mind in this matter. The man Tapilow's punishment was deserved."

I looked from one to the other of them in wonder.

"But I do not understand!" I exclaimed. "You mean to say, then, that even if Tapilow himself should wish it — "

Monsieur Decresson smiled grimly.

"What happens in the Café des Deux Épingles," he said, "happens outside the world. Without special permission it would not be possible for Monsieur Tapilow to speak to the police of this assault. Buy your *Figaro* every evening," he continued, "and soon you will read. In the meantime, I recommend you, monsieur, not to stay too long in Paris."

They took leave of me with some solemnity on the pavement outside the restaurant, but Monsieur Decresson, before stepping into his automobile, drew me a little on one side.

"Capitaine Rotherby," he said, "you have been dealt

with to-day as a very privileged person. You were brought to the Café des Deux Épingles a stranger, almost a guest, and your behavior there might very well have been resented by us."

"If I have not said much," I answered, "please do not believe me any the less grateful."

"Let that go," Monsieur Decresson said coldly. "Only I would remind you of this. You are a young man, but your experience has doubtless told you that in this world one does not often go out of one's way to serve a stranger for no purpose at all. There is a chance that the time may come when we shall ask you, perhaps through Louis here, perhaps through some other person, to repay in some measure your debt. If that time should come, I trust that you will not prove ungrateful."

"I think," I answered confidently, "that there is no fear of that."

Monsieur Decresson touched Louis on the shoulder and motioned him to enter the automobile which was waiting. With many bows and solemn salutes the great car swung off and left me there alone. I watched it until it disappeared, and then, turning in the opposite direction, started to walk toward the Ritz. Curiously enough it never occurred to me to doubt for a moment the assurance which had been given me. I had no longer the slightest fear of arrest.

On the way I passed the Café de Paris. Then I suddenly remembered that strange little note from the girl with the turquoises. I never stopped to consider whether or not I was doing a wise thing. I opened the swing doors and passed into the restaurant. It was almost empty, except for a few people who had sat late over their luncheon. I called Léon to me.

"Léon," I said, "you remember me? I am Captain Rotherby."

He held up his hand.

"It is enough, monsieur," he declared. "If monsieur would be so good."

He drew me a little on one side.

"Mademoiselle still waits," he said in an undertone. "If monsieur will ascend."

"Upstairs?" I asked.

Léon bowed and smiled.

"Mademoiselle is in one of the smaller rooms," he said. "Will monsieur follow me?"

"Why, certainly," I answered.

CHAPTER VII

A DOUBLE ASSIGNATION

I FOLLOWED Léon upstairs to the region of smaller apartments. At the door of one of these he knocked, and a feminine voice at once bade us enter.

Mademoiselle was sitting upon a lounge, smoking a cigarette. On the table before her stood an empty coffee-cup and an empty liqueur-glass. She looked at me with a little grimace.

"At last!" she exclaimed.

"It is the gentleman whom mademoiselle was expecting?" Léon asked discreetly.

"Certainly," she answered. "You may go, Léon."

We were alone. She gave me her fingers, which I raised to my lips.

"Mademoiselle," I said, "I owe you a thousand apologies. I can assure you, however, that I have come at the earliest possible moment."

She motioned me to sit down upon the lounge by her side.

"Monsieur had a more interesting engagement, perhaps?" she murmured.

"Impossible!" I answered.

Now I had come here with no idea whatever of making love to this young lady. My chief interest in her was because she, too, was an habitué of this mysterious café; and because, from the first, I felt that she had some other than the obvious reason for sending me that little note. Nevertheless, it was for me to conceal these things, and

I did not hesitate to take her hand in mine as we sat side by side. She did not draw it away, and she did not encourage me.

"Monsieur," she said, "do not, I beg of you, be rash. It was foolish of me, perhaps, to meet you here. We can talk for a few minutes, and afterwards, perhaps, we may meet again, but I am frightened all the time."

"Monsieur Bartot?" I asked.

She nodded.

"He is very, very jealous," she answered.

"You go with him every night to the restaurant in the Place d'Anjou?" I asked.

"I go there very often," she answered. "Monsieur, unless I am mistaken, is a stranger there."

I nodded.

"Last night," I told her, "I was there for the first time."

"You came," she said, toying with her empty liqueur-glass, "with Louis."

"That is so," I admitted.

"Louis brings no one there without a purpose," she remarked.

"You know Louis, then?" I asked.

She raised her eyebrows.

"All the world knows Louis," she continued. "A smoother-tongued rascal never breathed."

"Louis," I murmured, "would be flattered."

"Louis knows himself," she continued, "and he knows that others know him. When I saw monsieur with him I was sorry."

"You are very kind," I said, "to take so much interest."

She looked at me, for the first time, with some spice of coquetry in her eyes.

"I think that I show my interest," she murmured, "in

meeting monsieur here. Tell me," she continued, "why were you there with Louis?"

"A chance affair," I answered. "I met him coming out of the Opera. I was bored, and we went together to the Montmartre. There I think that I was more bored still. It was Louis who proposed a visit to the Café des Deux Épingles."

"Did you know," she asked, "that you would meet that man — the man with whom you quarrelled?"

I shook my head.

"I had no idea of it," I answered.

She leaned just a little towards me.

"Monsieur," she said, "if you seek adventures over here, do not seek them with Louis. He knows no friends, he thinks of nothing but of himself. He is a very dangerous companion. There are others whom it would be better for monsieur to make companions of."

"Mademoiselle," I answered, looking into her eyes, "these things are not so interesting. You sent me last night a little note. When may I see you once more in that wonderful blue gown, and take you myself to the theatre, to supper, — where you will?"

She shot a glance at me from under her eyelids. The blind was not drawn, and the weak sunlight played upon her features. She was over-powdered and over-rouged, made up like all the smart women of her world, but her features were still good and her eyes delightful.

"Ah, monsieur," she said, "but that would be doubly imprudent. It is not, surely, well for monsieur to be seen too much in Paris to-day? He was badly hurt, that poor Monsieur Tapilow."

"Mademoiselle," I assured her, "there are times when the risk counts for nothing."

"Are all Englishmen so gallant?" she murmured.

"Mademoiselle," I answered, "with the same inducement, yes!"

"Monsieur has learned how to flatter," she remarked.

"It is an accomplishment which I never mastered," I declared.

She sighed. All the time I knew quite well that she carried on this little war of words impatiently. There were other things of which she desired to speak.

"Tell me, monsieur," she said, "what had he done to you, this man Tapilow?"

I shook my head.

"You must forgive me," I said. "That is between him and me."

"And Monsieur Louis," she murmured.

"Louis knew nothing about it," I declared.

She seemed perplexed. She had evidently made up her mind that Louis had taken me there with the object of meeting Tapilow, and for some reason the truth was interesting to her.

"It was a quarrel about a woman, of course," she murmured, — "the friend of monsieur, or perhaps a relation. I am jealous! Tell me, then, that it was a relation."

"Mademoiselle," I answered gravely, "I cannot discuss with you the cause of the quarrel between that man and myself. Forgive me if I remind you that it is a very painful subject. Forgive me if I remind you, too," I added, taking her other hand in mine for a moment, "that when I saw you scribble those few lines and send them across to me, and when I read what you said and came here, it was not to answer questions about any other person."

She raised her eyes to mine. They were curiously and

wonderfully blue. Then she shook her head and withdrew her hands, sighing.

"But, monsieur," she said, "since then many things have happened. You must not show yourself about in Paris. It is better for you to go back to England."

"I am quite safe here," I declared.

"Then it has been arranged!" she exclaimed quickly. "Louis is, after all, monsieur's friend. He has perhaps seen —"

"We will not talk of these things," I begged. "I would rather —"

She started, and drew a little away, glancing nervously toward the door.

"I am terrified," she said. "Monsieur must come to my apartments one afternoon, where we can talk without fear. There is one more question, though," she continued rapidly. "Louis looked often at us. Tell me, did he say anything to you about Monsieur Bartot and myself?"

"Nothing," I answered, "except that Monsieur Bartot held a somewhat unique position in a certain corner of Paris, and that he was a person whom it was not well to offend."

"No more?" she asked.

"No more," I answered.

"I saw him point us out to you," she remarked.

"I asked him to show me the most beautiful woman in the room," I answered.

She shook her head.

"You are too much of a courtier for an Englishman," she said. "You do not mean what you say."

"Even an Englishman," I answered, "can find words when he is sufficiently moved."

I made a feint again to hold her hands, but she drew away.

"When are you going back to England?" she asked abruptly.

"To-morrow, I think," I answered, "if I am still free."

"Free!" she repeated scornfully. "If you are protected, who is there who will dare to touch you? Monsieur Decresson has all the police dancing to his bidding, and if that were not sufficient, Monsieur Bartot could rescue you even from prison. No, you are safe enough, monsieur, even if you remain here! It is Louis, eh, who is anxious for you to return to England?"

"My time was nearly up anyhow," I told her. "It is not until this moment that I have felt inclined to stay."

"Nevertheless," she murmured, "Monsieur goes to London to-morrow. Is it permitted to ask —"

"Anything," I murmured.

"If monsieur goes alone?"

"I fear so," I answered, "unless mademoiselle —"

She laid her fingers upon my lips.

"Monsieur does not know the elderly gentleman and the very beautiful girl who sat opposite him last night?" she asked, — "Monsieur Delora and his niece?"

Somehow I felt convinced, the moment that the question had left her lips, that her whole interest in me was centred upon my reply. She concealed her impatience very well, but I realized that, for some reason or other, I was sitting there by her side solely that I might answer that question.

"I heard their names last night for the first time," I declared. "It was Louis who told me about them."

She looked at me for several moments as though anxious to be sure that I had spoken the truth.

"Mademoiselle!" I said reproachfully. "Let us leave these topics. I am not interested in the Deloras, or Louis, or Monsieur Bartot. Last night is finished, and to-morrow I leave. Let us talk for a few moments of ourselves."

She held up her finger suddenly.

"Listen!" she exclaimed, in a voice of terror.

Footsteps had halted outside the door. She ran to the window and looked down. In the street below was standing an automobile with yellow wheels. I was looking over her shoulder, and she clutched my arm.

"It is he — Bartot!" she cried. "He is here at the private entrance. Some one has told him that I am here. Mon Dieu! It is he outside now!"

It was bad acting, and I laughed.

"Mademoiselle," I said, "if Monsieur Bartot is your lover, be thankful that you have nothing with which to reproach yourself."

I rang the bell. She looked at me for a moment with eyes filled with a genuine fear. Obviously she did not understand my attitude. From my trousers pocket I drew a little revolver, whose settings and mechanism I carefully examined. There was a loud knock at the door and the sound of voices outside. Monsieur Bartot entered, in a frock-coat too small for him and a tie too large. When he saw us he fell back with a theatrical start.

"Susette!" he exclaimed. "Susette! And you, sir!" he added, turning to me.

He slammed the door and stood with his back to it.

"What the devil is the meaning of this?" he asked, looking from one to the other of us.

I shrugged my shoulders.

"You had better ask mademoiselle," I answered.

"She is, I believe, an acquaintance of yours. As for me —"

"My name is Bartot, sir," he cried fiercely.

"An excellent name," I answered, "but unknown to me. I do not yet understand by what right you intrude into a private room here."

He laughed hardly.

"'Intrude'!" he cried. "One does not call it that. 'Intrude,' when I find you two together, eh?"

I turned to the girl, who, with her handkerchief dabbed to her eyes, was still affecting a perfect frenzy of fear.

"Has this person any claims upon you?" I asked. "He seems to me to be an exceedingly disagreeable fellow."

Bartot's face grew purple. His cheeks seemed to distend and his eyes grow smaller. It was no longer necessary for him to play a part. He was becoming angry indeed.

"Monsieur," he said, "I remember you now. It was you who tried to flirt with this lady last night in the Café des Deux Épingles. You have not even the excuse of ignorance. All the world knows that I have claims upon this lady."

I bowed.

"Claims," I answered, "which I can assure you I am not in a position to dispute."

"How is it, then," he asked fiercely, "that I find you two, strangers last night, together to-day here?"

I altered one of the cartridges in my revolver and let it go with a snap. Bartot took a quick step backwards.

"It is a long story," I said softly, "and I doubt whether it would interest you, Monsieur Bartot. Still, if you are really curious, mademoiselle will satisfy you later."

I saw a look pass between the two, and I no longer had any doubt whatever. I knew that they were in collusion, that I had been brought here to be pumped by mademoiselle.

"Monsieur," Bartot said, "you are apparently armed, and you can leave this room if you will, but I warn you that you will not leave Paris so easily."

The situation was quite plain to me. However little flattering it might be to my vanity, I should not have been in the least surprised if Monsieur Bartot had held out his hands, begged my pardon, and ordered a bottle of wine.

"Be reasonable, monsieur," I begged. "It is open to every one, surely, to admire mademoiselle? For the rest, I have been here only a few moments. So far as I am concerned," I added, glancing at the table, "mademoiselle has lunched alone."

"If I could believe that!" Bartot muttered, with a look of coming friendship in his eyes.

"Mademoiselle will assure you," I continued.

"Then what are you doing here?" he asked.

I raised my eyebrows.

"I was not aware," I said, "that this was a private restaurant."

"But these are private rooms," he answered. "Still, if it was a mistake, — I trust mademoiselle always."

She held out her hands to him with a theatrical gesture.

"Henri," she cried, "you could not doubt me! It is impossible!"

"You are right," he answered quickly. "I was too hasty."

I smiled upon them both.

"Mademoiselle," I said, "I am sorry that our pleasant

little conversation has been interrupted. Believe me, though, to be always your devoted slave."

I opened the door. Monsieur Bartot turned towards me. I am convinced that he was about to offer me his hand and to call for that bottle of wine. I felt, however, that flight was safest. I went out and closed the door.

"The bill, monsieur?" a waiter called after me as I descended the stairs.

I gave him five francs for a *pour boire*.

"Monsieur there will pay," I told him, pointing towards the room.

CHAPTER VIII

LOUIS INSISTS

I ARRIVED at the Ritz to find Louis walking impatiently up and down the stone-flagged pavement outside the entrance. He came up to me eagerly as I approached.

"I have been waiting for you for more than an hour!" he exclaimed.

I looked at him in some surprise. I had not yet grown accustomed to hear him speak in such a tone.

"Did I say that I was coming straight back?" I asked.

"Of course not," he answered. "After you left, though, I had some trouble with Monsieur Grisson. There is a chance that we may have to move Tapilow to a hospital, and he is just one of those fools who talk. Monsieur Grisson insists upon it that you leave Paris by the four o'clock train this afternoon."

I shook my head.

"I could not catch it," I declared. "It is half-past three now."

"On the other hand, you can and you must," Louis answered. "I took the liberty of telephoning in your name and ordering the valet to pack your clothes. Your luggage is in the hall there, and that automobile is waiting to take you to the Gare du Nord."

I opened my mouth to protest, but Louis' manner underwent a further change.

"Captain Rotherby," he said, "it is I and my friends who save you, perhaps, from a considerable inconvenience.

Forgive me if I remind you of this, but it is not fitting that you should argue with us on this matter."

Louis was right. For more reasons than he knew of, it was well that I should leave Paris.

"Are you coming with me?" I asked.

"I am crossing by the night boat," Louis answered. "I have not quite finished the work for which I came over. I have some things to buy."

I smiled.

"Upon my word," I said, "I had forgotten your profession."

I went back into the hotel and paid my bill. Louis drove with me to the station and saw to the registration of my luggage. Afterwards he found my reserved seat, in which I arranged my rug and books. Then I turned and walked down the corridor with him.

"I trust," he said, "that monsieur will have a pleasant journey and pleasant companions."

I glanced into the *coupé* which we were just passing. It seemed curious that even as the wish left his lips I should find myself looking into the dark eyes of the girl whose face had been so often in my thoughts during the last few days! Opposite her was the gray-bearded man Delora, already apparently immersed in a novel. Every seat in the compartment was laden with their small belongings, — dressing-bags, pillows, a large jewel-case, books, papers, flowers, and a box of chocolates. I turned to Louis.

"Again," I remarked, "we meet friends. What a small place the world is!"

We stepped down on to the platform. Louis, for some reason, seemed slightly nervous. He glanced up at the clock and watched the few late arrivals with an interest which was almost intense.

"Monsieur," he said, a little abruptly, "there is a question which I should like to ask you before you leave."

"There are a good many I should like to ask you, Louis," I answered, "but they will keep.   Go ahead."

"I should like to know," Louis said, "where you spent the hour which passed between your leaving the Café Normandy and arriving at the Ritz."

I hesitated for a moment.   After all, I had no reason to keep my movements secret.   It was better, indeed, to avoid complications so far as possible.

"You shall know if you like, Louis," I said.   "I kept my appointment with the young lady of the turquoises."

Louis' pale face seemed suddenly strained.

"It was my fault!" he muttered.   "I should not have left you!   You do not understand how those affairs are here in Paris!   If Bartot knew —"

"Bartot did know," I interrupted.

Louis' face was a study.

"Bartot came in while I was talking to mademoiselle," I said.

"There was a scene?"   Louis inquired breathlessly. "Bartot threatened monsieur?   Perhaps there were blows?"

"Nothing of the sort," I answered.   "Bartot blustered a little and mademoiselle wrung her hands, but they played their parts badly.   Between you and me, Louis, I have a sort of an idea that Bartot's coming was not altogether accidental."

"It was a trap," Louis murmured softly.   "But why?"

I shook my head.

"Louis," I said, "I am the wrong sort of man to be even a temporary dweller in this nest of intrigue.   I do not understand it at all.   I do not understand any of you.   I only know that I owe you and those other gentlemen a very considerable debt, and I have been solemnly warned against you by the young lady whom I met at the Café de Paris. I have been assured that association with you is the first step toward my undoing. Monsieur Bartot, for all his bluster, seemed very anxious to be friendly."

"It was the girl!" Louis exclaimed. "Bartot was too big a fool to understand!"

I sighed.

"I fear that I am in the same position as Monsieur Bartot," I said. "I do not understand!"

There was a warning cry. I had only just time to swing myself on to the slowly moving train. Louis ran for a moment by the side.

"Those people are harmless," he said. "They merely wished, if they could, to make use of you. Mademoiselle has tied other fools to her chariot wheels before now, that Bartot may grow fat. But, monsieur!"

I leaned over to catch his words.

"If Monsieur or Mademoiselle Delora should address you," he said, "you need have no fear. They are not of the same order as Bartot and Susette."

"I will remember," I answered, waving my farewells.

I regained my compartment, which I was annoyed to find had filled up till mine was the only vacant seat. I had not had time to buy any papers or magazines, but, after all, I had enough to interest me in my thoughts. Of Tapilow I scarcely thought at all. He and I had met, and I had kept my oath. So far as I was concerned, that was the end. I had not even any fears for my own safety as regards this matter. My interview with Decresson and his friend had had a curiously convincing effect upon me. I felt that I had been tried for my crime, and acquitted, in

the most orthodox fashion. For me the curtain had fallen
upon that tragedy. It was the other things which occupied
my mind. I seemed to have found my way into a maze, to
have become mixed up in certain affairs in a most mysterious and inexplicable way. What was the meaning of that
place to which Louis had introduced me? Was it some
sort of secret organization, — an organization which as-
sumed to itself, at any rate, the power to circumvent the
police? And Bartot, too! Had he really the power which
Louis had declared him to possess? If so, why had he
baited a clumsy trap for me and permitted me to walk
out of it untouched? What did they want from me, these
people? The thought was utterly confusing. I could
find absolutely no explanation. Then, again, another
puzzle remained. I remembered Louis' desire, almost
command, that I should return to London by this particular train. Had he any reason for it? Was it connected in
any way, I wondered, with the presence of this man and
girl in the next compartment? It seemed feasible, even if
inexplicable.

I rose and strolled down the corridor, looking in at the
coupé where these two people sat, with all the banal impertinence of the curious traveller. The girl met my eyes
once and afterwards simply ignored me. The man never
looked up from his magazine. I passed and repassed
three or four times. The effect was always the same. At
last I resumed my seat. At any rate, they showed no
pressing desire to make my acquaintance!

At Boulogne I descended at once into the saloon and
made a hasty meal. When I came up on deck in the
harbor I found that the chair which I had engaged was
lashed close to the open door of a private cabin, and in the
door of that cabin, standing within a few feet of me, was

the niece of Monsieur Delora. I racked my brains for something to say. She gave me no encouragement whatever. At last I descended to a banality.

"We shall have rather a rough crossing, I am afraid," I said, touching my cap.

She looked at me as though surprised that I should have ventured to address her. She did not take the trouble to be annoyed. She answered me, indeed, with civility, but in a manner which certainly did not encourage me to attempt any further conversation. There was a moment's pause. Then she turned away and spoke to some one behind her in the cabin. A moment or two later the door was closed and I was left alone. After that it seemed ridiculous to imagine that there was any special significance to be attached to the fact that we were fellow passengers.

The crossing was a rough one, and I saw nothing more of either Delora or the girl. I had very little hand baggage, and I was one of the first to reach the train, where I made myself comfortable in the corner seat of a carriage towards the rear end. The inspector, whom I knew very well, locked my door, and until the last moment it seemed as though I should have the compartment to myself. The train, indeed, was on the point of starting, and I had almost given up looking out for my fellow passengers when they came hurrying up along the platform. I saw them glancing into the windows of every carriage in the hope of finding a seat. Two porters carried their small baggage. An obsequious guard followed in the rear. Just as they were opposite to the carriage in which I was sitting the whistle blew.

"Plenty of room higher up!" the inspector exclaimed. "Take your seats, please."

"We will get in here," the girl answered, — "that is to say, unless it is a reserved carriage. Please to open the door at once."

The inspector hesitated, remembering the tip which I had given him, but he had no alternative. The guard produced his key and opened the door. It was not until that moment that the girl recognized me. She stepped back, and the look which she threw in my direction was certainly not flattering.

"Can you find us another carriage?" she asked the guard, imperiously.

"Quite impossible, miss," the man answered. "You must get in here or be left behind."

They had barely time to take their seats. As my place was next to the window, I felt bound to help the porter hand in the small packages. The man Delora, who was wrapped up in a fur coat, and who looked ghastly ill, thanked me courteously enough, but the girl ignored my assistance. They took the two corner seats at the further end of the carriage. Delora immediately composed himself to sleep.

"It was a wretched crossing!" he said to the girl, — "the most miserable crossing I have ever had! And these trains, — so small, so uncomfortable!"

She shrugged her shoulders.

"When one travels," she said, "I suppose that one must put up with inconveniences of all sorts."

I knew very well that the last part of her sentence not only had reference to me, but was intended for my hearing. I affected, however, to be absorbed in the magazine which I was reading, and under cover of which I was able to make a close observation of the man, who was sitting on the same side as myself. He had put up his feet and closed

his eyes, but he had evidently suffered badly from sea-
sickness, for his face remained almost deathly white, and
he shivered now and then as though with cold. He had
lost the well-groomed air which had distinguished him in
Paris. His features were haggard and worn, and he
looked at least ten years older. His clothes were excellently made, and the fur coat which he had wrapped
around himself was magnificent. For the rest, he seemed
tired out — a man utterly wearied of life. Before we had
reached the town station he was asleep.

The train rushed on into the darkness, and after a time
I ventured to glance toward the girl. She, too, was leaning
back in her place, but her face was turned a little away
from me towards the window, through which she was
gazing with the obvious intentness of one whose thoughts
are far away. I had all my life been used to observing
closely people of either sex who interested me, and I found
now, as I had found during those various accidental meet-
ings in Paris, that the study of this young woman afforded
me a peculiar pleasure. Apart from her more personal
fascination, she was faultlessly dressed. She wore a
black tailor-made suit, perhaps a little shorter than is
usual for travelling in England, patent shoes, — long and
narrow, — and black silk stockings. Her hat was a small
toque, and her veil one of those for which Frenchwomen
are famous, — very large, but not in the least disfiguring.
This, however, she had raised for the present, and I was
able to study the firm but fine profile of her features, to
notice the delicacy of her chin, her small, well-shaped
ears, her eyebrows — black and silky. Her eyes themselves were hidden from me, but their color had been the
first thing which had attracted me. They were of a blue
so deep that sometimes they seemed as black as her eye-

brows themselves. It was only when she smiled or came into a strong light that they seemed suddenly to flash almost to violet. Her figure was slim — she was, indeed, little more than a girl — but very shapely and elegant. She could scarcely be called tall, but there was something in her carriage which seemed to exaggerate her height. The very poise of her head indicated a somewhat contemptuous indifference to the people amongst whom she moved.

I had kept my scrutiny under control, prepared for any sudden movement on the part of the girl; but after all she was too quick for me. She turned from the window with a perfectly natural movement, and yet so swiftly that our eyes met before I could look away. She leaned a little forward in her place, and her forehead darkened.

"Perhaps, sir," she said, "you will be good enough to tell me the meaning of your persistent impertinence?"

CHAPTER IX

A TRAVELLING ACQUAINTANCE

HER words were so unexpected that for a moment or two I was speechless. On the whole, I scarcely felt that I deserved the cold contempt of her voice or the angry flash in her eyes.

"I am afraid I don't understand you," I said. "If you refer to the fact that I was watching you with some interest at that moment, I suppose I must plead guilty. On the other hand, I object altogether to the term 'impertinence.'"

"And why do you object?" she asked, looking at me steadily, and beating with her little hand the arm-rest by her side. "If your behavior is not impertinence, pray what is it? We meet at the Opera. You look. It is not enough for you that you look once, but you look twice, three times. You come out on to the pavement to hear the address which my uncle gives the chauffeur. We go to a restaurant for supper, where only the few are admitted. You are content to be brought by a waiter, but you are there! You travel to England by the same train, — you walk up and down past my compartment. You presume to address me upon the boat. You give a fee to the guard that he should put us in your carriage. Yet you object to the term 'impertinence'!"

"I do," I answered, "most strongly. I consider your use of the word absolutely uncalled for."

She looked across at the sleeping man. He was breathing heavily, and was evidently quite unconscious of our conversation.

"Your standard of manners is, I am afraid, a peculiar one," she said. "In Paris one is used always to be stared at. Englishmen, I was told, behaved better."

She took up a magazine and turned away with a shrug of the shoulders. I leaned a little further forward in my place, and lowered my voice so as not to disturb the sleeping man.

"You are really unjust to me," I said. "I will plead guilty to noticing you at the Opera House, but I did so as I would have done any well-dressed young woman who formed a part of the show there. So far as regards my visit to the Café des Deux Épingles, I went at the suggestion of Louis, whom I met by accident, and who is the *maître d'hôtel* at my favorite restaurant. I had no idea that you were going to be there. On the contrary, I distinctly heard your companion tell your chauffeur to drive to the Ritz. I came on this train by accident, and although it is true that I spoke to you as I might have done to any other travelling companion, I deny that there was anything in the least impertinent either in what I said or how I said it. So far as regards your coming into this carriage," I added, "I feed the guard to keep it to myself, and although I will not say that your presence is unwelcome, it is certainly unsought for."

She was silent for a moment, watching me all the time intently. My words seemed to have given her food for thought.

"Listen," she said, leaning forward. "Do you mean to say that that was your first visit to the Café des Deux Épingles?"

"Absolutely my first visit," I answered. "I met Louis by accident that night. He knew that I was bored, and he took me there."

I LEANED A LITTLE FURTHER FORWARD IN MY PLACE, AND LOWERED MY
VOICE SO AS NOT TO DISTURB THE SLEEPING MAN.

Page 66

"You met him at the Opera and you asked him who we were," she remarked.

"That is quite true," I admitted, "but I scarcely see that there was anything impertinent in that. Afterwards we spoke together for a little time. I told him that I was alone in Paris and bored. It was because I was alone that we went out together."

Her forehead was wrinkled with perplexity. Her eyes seemed always to be seeking mine, as though anxious to learn whether I were indeed speaking the truth.

"I do not understand at all," she said. "You mean to tell me, then, that you know nothing of Louis except as a *maître d'hôtel*, that you were a chance visitor to Paris this week?"

"Absolutely," I answered.

Suddenly a thought seemed to occur to her. She drew away from me. In her eyes I seemed to see reflected the tragedy of those few moments in the Café des Deux Épingles.

"How can I believe you?" she exclaimed. "Remember that I saw you strike that man! It was horrible! I have never seen anything like it! You were like a wild animal! They tell me that he was very badly hurt. Is it true?"

"I believe so," I answered. "I am afraid that I hope so."

"And you," she continued, "go free! You have not even the air of one who flies for his life. Yet you tell me that you are not one of those — those —"

"Those what?" I asked eagerly.

"Those who frequent the Café des Deux Épingles," she said slowly, — "those who take advantage of the peculiar protection which some of those behind the scenes there are able to extend to their friends."

I shook my head.

"I know nothing of the place beyond that brief visit," I answered. "I know nothing of Louis except as a *maître d'hôtel* in my favorite restaurant. I know nothing of the people who frequent the Café des Deux Épingles except those I saw there that night. You," I added, "were one of them. I can assure you that when I went with Louis to that place I had not the slightest idea that I should meet the person whom I did meet."

"What is your name?" she asked abruptly.

I handed her my card. She read it with a perplexed face. The man opposite to her moved uneasily in his sleep. She crumpled the card up in her hands and remained for a few moments apparently deep in thought.

"You are an Englishman?" she asked, after a short pause.

"Decidedly!" I answered.

"I have not known many Englishmen," she said slowly. "I have lived in the country, near Bordeaux, and in Paris, most of my days. It is very certain, though, that I have never seen an Englishman like you. I was looking into your eyes when that man came into the room. I saw you rise to strike him."

She shuddered. I leaned across towards her.

"Listen," I said, "I do not wish you to think me worse than I am. You sympathize with that man whom I struck down. You look upon me as a sort of would-be assassin. You need not. I tell you, upon my honor, that if ever a man in this world deserved death, he deserved it."

"From you?" she asked.

"From me!" I answered firmly. "It was not, perhaps, a personal matter, but I have a brother, — listen, mademoiselle!" I continued. "He is a cripple. He was thrown from his horse — he was master of hounds in those days — and he has never been able to walk since. He was married to a woman whom he loved, a poor girl whom he had made wealthy, and to whom he had given a great position. She loved him, and she was content, after his accident, to give her life to him. Then that man came, the man whom you saw me punish. I tell you that this was no chance affair," I went on. "He set himself deliberately to win her heart. How far he succeeded I do not know. I can only tell you that she left my brother's home with him. The man was his guest at the time, — was his guest from the beginning of the affair."

The girl's eyes blazed. Even in that dim light I could see the dark blue fire in them.

"You did well !" she said. "For that I have no more to say. One who wrongs the helpless should be punished. But I do not understand this," she added. "I do not understand why those people at the Café des Deux Épingles should shield you when you are not one of them, — when you have no knowledge of any of them save the very slightest. They are not philanthropists, those people. Some day or other you will have to pay the price !"

I shrugged my shoulders.

"I have never refused to pay my just debts," I said. "If any one of them comes to me with a definite request which I can grant, you may be very sure that I shall grant it."

"You are not already their servant, then ?" she asked. "You are sure, quite sure of that ?"

"In what way ?" I asked.

"You look honest," she said. "Perhaps you are. Perhaps I have doubted you without a cause. But I will ask you this question. Has it been suggested to you by any of them that you should watch us — my uncle and me?"

"On my honor, no!" I answered earnestly.

She was evidently puzzled. Little by little the animosity seemed to have died away from her face. She looked at the sleeping man thoughtfully, and then once more at me.

"Tell me," she said, — "do not think, please, that I am inquisitive, but I should like to believe that you are not one of those whom we need fear, — is Louis indeed an ordinary acquaintance of yours?"

"He is scarcely that," I answered. "He is simply the *maître d'hôtel* at a restaurant I frequent. I had never in my life seen him before, except in his restaurant. When he spoke to me at the Opera I did not for some time recognize him."

She appeared to be convinced, but still a little bewildered. She was silent.

"Don't you think," I said, after a short pause, "that it is almost my turn now to ask a few questions?"

She seemed surprised.

"Why not?" she asked.

"Tell me, you are not English," I said, "and you are not French. Yet you speak English so well."

She smiled.

"My father was a Frenchman and my mother a Spaniard," she answered. "I was born in South America, but I came to Europe when very young, and have lived in France always. My people" — she looked towards the sleeping man as though to include him — "are all coffee planters."

"You are going to stay long in London?" I asked.

"My uncle sells his year's crops there," she answered. "When he has finished his business we move on."

"Will you tell me, then," I asked, "why you, too, were at the Café des Deux Épingles? You admit that it is the resort of people of mysterious habits. What place had you there?"

She looked away from me for a moment. My question seemed to disconcert her, perhaps by reason of its directness.

"Well," she said, "my uncle has lived for many years in Paris. He knows it as well as the Parisians themselves. He has always had a taste for adventure, and I fancy that he has friends who are interested in the place. At any rate, I have been there with him two or three times, and he is always welcome."

"From what I have heard," I remarked, "I should imagine that you and I are the only people who have been allowed to go there without qualifications."

She glanced as though by accident at the sleeping man opposite. Then, as though conscious of what she had done, a spot of color burned in her cheeks. Since the anger which had first inspired her to speech had died away, her manner had been a little shy. I realized more and more that she must be quite young.

"Perhaps," she answered. "I do not understand the place or its habitués. I only know that while one is there, one must be careful."

"Tell me," I asked, "what are you going to do in London while your uncle looks after his business?"

"Amuse myself as best I can, I suppose," she answered carelessly. "There are always the shops, and the theatres in the evening."

"Where are you going to stay?" I inquired.

"At the Milan, I think," she answered.

Somehow her answer to my question struck me as ominous. To the Milan, of course, where Louis was all the time predominant! The girl might be innocent enough of all wrong-doing or knowledge of wrong-doing, but could one think the same of her uncle? I glanced at him in- stinctively. In sleep, his features were by no means prepossessing.

"I may come across you, then," I ventured.

She smiled at me. It was wonderful what a difference the smile made in her face. To me she seemed at that moment radiantly beautiful.

"It would be very pleasant," she said. "I know no one in London. I expect to be alone a great deal. You live in London?" she asked.

"As much there as anywhere," I answered. "I have never settled down since I sent in my papers."

"Why did you do that?" she asked.

"I was badly knocked about at Ladysmith," I answered, "and I could not get round in time. I have n't altogether finished soldiering, though," I added. "At least, I hope not."

"But where do you call your home, then?" she asked timidly.

"I am not one of those fortunate persons who possess one," I answered. "I spend a great deal of time in Norfolk with my brother, and I have just a couple of rooms in town."

The train had slackened speed. All around us was a wide-spreading arc of yellow lights. The clearness had gone from the atmosphere. The little current of air which came in through the half-open window was already murky and depressing.

"It is London?" she asked.

"We shall be there in ten minutes," I answered, look- ing out.

A TRAVELLING ACQUAINTANCE 73

She leaned over and waked her uncle. He sat up drowsily.

"We shall be there in ten minutes," she said.

"So soon!" he answered. "Do you know on which side we arrive, sir?" he asked me.

"On your side," I answered.

He rose to his feet, and commenced to wrap a scarf around his neck.

"You will be smothered," the girl remarked.

"I am cold," he answered, in a low tone. "I am always cold after I have crossed the Channel. Besides, it is the damp air. You, too, will find it so in London, Felicia. You must be careful."

Already he was peering out of the window into the darkness. I could not help wondering whether it was seasickness alone which was responsible for his haggard features, for that grim look of covert fear which seemed to have settled around his mouth and eyes. To me he seemed like a man who is about to face the unknown, and who fears!

The train began to slacken pace. We drew into the station. I noticed that a man was standing by himself at this remote end of the platform, and that as we passed he seemed to look intently into our carriage.

"Can I be of any service to you?" I asked the girl, as I collected my small belongings. "I suppose, though, that your uncle is used to the journey."

She glanced towards the man opposite. He turned to me, and I found his appearance almost terrifying. He seemed to be suffering from more than physical sickness.

"I thank you, sir," he said rapidly. "You could, if you would, be of immense service."

"I should be delighted," I answered. "Tell me in what way?"

"I am exceedingly ill," the man said, with a groan. "I suffer from heart attacks, and the crossing has altogether upset me. If you could remain with my niece while our luggage is examined, and send her afterwards to the Milan Hotel, you would do a real favor to a sick man. I could myself take a hansom there without waiting for a moment, and get to bed. Nothing else will do me any good."

I glanced across at the girl. She was watching her uncle with distressed face.

"If you will allow me," I said, "it will give me very great pleasure to look after you. I am going to the Milan myself, and I, too, have luggage to be examined."

"It is very kind of you," she said hesitatingly. "Don't you think, though," she added, turning to her uncle, "that I had better go with you? We could send a servant for the luggage afterwards."

"No, no!" he objected impatiently. "I shall call at the chemist's. I shall get something that will put me right quickly."

"It is settled, then," I declared.

Apparently Delora thought so. The train had scarcely come to a standstill, but already he had descended. Avoiding the platform, he crossed straight on to the roadway, and was lost amidst the tangle of cabs. I turned to the girl, affecting not to notice his extraordinary haste.

"We will have our small things put into an omnibus," I said. "There will be plenty of time afterwards to come back and look for our registered luggage."

"You are very kind," she murmured absently.

Her eyes were still watching the spot where her companion had disappeared.

CHAPTER X

DELORA DISAPPEARS

I was fortunate enough to find a disengaged omnibus, and filled it with our rugs and smaller belongings. Then we made our way slowly back to the little space prepared for the reception of the heavier baggage, and around which a barrier had already been erected. There was a slight nervousness in my companion's manner which made conversation difficult. I, too, could not help feeling that the situation was a difficult one for her.

"I am afraid," I remarked, "that you are worried about your uncle. Is his health really bad, or is this just a temporary attack? I thought he looked well enough in the train on the other side."

"He suffers sometimes," she answered, "but I do not think it is anything really serious."

"He will be all right by the time we get to the hotel," I declared.

"Very likely," she answered. "For myself, I think that I always feel a little nervous when I arrive at a strange place. I have never been here before, you know, and I could not help wondering, for a moment, what would become of me if my uncle were really taken ill. Everyone says that London is so big and cold and heartless."

"You would have nothing to fear," I assured her. "You forget, too, that your uncle has friends here."

We leaned over the barrier and watched the luggage being handed out of the vans and thrown on to the low wooden platforms. By my side a dark young man, with sallow features and *pince nez*, was apparently passing his time in the same manner. My companion, who was restless all the time, glanced at him frequently, or I should scarcely have noticed his existence. In dress and appearance he resembled very much the ordinary valet in private service, except for his eye-glasses, and that his face lacked the smooth pastiness of the class. For some reason or other my companion seemed to take a dislike to him.

"Come," she said to me, "we will move over to the other side. I think we shall get in quicker."

I followed her lead, and I saw her glance back over her shoulder at the young man, who seemed unaware, even, of her departure.

"I do hate being listened to," she said, "even when one is talking about nothing in particular!"

"Who was listening to us?" I asked.

"The young man next to you," she answered. "I could see him look up in that horrid stealthy way from under his eyelids."

I laughed.

"You are a very observant person," I remarked.

She drew a little closer to me. Somehow or other I found the sense of her near presence a delightful thing. All her garment seemed imbued with a faint perfume, as though of violets.

"I think that I have only become so quite lately," she said. "Perhaps it is because I have lived such a quiet life, and now things are so different. My uncle has been so mysterious, especially during the last few days, and I suppose it has made me suspicious. Wherever we go, I always seem to fancy that some one is watching us. Besides, I am sure that that young man was a South American, and I hate South Americans!"

"I fancy," I said, "that the attention he bestowed upon us was due to a more obvious cause."

"Please do not talk like that," she begged. "I do not wish for compliments from you. I have been told always that Englishmen are so truthful. One has compliments from Frenchmen, from Spaniards, and from South Americans. They fall like froth from their lips, and one knows all the time that it means nothing, and less than nothing. It is such a pity!"

"Why a pity?" I asked, more for the sake of keeping her talking than anything. "Certainly it is a picturesque habit of speech."

She shrugged her shoulders.

"I do not like it," she said quietly. "By degrees, one comes to believe nothing that any man says, even when he is in earnest. Remember, Capitaine Rotherby, I hope that I shall never hear a compliment from you."

"I will be careful," I promised her, "but you must remember that there is sometimes a very fine distinction. I may be driven to say something which sounds quite nice, because it is the truth."

She laughed at me with her eyes, a habit of hers which from the first I had admired. For the moment she seemed to have forgotten her anxieties.

"You are worse than these others," she murmured. "I believe — no, I am quite sure, that you are more dangerous! Come, they are ready for us."

The barriers were thrown open, and a little stream of people entered the enclosed space. My companion's trunks were all together, and easily found. The officer bent over, chalk in hand, and asked a few courteous questions. At that moment I became aware that the young man in eye-glasses was standing once more by my side. Her trunks were promptly marked, and I directed the porter to take them to our omnibus. Then we moved on a little to where my things were. The young man sauntered behind us, and stopped to light a cigarette. My companion's fingers fell upon my arm.

"He is everywhere!" she murmured. "What does he want?"

I turned round sharply and caught him in the act of inspecting my labels. I was beginning now to lose my temper.

"May I ask," I said, standing in his way, "to what we owe — this young lady and I — your interest in us and our concerns?"

He stared at me blankly.

"I do not understand you, sir," he said.

I was foolish enough to lose my temper. A policeman was standing within a few feet of us, and I appealed to him.

"This person annoys us," I said, pointing him out, "by following us everywhere we go. The young lady is carrying a jewel-case, and I have papers of some importance myself. Will you kindly ask him to move on, or ascertain whether he is a *bona fide* traveller?"

The young man smiled faintly. The policeman answered me civilly, but I knew at once that I had made a mistake.

"This gentleman is well known to us, sir," he said. "I do not think you will find him causing you any trouble."

"I hope, at any rate," I said, turning away, "that we have seen the last of him."

Apparently we had, — for the moment, at any rate. I claimed my own belongings, and had them sent down to the omnibus Then I handed my companion in, and was on the point of joining her, when I saw walking along the platform, within a few feet of us, the policeman to whom I had appealed. I turned back to him.

"I wonder," I said, drawing him a little on one side, "if you would care to earn a sovereign without committing a breach of duty?"

He looked at me stolidly. Apparently he thought that silence was wisest.

"You said that that young man who followed us about here was well known to you," I said. "Who is he?"

"It is not my place to tell you, sir," the man answered, and passed on.

I stepped into the 'bus and we drove off. As we turned out of the station I caught a last glimpse of our shadower. He was standing close to the main exit with his hands behind him, looking up to the sky as though anxious to discover whether it were still raining. He looked into our 'bus as it clattered by, and my companion, who caught sight of him, leaned back in her seat.

"I am sure," she declared firmly, "that that is a detective."

I was equally certain of it, but I only laughed.

"If he is," I said, "it is certainly not you who needs to be anxious. There can be no question as to whom he is watching. You must remember that although those mysterious people up at the Place d'Anjou may be powerful in their way, they would have to be very clever indeed to protect me absolutely. It is pretty well known over here that I had threatened to kill Tapilow wherever I met him."

She looked at me for a moment, doubtfully, and then she shook her head.

"It is not you whom they are watching," she said.

"Who, then?" I asked.

"My uncle and me," she answered.

I looked at her curiously.

"Tell me," I said, "why you think that? Your uncle is a man of position, and has legitimate business here. Why should he be watched by detectives?"

She shook her head.

"I suppose it is because we are foreigners," she said, "but ever since my uncle fetched me from Bordeaux we seem to have been watched by some one wherever we go."

"You will not suffer much from that sort of thing over here," I remarked cheerfully. "England is not a police-ridden country like Germany, or even France."

"I know," she answered, "and yet I have told you before how I feel about arriving in England. There seems something unfriendly in the very atmosphere, something which depresses me, which makes me feel as though there were evil times coming."

I laughed reassuringly.

"You are giving way to fancies," I said. "I am sure that London is doing its best for you. See, the rain is all over. We have even continental weather to welcome you. Look at the moon. For London, too," I added, "the streets seem almost gay."

She leaned out of the window. A full moon was shining in a cloudless sky. The theatres were just over. The pavements were thronged with men and women, and the streets were blocked with carriages and hansoms on their way to the various restaurants. At the entrance to the Milan our omnibus was stopped for several moments whilst motors and carriages of all descriptions, with their load of men and women in evening clothes, passed slowly by and turned in at the courtyard. We found ourselves at last at the doors of the hotel, and I received the usual welcome from my friend the hall-porter.

"Back again once more, you see, Ashley," I remarked. "I have brought Miss Delora on from the station. Her uncle is here already. We came over by the same train."

The reception clerk stepped forward and smilingly acknowledged my greeting. He bowed, also, to my companion.

"We are very pleased to see you, Miss Delora," he said. "We were expecting you and Mr. Delora to-night."

"My uncle came on at once from the station," she said. "He was not feeling very well."

The clerk bowed, but seemed a little puzzled.

"Will you tell me where I can find Mr. Delora?" she asked.

"Mr. Delora has not yet arrived, madam," the clerk answered.

She looked at him for a moment, speechless.

"Not arrived?" I interrupted. "Surely you must be mistaken, Dean! He left Charing Cross half an hour before us."

The clerk shook his head.

"I am quite sure, Captain Rotherby," he said, "that Mr. Delora has not been here to claim his rooms. He may have entered the hotel from the other side, and be in the smoking-room or the American bar, but he has not been here."

There was a couch close by, and my companion sat down. I could see that she had turned very white.

"Send a page-boy round the hotel," I told the hall-porter, "to inquire if Mr. Delora is in any of the rooms. If I might make the suggestion," I continued, turning towards her, "I would go upstairs at once. You may find, after all, that Mr. Dean has made a mistake, and that your uncle is there."

"Why, yes!" she declared, jumping up. "I will go at once. Do you mind — will you come with me?"

"With pleasure!" I answered.

I paused for a moment to give some instructions about my own luggage. Then I stepped into the lift with the clerk and her.

"Your uncle, I hope, is not seriously indisposed, Miss Delora?" he asked.

"Oh, no!" she answered. "He found the crossing very rough, and he is not very strong. But I do not think that he is really ill."

"It is a year since we last had the pleasure," the clerk continued.

She nodded.

"My uncle was over then," she remarked. "For me this is the first time. I have never been in England before."

The lift stopped.

"What floor are we on?" the girl asked.

"The fifth," the clerk answered. "We have quite comfortable rooms for you, and the aspect that your uncle desired."

We passed along the corridor and he opened the door, which led into a small hall and on into a sitting-room. The clerk opened up all the rooms.

"You will see, as I told you before, Miss Delora," he said, "that there is no one here. Your uncle's rooms open out from the right. The bathroom is to the left there, and beyond are your apartments."

She peered into each of the rooms. They were indeed empty.

"The apartments are very nice," she said, "but I do not understand what has become of my uncle."

"He will be up in a few minutes, without a doubt," the clerk remarked. "Is there anything more that I can do for you, madam? Shall I send the chambermaid or the waiter to you?"

"Not yet," she answered. "I must wait for my uncle. Will you leave word below that he is to please come up directly he arrives?"

"Certainly, madam!" the clerk answered, turning towards the door.

I should have followed him from the room, but she stopped me.

"Please don't go," she said. "I am very foolish, I know, but I am afraid!"

"I will stay, of course," I answered, sitting down by her side upon the couch, "but let me assure you that there is nothing whatever to fear. Your uncle may have had a slight cab accident, or he may have met with a friend and stopped to talk for a few minutes. In either case he will be here directly. London, you know, is not the city of mysteries that Paris is. There is very little, indeed, that can happen to a man between Charing Cross Station and the Milan Hotel."

She leaned forward a little and buried her face in her hands.

"Please don't!" I begged. "Indeed, I mean what I say! There is no cause to be anxious. Your uncle spoke of stopping at a chemist's. They may be making up his prescription. A hundred trivial things may have happened to keep him."

"You do not know!" she murmured.

CHAPTER XI

THERE was no doubt about it that Delora had disappeared. I followed the reception clerk downstairs myself within the space of a few minutes, and made the most careful inquiries in every part of the hotel. It did not take me very long to ascertain, beyond the shadow of a doubt, that he was not upon the premises, nor had he yet been seen by any one connected with the place. I even walked to the corner of the courtyard and looked aimlessly up and down the Strand. Within those few hundred yards which lay between where I was standing and Charing Cross something had happened which had prevented his reaching the hotel. It may have been the slightest of accidents. It might be something more serious. Or it might even be, I was forced to reflect, that he had never intended coming! Presently I returned to the suite of rooms upon the fifth floor to make my report to Miss Delora. I found her calmer than I had expected, but her face fell when I was forced to confess that I had heard no news.

"I am sorry," I said, "but there is no doubt that up to the present, at any rate, your uncle has not been here. I am quite sure, though," I added, "that there is no cause for alarm. A hundred slight accidents might have happened to detain him for half an hour or so."

She glanced at the clock.

"It is more than that," she said softly.

"Tell me," I asked, "would you like me to communicate with the police? They are in touch with the hospitals, and if any misfortune has happened to your uncle — which, after all, is scarcely likely — we should hear of it directly."

She shook her head vigorously. The idea, for some reason, seemed to displease her.

"No!" she said. "Why should we appeal to the police? What have they to do with my uncle? I am quite sure that he would not wish that."

"I presume," I said, "that nothing of this sort has ever happened before? — I mean that he has not left you without warning?"

"Not under the same circumstances," she admitted. "And yet, he has a very queer way of absenting himself every now and then."

"For long?" I asked.

"It depends," she answered. "Never for any length of time, though."

"After all," I remarked, "you cannot have seen such a great deal of him. He lives in South America, does he not, and you have never been out of France?"

"It is true," she murmured.

"I noticed," I continued thoughtfully, "that he seemed disturbed as we neared London."

She drew out the pins from her hat, and with a little gesture of relief threw it upon the table.

"Please sit down for a minute," she said. "I want to think."

She leaned forward upon the couch, her head buried in her hands. I felt that she desired silence, so I said nothing. Several moments passed, then there came a sudden and unexpected interruption. The bell of the telephone instrument, which stood between us upon the table, commenced to ring. Her hands fell from before her face. She looked across at me with parted lips and wide-open eyes. I made a movement towards the instrument, but she checked me.

"Stop!" she said. "Wait a moment! Let me think!"

She had risen to her feet. We stood looking at one another across the table. Between us was the telephone instrument and the bell which had just rung out its summons.

"Are you not going to answer it?" I asked.

"I am afraid!" she answered. "I do not know what has come over me. I am afraid! Take up the receiver. Tell me who it is who speaks."

"You are sure that you wish it?" I asked.

"At once!" she insisted. "They will have gone away."

The bell rang again. I took the receiver into my hands.

"Who is there?" I asked.

"Is that the apartment of Mr. Delora?" was the reply.

"Yes!" I said.

"I wish to speak to Miss Felicia Delora," the voice said.

"Who are you?" I asked.

"It does not matter," was the answer. "Be so good as to tell her to come to the telephone — Miss Felicia Delora."

I held the receiver away from me and turned to her.

"Some one wishes to speak to you," I said.

"Who is it?" she asked.

"The person gave no name," I answered.

"Did you recognize the voice?" she asked.

I hesitated.

"I was not sure," I said.   "It was like your uncle's."

She took the instrument into her hand. What passed between her and the person at the other end I had, of course, no means of telling. All I know was that she said, at short intervals, — "Yes! No! Yes! I promise!" Then she laid the instrument down and looked at me.

"The mystery is solved," she said. "My uncle has met some friends, and stayed with them for a little time to discuss a matter of business. I am sorry to have been so troublesome to you. My anxieties, of course, are at an end now."

I bowed, and moved toward the door.

"If there is anything else that I can do — " I said.

"I shall ask you," she answered, looking at me earnestly. "I shall, indeed."

"My number is 128," I said. "I am two floors above you. Please do not forget to make use of me if you need a friend."

"I shall not forget," she answered softly.

Then, as though moved by a sudden impulse, she held out her hand, — a small white hand with rather long fingers, manicured to a perfection unusual in this country. She wore only one ring, in which was set a magnificent uncut emerald. I held her fingers for a moment, and raised them to my lips.

"I shall be always at your service," I answered quietly, "however much — or however little you may care to tell me. Good night!"

I went to my rooms and washed. Afterwards I descended and ordered some supper in the café.

"Louis is not back yet?" I remarked to the waiter who attended to me.

"Not yet, monsieur," the man answered. "We expect

him some time to-morrow. Monsieur is also from Paris?"

I nodded, and did not pursue the subject. On my way back to my rooms half an hour later I stopped to speak for a few minutes with the hall-porter.

"Mr. Delora has not arrived yet, sir," he remarked.

"No!" I answered. "I dare say there has been some slight mistake. I fancy that he has telephoned to his niece."

The hall-porter looked a little puzzled.

"It is rather a curious thing, sir," he said, "but there seem to be a good many people who are wanting to see Mr. Delora. We have had at least a dozen inquiries for him during the last few days, and all from people who refuse to leave their names."

I nodded.

"Business friends, perhaps," I remarked. "Mr. Delora comes over to keep friends with his connections here, I suppose."

The hall-porter coughed discreetly but mysteriously.

"No doubt, sir," he remarked.

I went on my way to my rooms, not caring to pursue the conversation. Yet I felt that there was something beneath it all. Ashley knew or guessed something which he would have told me with very little encouragement. Over a final cigarette I tried to think the matter out. Here were these people, remarkable for nothing except the obviously foreign appearance of the man, and the good taste and beauty of the girl. I had seen them at every fashionable haunt in Paris, and finally at a restaurant which Louis had frankly admitted to be the meeting-place of people whose careers were by no means above suspicion. I had crossed with them to England, and if their presence on the train were not the cause for Louis' insisting upon my hurried departure from Paris, it at any rate afforded him gratification to think that I might, perhaps, make their acquaintance. During the whole of the journey neither of them had made the slightest overture towards me. That we had come together at all was, without doubt, accidental. I did not for a moment doubt the girl's first attitude of irritation towards me. It was just as certain that her uncle had shown no desire whatever to make my acquaintance. I remembered his curious agitation as we had reached London, his muttered excuse of sea-sickness, and his somewhat extraordinary conduct in leaving his niece alone with me — a perfect stranger — while he hurried off to the hotel at which he had never arrived. Presumably, if that was indeed he who had spoken to the girl upon the telephone, she understood more about the matter than I did. He may have given her some explanation which accounted for his absence. If so, he had obviously desired it to remain a secret. What was the nature of this mystery? Of what was it that he was afraid? Who was this young man who, after his departure, had taken so much interest in his niece and myself at Charing Cross? Was it some one whom he had desired to evade? — a detective, perhaps, or an informer? The riddle was not easy to solve. Common-sense told me that my wisest course was to fulfil my original intention, and take the first train on the morrow to my brother's house in Norfolk. On the other hand, inclination strongly prompted me to stay where I was, to see this thing through, to see more of Felicia Delora! I was thirty years old, free and unencumbered, a moderately impressionable bachelor of moderate means. Until the time when the shadow of this tragedy had come into my life, which had found its culmination in the little restaurant of the Place d'Anjou, things had moved smoothly enough with me. I had had the average number of flirtations, many pleasant friendships. Yet I asked myself now whether there was any one in the past who had ever moved me in the same way as this girl, who was still almost a perfect stranger to me. I hated the man, her uncle. I hated the circumstances under which I had seen her. I hated the mystery by which they were surrounded. It was absolutely maddening for me to reflect that two floors below she was spending the night either with some mysterious and secret knowledge, or in real distress as to her uncle's fate. After all, I told myself a little bitterly, I was a fool! I was old enough to know better! The man himself was an adventurer, — there could be no doubt about it. How was it possible that she could be altogether ignorant of his character?

Then, just as I was half undressed, there came a soft knock at my door. I rose to my feet and stood for a moment undecided. For some time my own personal danger seemed to have slipped out of my memory. Now it came back with a sudden terrible rush. Perhaps the man Tapilow was dead! If so, this was the end!

I went out into the little hall and opened the door. The corridors outside were dimly lit, but there was no mistaking the two men who stood there waiting for me. One was obviously a police inspector, and the man by his side, although he wore plain clothes, could scarcely be anything but a detective.

CHAPTER XII

FELICIA DELORA

I LOOKED at the two men, and they returned my gaze with interest.

"Are you Captain Rotherby, sir?" the inspector asked. I nodded.

"That is my name," I said.

"We shall be glad to have a few words with you, sir," he declared.

"You had better come inside," I answered, and led the way into my sitting-room.

"We have been sent for," the inspector continued, "to inquire into the disappearance of Mr. Delora, — the gentleman who was expected to have arrived at this hotel this evening," he added, referring to his notes.

To me, who with a natural egotism had been thinking of my own affairs, and had been expecting nothing less than arrest, this declaration of the object of their visit had its consolations.

"We understand," the inspector continued, "that you travelled with Mr. Delora and his niece from Folkestone to Charing Cross."

"That is quite true," I answered. "The guard put them in my carriage."

"Did you converse with them during the journey, sir?"

"The man was asleep all the way," I answered. "He never even opened his eyes till we were practically in London."

"You talked, perhaps, with the young lady?" the man inquired.

"If I did," I answered serenely, "it seems to me that it was my business."

The police inspector was imperturbable.

"When was the last time you saw this Mr. Delora?" he asked.

"At Charing Cross Station," I answered. "He left the carriage directly the train stopped and went to get a hansom. He had been sea-sick coming over, and was anxious to get to the hotel very quickly."

"Leaving his niece alone?" the man asked.

"Leaving her in my care," I answered. "We were all coming to the same hotel, and the young lady and I had been in conversation for some time."

"He asked you, then, to take care of her?" the man inquired.

"The request as he made it," I answered, "was a perfectly natural one. By the bye," I continued, "who sent for you?"

"We were advised of Mr. Delora's disappearance by the proprietor of the hotel," the inspector answered.

"How do you know that it is a disappearance at all?" I asked. "Mr. Delora may have met some friends. He is not obliged to come here. In other words, if he chooses to disappear, he surely has a perfect right to! Are you acting upon Miss Delora's instructions?"

"No!" the inspector answered. "Miss Delora has not moved in the matter."

"Then I consider," I declared, "that your action is premature, and I have nothing to say."

The inspector was temporarily nonplussed. My view of the situation was perfectly reasonable, and my assumption that there was some other reason for their visit was not without truth. The man in the plain clothes, who had been listening intently but as yet had not spoken, intervened.

"Captain Rotherby," he said, "I am a detective from Scotland Yard, — in fact I am the head of one of the departments. We know you quite well to be a young gentleman of family, and above suspicion. We feel sure, therefore, that we can rely upon you to help us in any course we may take which is likely to lead to the detection of crime or criminals."

"Up to a certain point," I assented, "you are perfectly right."

"There are circumstances connected with these people the Deloras, uncle and niece," the detective continued, "which require investigation."

"I am sorry," I answered, "but I cannot at present answer any more questions, except with Miss Delora's permission."

"You can tell me this, Captain Rotherby," the detective asked, looking at me keenly, "do you know whether Miss Delora has been in comumnication with her uncle since she reached the hotel?"

"I have no idea," I answered.

"There is a telephone in her room," the detective continued, without removing his eyes from my face. "We understand from the hall-porter that a message was received by her soon after her arrival."

"Very likely," I answered. "I should suggest that you go and interview Miss Delora. She will probably tell you all about it."

They were both silent. I felt quite certain that they had already done so. At that moment my own telephone bell rang. The two men exchanged quick glances. I took up the receiver.

"Is that Capitaine Rotherby?"

I recognized the voice at once. It was Miss Delora speaking.

"Yes!" I answered.

"I thought I should like to let you know," she continued, "that I am no longer in the least anxious about my uncle. He is always doing eccentric things, and I am sure that he will turn up, — later to-night, perhaps, or at any rate to-morrow. I do not wish any inquiries made about him. It would only annoy him very much when he came to hear of it."

"I am very glad to hear you say so, Miss Delora," I answered. "To tell you the truth, there are some men here at present who are asking me questions. I have told them, however, that you are the only person to whom they should apply."

Her voice, when she answered me, showed some signs of agitation.

"I have not asked the help of the police," she declared, "and I do not need it! They would have come to my rooms, but I refused to receive them."

"I quite agree with you, Miss Delora," I answered. "Good night!"

"Good night, Capitaine Rotherby!" she said softly.

I laid down the receiver.

"You have probably overheard my conversation," I said to the inspector. "After that, I can only wish you good night!"

He moved at once to the door in stolid, discontented fashion. The detective, however, lingered.

"Captain Rotherby," he said, "I cannot blame you for

your decision. I think, however, it is only fair to warn you that you will probably find yourself better off in the long run if you do not mix yourself up in this affair."

"Indeed!" I answered.

"There are wheels within wheels," the man continued. "I have no charge to make against Mr. Delora. I have no charge to make against any one. But I think that so far as you are concerned, you would be well advised to remember that these are merely travelling companions, and that even the most accomplished man of the world is often deceived in such. Good night, sir!"

They left me then without another word. I heard their footsteps die away along the corridor, the ring of the lift bell, the clatter of its ascent and descent. Then I undressed and went to bed.

I awoke the next morning rather late, dressed and shaved in my rooms, and descended to the café for breakfast. The waiter who usually served me came hurrying up with a welcoming smile.

"Monsieur Louis," he announced, "returned early this morning."

"He is not here now?" I asked, looking around the room.

The waiter smiled deprecatingly.

"But for the early breakfast, no, sir!" he said. "Monsieur Louis will come at one o'clock, perhaps, — perhaps not until dinner-time. He will be here to-day, though."

I unfolded my paper and looked through the list of accidents. There was nothing which could possibly have applied to Mr. Delora. I waited until eleven o'clock, and then sent up my name to Miss Delora. A reply came back almost at once, — Miss Delora had gone out an hour ago, and had left no word as to the time of her return.

Once more I was puzzled. Why should she go out unless she had received some news? She had told me that she had no friends in London. It was scarcely likely that she would go out on any casual expedition in her present state of uncertainty. I made my way to the manager's office, whom I knew very well, and with whom I had often had a few minutes' talk. He received me with his usual courtesy, and gave me a handful of cigarettes to try. I lit one, and seated myself in his easy-chair.

"Mr. Helmsley," I said, "you know that I am not, as a rule, a curious person, and I should not like to ask you any questions which you thought improper ones, but you have some guests staying here in whom I am somewhat interested."

Mr. Helmsley nodded, and by his genial silence invited me to proceed.

"I mean Mr. Delora and his niece," I continued.

The smile faded from the manager's face.

"The gentleman who did not arrive last night?" he remarked.

I nodded.

"I travelled up with them," I said, "from Folkestone, and certainly Mr. Delora's behavior was a little peculiar as we neared London. He seemed nervous, and anxious to quit the train at the earliest possible moment. I brought his niece on here, as you know, found that he had not arrived, and I understand that, up to the present, nothing has been heard of him."

"It is quite true," Mr. Helmsley admitted thoughtfully. "The matter was reported to me last night, and very soon afterwards an inspector from Scotland Yard called. I gave him all the information I could, naturally, but on reference to the young lady she declined to consider the matter seriously at all. Her uncle, she said, had probably met some friends, or had made a call upon the way. Under the circumstances, there was nothing else to do but to drop the matter, so far as any direct inquiries were concerned.

I nodded.

"But the man himself?" I asked. "What do you know of him?"

"I have always understood," Mr. Helmsley said slowly, "that he was a gentleman from South America who had large coffee plantations, and who came over every year to sell his produce. He has stayed at the hotel about this time for the last four years. He has always engaged a good suite of rooms, has paid his accounts promptly, — I really do not know anything more about him."

"Has his niece accompanied him always?" I asked.

"Never before," Mr. Helmsley answered, — "at least, not to my recollection."

"You do not know what part of South America he comes from?" I asked.

"I have no idea," Mr. Helmsley declared. "His letters are always forwarded to an agent."

"So practically you can tell me nothing," I said, rising.

"Nothing at all, I fear," Mr. Helmsley answered. "I shall make it a point of calling upon the young lady within an hour or so, to inquire again about her uncle."

"The young lady has gone out," I remarked. "I have just sent my own name up."

Mr. Helmsley raised his eyebrows. He, too, was surprised.

"Then she has probably heard something," he remarked.

"Perhaps," I answered. "By the bye, I understand that Louis is back."

"He came by the night train," Mr. Helmsley answered. "I scarcely expected him so soon. You will probably see him in the café at luncheon-time."

I took my leave of the manager and returned to my own side of the hotel.

"If Miss Delora should come in," I said to the hall-porter on my way to the lift, "please let me know. I shall be in my room, writing letters."

"Miss Delora came in just after you crossed the court-yard, sir," the man answered. "She is in her room now."

"Alone?" I asked.

"I believe that she came in with a gentleman, sir. Shall I ring up and ask for her?"

I hesitated for a moment. I was recalling to myself her statement that she had no friends in London whatsoever.

"Yes!" I answered. "Send up my name, and say that I should like to see her."

The man went to the telephone, and emerged from the box a moment later.

"Miss Delora would be much obliged," he said, "if you would kindly go to her room in a quarter of an hour."

I nodded, and turned away for the lift. The cigarette between my lips was suddenly tasteless. I was experiencing a new sensation, and distinctly an unpleasant one. With it was coupled an intense curiosity to know the identity of the man who was even now with Felicia!

CHAPTER XIII

LOUIS, MAÎTRE D'HÔTEL

I MEASURED out that quarter of an hour into minutes, and almost into seconds. Then I knocked at the door of the sitting-room, and was bidden enter by Felicia Delora herself. She was alone, but she was dressed for the street, and was apparently just leaving the hotel again. Her clothes were of fashionable make, and cut with the most delightful simplicity. Her toilette was that of the ideal Frenchwoman who goes out for a morning's shopping, and may possibly lunch in the Bois. She was still very pale, however, and the dark lines under her eyes seemed to speak of a sleepless night. I fancied that she welcomed me a little shyly. She dropped her veil almost at once, and she did not ask me to sit down.

"I hope that you have some news this morning of your uncle, Miss Delora?" I asked.

She shook her head.

"I have not heard — anything of importance," she answered.

"I am sorry," I said. "I am afraid that you must be getting very anxious."

She bent over the button of her glove.

"Yes," she admitted. "I am very anxious! I am very anxious indeed. I scarcely know what to do."

"Tell me, then," I said, "why do you not let me go with you to the police and have some inquiries made?

If you prefer it, we could go to a private detective. I really think that something ought to be done."

She shook her head.

"I dare not," she said simply.

"Dare not?" I repeated.

"Because when he returns," she explained, "he would be so very, very angry with me. He is a very eccentric man — my uncle. He does strange things, and he allows no one to question his actions."

"But he has no right," I declared hotly, "to leave you like this in a strange hotel, without even a maid, without a word of farewell or explanation. The thing is preposterous!"

She had finished buttoning her gloves, and looked up at me with a queer little smile at the corner of her lips and her hands behind her.

"Capitaine Rotherby," she said, "there are so many things which it seems hard to understand. I myself am very unhappy and perplexed, but I do know what my uncle would wish me to do. He would wish me to remain quite quiet, and to wait."

I was silent for a few moments. It was difficult to reason with her.

"You have been out this morning," I said, a little abruptly.

"I have been out," she admitted. "I do not think, Capitaine Rotherby, that I must tell you where I have been, but I went to the one place where I thought that I might have news of him."

"You brought back with you a companion."

"No, not a companion," she interposed gently. "You must not think that, Capitaine Rotherby. He was just a person who — who had to come. You are not cross with me," she asked, lifting her eyes a little timidly to mine, "that there are some things which I do not tell you?"

"No, I am not cross!" I answered slowly. "Only, if you felt it possible," I added, "to give me your entire confidence, it seems to me that it would be better. I will ask you to believe," I continued, "that I am not merely a curious person. I am — well, more than a little interested."

She held out both her hands and raised her eyes to mine. Through the filmy lace of her veil I could see that they were very soft, almost as though tears were gathering there.

"Oh! I do believe you, Capitaine Rotherby," she said, "and I would be very, very happy if I could tell you now all the things which trouble me, all the things which I do not understand! But I may not. I may not — just now."

"Whenever you choose," I answered, "I shall be ready to hear. Whenever you need my services, they are yours."

"You do trust me a little, then?" she asked quickly.

"Implicitly!" I answered.

"You do not mind," she continued, "that I tell you once more that I am going out, and that I must go out alone?"

"Why, no!" I answered. "If you do not need me, there is an end of it."

"You are very good to me," she said. "Perhaps this afternoon, if you have a few minutes to spare, we might talk, eh?"

"At any time you say," I answered.

"At four o'clock, then," she said, "you will come here and sit with me for a little time. Perhaps this evening, if you have nothing to do —" she asked.

"I have nothing to do," I interrupted promptly.

"I do not know how I shall feel," she said, "about going out, but I would like to see you, anyhow."

"I shall come," I promised her. "Some time within the next few days I must go down to Norfolk —"

"To Norfolk?" she interrupted quickly. "Is that far away?"

"Only a few hours," I answered.

"You will stay there?" she exclaimed.

I shook my head.

"I think not," I answered. "I think I shall come back directly I have seen my brother."

She lifted her eyes to mine.

"Why?" she whispered.

"In case I can be of service to you!" I answered.

"You are so very good, so very kind," she said earnestly; "and to think that when I first saw you, I believed — but that does not matter!" she wound up quickly. "Please come to the lift with me and ring the bell. I lose my way in these passages."

I watched her step into the lift, her skirts a little raised, she herself, to my mind, the perfection of feminine grace from the tips of her patent shoes to the black feathers in her hat. She waved her hand to me as the lift shot down, and I turned away . . .

At exactly half-past one I went down to the café for lunch. The room was fairly full, but almost the first person I saw was Louis, suave and courteous, conducting a party of guests to their places. I took my seat at my accustomed table, and watched him for a few moments as he moved about. What a waiter he must have been, I thought! His movements were swift and noiseless. His eyes seemed like points of electricity, alive to the smallest fault on the part of his subordinates, the slightest frown on the faces of his patrons. There was scarcely a person lunching there who did not feel that he himself was receiving some part of Louis' personal attention. One saw him in the distance, suggesting with his easy smile a suitable luncheon to some bashful youth; or found him, a moment or two later, comparing reminiscences of some wonderful sauce with a *bon viveur*, an habitué of the place. Such a man, I thought, was wasted as a *maître d'hôtel*. He had the gifts of a diplomatist, the presence and inspiration of a genius.

I had imagined that my entrance into the room was unnoticed, but I found him suddenly bowing before my table.

"The *Plat du Jour*," he remarked, "is excellent. Monsieur should try it. After a few days of French cookery," he continued, "a simple English dish is sometimes an agreeable relief."

"Thank you, Louis," I answered. "Tell me what has become of Mr. Delora?"

My sudden attack was foiled with the consummate ease of a master — if, indeed, the man was not genuine.

"Mr. Delora!" he repeated. "Is he not staying here, — he and his niece? I have been looking for them to come into luncheon."

"His niece is here," I answered. "Mr. Delora never arrived."

Louis then did a thing which I have never seen him do before or afterwards, — he dropped something which he was carrying! It was only a wine carte, and he stooped and picked it up at once with a word of graceful apology. But I noticed that when he once more stood erect, the exercise of stooping, so far from having brought any flush into his face, seemed to have driven from it every atom of color.

"You mean that Mr. Delora went elsewhere, Monsieur?" he asked.

I shook my head.

"They travelled up from Folkestone," I said, "in my carriage. At Charing Cross Mr. Delora, who had been suffering, he said, from sea-sickness, and who was certainly very nervous and ill at ease, jumped out before the train had altogether stopped and hurried off to get a hansom to come on here. It had been arranged that I should bring his niece and follow him. When we arrived he had not come. He has not been here since. I have just left his niece, and she assured me that she had no idea where he was."

Louis stood quite still.

"It is a most singular occurrence," he said.

"It is the strangest thing I have ever heard of in my life," I answered.

"Monsieur is very much interested, doubtless," Louis said thoughtfully. "He travelled with them, — he expressed, I believe, an admiration for the young lady. Doubtless he is very much interested."

"So much so, Louis," I answered, "that I intend to do everything I can to solve the mystery of Delora's disappearance. I am an idle man, and it will amuse me."

Louis shook his head.

"Ah!" he said, "it is not always safe to meddle in the affairs of other people! There are wheels within wheels. The disappearance of Mr. Delora may not be altogether so accidental as it seems."

"You mean — " I exclaimed hastily.

"But nothing, monsieur," Louis answered, with a

little shrug of the shoulders. "I spoke quite generally. A man disappears, and every one in the world immediately talks of foul play, of murder, — of many such things. But, after all, is that quite reasonable? Most often the man who disappears, disappears of his own accord, — disappears either from fear of things that may happen to him, or because he himself has some purpose to serve."

"You mean to suggest, then, Louis," I said, "that the disappearance of Mr. Delora is a voluntary one?"

Once more Louis shrugged his shoulders.

"Who can tell, monsieur?" he answered. "I suggest nothing. I spoke only as one might speak, hearing of this case. One moment, monsieur."

He darted away to welcome some new-comers, ushered them to their table, suggested their lunch, passed up and down the room, stopping here and there to bow to a patron, to examine the dishes standing ready to be served, to correct some fault of service. It seemed to me, as I watched him, that he did a hundred things before he returned. Yet in a very few moments he was standing once more before my table, examining with a complacent air the service of my luncheon.

"Monsieur will find the *petits carots* excellent," he declared. "My friend Henry, he tries to serve this dish, but it is not the same thing; no! Always the vegetables must be served in the country where they are grown. Monsieur will drink something?"

"A pint of Moselle," I ordered. "I dare not order whiskey and soda before you, Louis."

He made a little grimace.

"It is as monsieur wishes," he declared, "but it is a drink without *finesse*, — a crude drink for a man of monsieur's tastes. It shall be the Moselle No. 197," he added, turning to the waiter. "Do not forget the number. 197," he added, turning to me, "is an absolutely light wine, — for luncheon, delicious!"

We were alone once more. Louis bent, smiling, over my table.

"Monsieur is much interested," he said, "in the disappearance of an acquaintance, a passing travelling companion, but he does not ask of affairs which concern him more gravely."

"Of Tapilow!" I exclaimed quickly.

Louis nodded.

"Tapilow is in an hospital and he will live," Louis declared slowly, "but all his life he will limp, and all his life he will carry a scar from his forehead to his mouth."

I nodded meditatively.

"It is, perhaps," I answered, "a more complete punishment."

I fancied that in Louis' green eyes there shot for a moment a gleam of something like admiration.

"Monsieur has courage," he murmured.

"Why not?" I answered. "We all of us have a certain amount of philosophy, you know, Louis. It was inevitable that when that man and I met, I should try to kill him. I had no weapon that night. I simply took him into my hands. But there, you know the rest. If he had died, I might have had to pay the penalty. It was a risk, but you see I had to take it. The thing was inevitable. The wrong that he had done some one who is very dear to me was too terrible, too hideous, for him to be allowed to go unpunished."

"When he recovers," Louis remarked thoughtfully, "monsieur will have an enemy."

"A great man, Louis, once declared," I reminded him, "that one's enemies were the salt of one's life. One's friends sometimes weary. One's enemies give always a zest to existence."

Again Louis was summoned away. I ate my lunch and sipped my wine. Louis was right. It was excellent, yet likely enough to be overlooked by the casual visitor, for it was of exceedingly moderate price.

So Tapilow was not likely to die! So much the better, perhaps! The time might have come in my life when the whole of that tragedy lay further back in the shadows, and when the thought that I had killed a man, however much he had deserved it, might chill me. I understood from Louis' very reticence that I had nothing now to fear from the law. So far as regards Tapilow himself, I had no fear. It was not likely that he would ever raise his hand against me.

I dismissed the subject from my thoughts. It was just then I remembered that, after all, I had not gathered from Louis a single shred of information on the subject in which I was most interested. I almost smiled when I remembered how admirably he had contrived to elude my curiosity. The only thing which I gathered from his manner was that Mr. Delora's disappearance was un-expected by him. Never mind, the end was not yet! I ordered coffee and a liqueur, and laid my cigarette case upon the table. I would wait until Louis chose to come to me once more. There were certain things which I intended to ask him point blank.

CHAPTER XIV

LOUIS EXPLAINS

LOUIS returned of his own accord before long.

"Monsieur has been well served?" he asked genially.

"Excellently, Louis," I answered, "so far as the mere question of food goes. You have not, however, managed to satisfy my curiosity."

"Monsieur?" he asked interrogatively.

"Concerning the Deloras," I answered.

Louis shrugged his shoulders.

"But what should I know?" he asked. "Mr. Delora, he has come here last year and the year before. He has stayed for a month or so. He understands what he eats. That is all. Mademoiselle comes for the first time. I know her not at all."

"What do you think of his disappearance, Louis?" I asked.

"What should I think of it, monsieur? I know nothing."

"Mr. Delora, I am told," I continued, "is a coffee planter in South America."

"I, too," Louis admitted, "have heard so much."

"How came he to have the *entrée* to the Café des Deux Épingles?" I asked.

Louis smiled.

"I myself," he remarked, "am but a rare visitor there. How should I tell?"

"Louis," said I, "why not be honest with me? I am certainly not a person to be afraid of. I am very largely in your hands over the Tapilow affair, and, as you know, I have seen too much of the world to consider trifles. I do not believe that Mr. Delora came to London to sell his crop of coffee. I do not believe that you are ignorant of his affairs. I do not believe that his disappearance is so much a mystery to you as it is to the rest of us — say to me and to mademoiselle his niece."

Louis' face was like the face of a sphinx. He made no protestations. He denied nothing. He waited simply to see where I was leading him.

"I am not sure, Louis," I said, "that I do not believe that you had some object in taking me to the Café des Deux Épingles that night. Be honest with me. I can be a friend. I have influence here and there, and, as I think you know, I love adventures. Tell me what you know of this affair. Tell me if you had any motive in taking me to the Café des Deux Épingles that night?"

Louis looked around the room with keen, watchful eyes. Without abandoning his attitude of graceful attention to what I was saying, he seemed in those few moments to be absorbing every detail of the progress of the affairs in the restaurant itself. The arrangement of the service at some tables a little way off seemed to annoy him. He frowned and called one of his subordinates, speaking in a rapid undertone to him, and with many gestures. The man hurried away to obey his instructions, and Louis turned to me.

"Monsieur," said he, "there are many times when it is not wise or politic to tell the truth. There are many times, therefore, when I have to speak falsehoods, but I will confess that I do not like it. Always I would prefer the truth, if it were possible. When I saw you at the Opera in Paris I thought of you only as one of my best and most valued patrons. It was only as we stood there talking that another idea came into my head. I acted upon it. There was a reason why I took you to the Café des Deux Épingles!"

"Go on, Louis," I said. "Go on."

"I took you there," Louis continued, "because I knew that some time during the night Tapilow would come. Already I knew what would happen if you two met."

"You wished it to happen, then?" I exclaimed.

Louis bowed.

"Monsieur," he said, "I did wish it to happen! The person of whom we have spoken is no friend of mine, or of my friends. He had entered into a scheme with certain of them, and it was known that he meant to play them false. He deserved punishment, and I was content that he should meet it at your hands."

"Is that all, Louis?" I asked.

"Not all, monsieur," he continued. "I said to myself that if monsieur quarrels with his enemy, and trouble comes of it, it will be I — I and my friends — who can assist monsieur. Monsieur will owe us something for this, and the time may come — the time, indeed, may be very close at hand — when the services of monsieur might be useful."

"Come, Louis," I said, "this is better. Now I am beginning to understand. Go on a little further, if you please. I acknowledge your claim upon me. What can I do?"

"Monsieur likes excitement," Louis murmured.

"Indeed I do!" I answered fervently.

Louis hesitated.

"If there were some plot against this man Delora," he said, "to prevent his carrying out some undertaking, monsieur would help to frustrate it?"

"With all my heart," I answered. "There is only one thing I would ask. What is Mr. Delora's undertaking? — To sell his coffee?"

Louis' inimitable smile spread over his face.

"Ah!" he said, "monsieur is pleased to be facetious!"

Then I knew that I was on the point of learning a little, at any rate, of the truth.

"Mr. Delora has other schemes," Louis said slowly.

"So I imagined," I answered.

I saw Louis half turn his head. There was no change in his tone nor in his expression. Naturally, therefore, his words sounded a little strangely.

"My conversation with monsieur, for the moment, is finished," he said. "There is some one quite close who would give a great deal to overhear. It follows, therefore, that one says nothing. If monsieur will grant me a quarter of an hour at any time, in his room, after four o'clock —"

"At half-past four, Louis," I answered.

Louis gave a final little twist to my tablecloth and departed with a bow. I saw then that at the table next to mine, hidden from me, for the moment, by Louis himself, was seated the man who had stood by our side at Charing Cross!

After luncheon I took a taxicab, called on my tailor, looked in at the club, and bought some cigarettes. The whole of London seemed covered with dust sheets, to smell of paint. My club was in the hands of furbishers. My tobacconist was in his house-boat on the Thames. I met only one or two acquaintances, who seemed so sorry for themselves that their depression was only heightened by recognizing me. The streets were given over to a strangely clad crowd of pilgrims from other lands, —

American women with short coats, *pince nez*, and Baedekers, dragging along their mankind in neat suits and outrageous hats.   One seemed to recognize nothing familiar even in the shop-windows.   I was glad enough to get back to the Milan, especially so as in the lift I came upon Felicia.   She started a little at seeing me, and seemed a little nervous.   When the lift stopped at her floor I got out too.

"Let me walk with you to your room," I said.   "It is nearly four o'clock."

"If you please," she answered.   "I wanted to speak to you, Capitaine Rotherby.   There was something I forgot to say before I went out this morning."

I sighed.

"There is always a good deal that I forget to say when I am with you!" I answered.

She smiled.

"You, too!" she exclaimed.   "You are beginning to say the foolish things!   But never mind, we do not joke now.   I speak seriously.   Louis — Louis is back, eh?"

"Certainly," I answered.   "He was in the café at luncheon time."

"Capitaine Rotherby," she said, as we passed into her room together, "Louis is a very strange person.   I think that he has some idea in his head about you just now. Will you promise me this, — that you will be careful?"

"Careful?" I repeated.   "I don't quite understand; but I'll promise all the same."

She took hold of the lapels of my coat as though to pull me down a little towards her.   I felt my heart beat quickly, for the deep blue light was in her eyes.

"Ah, Capitaine Rotherby," she said, "you do not understand!   This man Louis — he is not only what he seems!

I think that he took you to the Café des Deux Épingles that night with a purpose. He thinks, perhaps, that you are in his power, eh, because you did fight with the other man and hurt him badly? And Louis knows!"

"Please go on," I said.

"I want you to be careful," she said. "If he asks you to do anything for him, be sure that it is something which you ought to do, — which you may do honorably! You see, Capitaine Rotherby," she went on, "Louis and his friends are not men like you. They are more subtle, — they have, perhaps, more brain, — but I do not think that they are honest! Louis may try to frighten you into becoming like them. He may try very many inducements," she went on, looking up at me. "You must not listen. You must promise me that you will not listen."

"I promise with all my heart," I answered, "that neither Louis nor any one else in the world shall make me do anything which I feel to be dishonorable."

"Louis is very crafty," she whispered. "He may make a thing seem as though it were all right when it is not, you understand?"

"Yes, I understand!" I answered. "But tell me, how did you get to know so much about Louis?"

"It does not matter — that," she answered, a little impatiently. "I have heard of Louis from others. I know the sort of man he is. I think that he will make some proposal to you. Will you be careful?"

"I promise," I answered. "May I see you again to-day? Remember," I pleaded, "that I am staying here only for your sake. I ought to have gone to Norfolk this afternoon."

She drew a little sigh.

"I wonder!" she said, half to herself. "I think, perhaps, — yes, we will dine together, monsieur, you and

I!" she said. "You must take me somewhere where it is quite quiet — where no one will see us!"

"Not down in the café, then?" I asked smiling.

She held up her hands in horror.

"But no!" she declared. "If it is possible, let us get away somewhere without Louis knowing."

"It can be arranged," I assured her. "May I come in and see you later on, and you shall tell me where to meet you?"

She thought for a minute.

"At seven o'clock," she answered. "Please go away now. I have a dressmaker coming to see me."

I turned away, but I had scarcely gone half a dozen paces before she called me back.

"Capitaine Rotherby," she said, "there is something to tell you."

I waited expectantly.

"Yes?" I murmured.

She avoided meeting my eyes.

"You need not trouble any further about my uncle," she said. "He has returned."

"Returned!" I exclaimed. "When?"

"A very short time ago," she answered. "He is very unwell. It will not be possible for any one to see him for a short time. But he has returned!"

"I am very glad indeed," I assured her.

Her face showed no signs of exultation or relief. I could not help being puzzled at her demeanor. She gave me no further explanation.

There was a ring at the door, and she motioned me away.

"The dressmaker!" she exclaimed.

I went upstairs to my rooms to wait for Louis.

CHAPTER XV

Louis appeared, as ever, punctual to the moment. He carried a menu card in his hand. He had the air of having come to take my orders for some projected feast. I closed the door of the outer hall and the door of my sitting-room.

"Now, Louis," I said, "we are not only alone, but we are secure from interruption. Tell me exactly what it is that you have in your mind."

Louis declined the chair to which I waved him. He leaned slightly back against the table, facing me.

"Captain Rotherby," he said, "I have sometimes thought that men like yourself, of spirit, who have seen something of the world, must find it very wearisome to settle down to lead the life of an English farmer gentleman."

"I am not proposing to do anything of the sort," I answered.

Louis nodded.

"For you," he said, "perhaps it would be impossible. But tell me, then, what is there that you care to do? I will tell you. You will give half your time to sport. The rest of the time you will eat and drink and grow fat. You will go to Marienbad and Carlsbad, and you will begin to wonder about your digestion, find yourself growing bald, — you will realize that nothing in the world ages a man so much as lack of excitement."

"I grant you everything, Louis," I said. "What excitement have you to offer me?"

"Three nights ago," Louis said, "I saw you myself take a man into your hands with the intention of killing him. You broke the law!"

"I did," I admitted, "and I would do it again."

"Would you break the law in other ways?" Louis asked.

"Under similar circumstances, yes!" I answered.

"Listen, monsieur," Louis continued. "It is our pleasure to save you from the unpleasant consequences which would certainly have befallen you in any other place than the Café des Deux Épingles after your — shall we say misunderstanding? — with James Tapilow."

"I admit my indebtedness, Louis," I answered.

"Will you do something to repay it?" Louis asked, raising his eyes to mine.

"You will have to tell me what it is first," I said.

"It is concerned with the disappearance of Mr. Delora," Louis said.

"But Mr. Delora has returned!" I exclaimed. "His niece told me so herself. He has returned, but he is very unwell — confined to his room, I believe."

"It is the story which has been agreed upon," Louis answered. "We were obliged to protect ourselves against the police and the newspaper people, but, nevertheless, it is not the truth. Mr. Delora has not returned!"

"Does mademoiselle know that?" I asked quickly.

"She does not," Louis admitted. "She has been told exactly what she told you, — that her uncle had returned, but that he was ill and must be kept quiet for a little time. It was necessary that she should believe his room occupied, for reasons which you will understand later. She shall be told the truth very soon."

I was conscious of a distinct sense of relief. The

thought that she might have told me a falsehood had given me a sudden stab.

"Where is Mr. Delora, then?" I asked.

"That we can guess," Louis said. "We want you to go to him."

"Very well, Louis," I said. "I am perfectly agreeable, only you must tell me who this Mr. Delora is, why he is in hiding, and who you mean when you say 'we'."

"Monsieur," Louis said, "if it rested with me alone I would tell you all these things. I would give you our confidence freely, because we are a little company who trust freely when we are sure. The others, however, do not know you as I know you, and I have the right to divulge only certain things to you. Mr. Delora has come to this country on a mission of peculiar danger. He has a secret in his possession which is of immense value, and there are others who are not our friends who know of it. Mr. Delora had a signal at Charing Cross that there was danger in taking up his residence here. That is why he slipped away quietly and is lying now in hiding. If monsieur indeed desires an adventure, I could propose one to him."

"Go ahead, Louis," I said.

"Let it be understood that Mr. Delora has returned. — As I have already told you, he has not returned. The door of his room is locked, and no one is permitted to enter. It is believed that to-night an attempt will be made to force a way into that room and to rob its occupant."

"The room is empty, you say? There is no one there?" I interrupted.

"Precisely, monsieur," Louis said, "but if some one were there who was strong and brave it might be possible to teach a lesson to those who have played us false, and who have planned evil things! If that some one were you, Captain Rotherby, we should consider — Monsieur De-cresson and the others would consider — that your debt to them was paid!"

I whistled softly to myself. I began to see Louis' idea. I was to enter, somehow or other, the room in which Mr. Delora was supposed to be, to remain there concealed, and to await this attack which, for some reason or other, they were expecting. And then, as the possibilities con-nected with such an event spread themselves out before me, my sense of humor suddenly asserted itself, and, to Louis' amazement, I laughed in his face. I came back from this world of fanciful figures, of mysterious robberies, of attempted assassinations, to the world of every-day things. It was Louis — the *maître d'hôtel*, the man who had ordered my *Plat du Jour* and selected my Moselle — who spoke of these things so calmly in my own sitting-room, with a menu card in his hand, and a morocco-bound wine list sticking out of his breast pocket. I was not in any imaginary city but in London, — city of tragedies, indeed, but tragedies of a homelier sort. It was not pos-sible that such things could be happening here, in an atmosphere which, through familiarity, had become almost commonplace. Was I to believe that Louis, my favorite *maître d'hôtel*, my fellow schemer in many luncheon and dinner parties, my authority upon vintages, my gastronomic good angel, was one of a band of conspirators, who played with life and death as though they had been the balls of a juggler? Was I to believe that there existed even in this very hotel, which for years had been my home, the seeds of these real tragical happenings which sometimes, though only half disclosed, blaze out upon the world as a revela-tion of the great underground world of crime? I found it almost impossible to take Louis seriously. I could not focus my thoughts.

"Louis," I said, "is this a great joke, or are you talking to me in sober, serious earnest?"

"I am talking in earnest, monsieur," Louis said slowly. "I have not exaggerated or spoken a word to you which is not the truth."

"Let me understand this thing a little more clearly," I said. "What has Ferdinand Delora done that he need fear a murderous assault? What has he done to make enemies? Is he a criminal, or are those who seek him criminals?"

"He carries with him," Louis said slowly, "a secret which will produce a great fortune. There are others who think that they have a right to share in it. It is those others who are his enemies. It is those others who hope to attain by force what they could gain by no other means."

A sudden inspiration prompted my next question.

"Was Tapilow one of those?" I demanded.

Louis nodded gravely.

"Monsieur Tapilow was one of those who claimed a share, but he was not willing to run the smallest risk," he assented.

"And for that reason," I remarked, "he is well out of the way! I understand. There is one more question, Louis, and it is one which you must answer me truthfully. You can imagine what it is when I tell you that it concerns mademoiselle!"

"Mademoiselle is innocent of the knowledge of any of these things," Louis declared earnestly. "She is a very charming and a very beautiful young lady, but if ever a young lady needed friends, she does!"

"Why is she here at all?" I demanded. "Why was she not left behind in Paris? If there is no part for her to play in this little comedy, it seems to me that she would have been much better out of the way."

"Captain Rotherby," Louis said, "there was a reason, and some day you will understand it — why it was necessary that she should come to London with her uncle. I can tell you no more. You must not ask me any more."

I looked into Louis' impenetrable face. I could learn nothing there. His words had left me partly unconvinced. Somehow I felt that the only time he had spoken the entire truth was when he had spoken of Felicia. Yet it was certainly true that I owed these people something, and I had no wish to shrink from paying my debt.

"Tell me," I said, "if I take Delora's place to-night, and if your scheme is successful, does that free him? Will he be able to come back? Will it be for the benefit of mademoiselle?"

"But most certainly!" Louis answered earnestly. "It is not an organization against which we fight. It is one or two desperate men who believe themselves robbed. Once they are out of the way, Delora can walk the streets a free man. There would be nothing," he added, "to prevent your seeking his friendship or the friendship of his niece."

"Very well," I agreed. "I will spend the night in Mr. Delora's rooms. I shall leave it to you to make all the arrangements."

Louis looked at me with a curious expression in his face.

"You understand, monsieur," he said slowly, "that there may be danger?"

"Naturally I understand," I said. "If it comes to a fight, I shall be prepared, and I have had a little experience."

"However well armed you may be," Louis said, "there will be a risk. Our enemies are swift and silent. One of them, at any rate, is an accomplished criminal. They are too clever for us unaided. I could take Mademoiselle Delora to Scotland Yard to-day, and I could tell them what we fear. They might patrol the hotel with the police, and even then you would wake in the night and find some one by your bedside."

"By the bye, Louis," I said, "why all this mystery? According to you, Delora is an honest man. Why don't you go to the police?"

Louis shook his head.

"We are not free to do that," he said. "Delora is honest, but it is a great secret which he controls, and the only chance of using it successfully is to keep it a secret from the whole world!"

"How am I to be introduced into the room, Louis?" I asked.

"That," he answered, "will be easy. There are two lifts, as you know, — one from the smoking-room and one from the entrance hall. The number of Mr. Delora's apartment is 157. Here, by the bye, monsieur, is a key."

I took it and put it in my waistcoat pocket.

"You will ascend by the lift from the smoking-room to the top floor," Louis continued. "You can then descend by the other lift to the fifth floor, and walk boldly into the sitting-room. The door on the right will be Mr. Delora's bedroom, and of that there will be, after midnight, a key upon the mantelpiece in the sitting-room."

"But Miss Delora?" I asked. "What of her? The sitting-room connects, also, with her apartments."

"Mademoiselle will be told something of this during the evening," Louis answered. "It will be better. She will have retired and be locked in her room long before it will be necessary for you to ascend."

"Very well," I said. "But now for the practical side of it. If anything really happens, what is to be my excuse for occupying those apartments to-night?"

"I will provide you with a sufficient one later on," Louis promised. "You will dine downstairs?"

"Possibly," I answered.

"In which case we can have a little conversation," Louis remarked.

"Louis," I said, "what sort of an affair is this, really, in which I am mixing myself up? Am I one of a gang of magnificent criminals, a political conspirator, or a fool?"

Louis smiled.

"Monsieur," he said, "I found you very weary of life. I will put you in the way of finding excitement. Monsieur should ask no more than that. There are many men of his temperament who would give years of their life for the chance."

He left me with his usual polite bow. I strolled after him down the corridor a moment or so later, but I just missed the lift in which he descended. Looking down, I saw that it had stopped at the fifth floor. It seemed as though Louis had gone to visit number 157!

CHAPTER XVI

TWO OF A TRADE

I SMOKED two pipes, one after the other, in a vain attempt to draw out some definite sequence of facts from the tangled web of happenings into which I seemed to have strayed. I came to the conclusion that Fate, which had bestowed on me a physique of more than ordinary size, a sound constitution, and muscles which had filled my study with various kinds of trophies, had not been equally generous in her dispensation of brains. Try as I would, I could make nothing of the situation in which I found myself. The most reasonable thing seemed to be to conclude that Louis was one of a gang of thieves, that I was about to become their accomplice, and that Felicia was simply the Delilah with whom these people had summoned me to their aid. Such a conclusion, however, was not flattering, nor did it please me in any way. Directly I allowed myself to think of Felicia, I believed in her. There were none of the arts of the adventuress about her methods, her glances, or her words. She did not, for instance, in the least resemble the young lady with the turquoises, who had also been good enough to take an interest in me! I gave the whole thing up at last. Perhaps by the morrow I should know more, — if, indeed, I thought, a little grimly, I knew anything! I could not help feeling that this little enterprise to which I had committed myself might turn out to be a serious affair. Even

Louis had not tried to minimize the risks. I felt, however, that if it led me to any better understanding of the situation, I could welcome whatever danger it involved.

A little before six o'clock I turned to look at the weather, which had been threatening all day, meaning to take a stroll. The rain, however, was coming down in sheets, so I descended instead to the little smoking-room, thinking that I might find there some one whom I knew. I had already ensconced myself in an easy-chair and ordered a whiskey and soda, when I became conscious that the very person with whom my thoughts were occupied was in the room and within a few feet of me.

Felicia was sitting on a couch, and by her side a man whom I recognized at once. It was the companion of my lady of the turquoises! Apparently they had not noticed my entrance. They continued for several moments to be unaware of it. Felicia was paler than ever. She seemed to be struggling, as she sat there, to conceal her fear and aversion for the man who leaned toward her, talking in rapid French, with many gesticulations. He was badly dressed in a travelling suit of French cut, with a waistcoat buttoned almost to the chin. A floppy black tie hung down over the lapels of his coat. His black moustache, which seemed to have suffered from the crossing, was drooping, and gave to his mouth a particularly sinister expression. He had a neck of unusual size, and the fat ran in ridges to the back of his scalp, worked up by his collar as he moved his head rapidly with every sentence. He seemed altogether unable to sit still or control himself. His boots — brown tops with narrow patent vamps — beat a tattoo upon the floor. No wonder that Felicia shrunk into the corner of her lounge! I felt that it was impossible for me to sit and watch them any longer. I rose to my feet.

Felicia saw me first, — then her companion. Felicia's first expression, to my intense joy, was one of relief. Her companion, on the other hand, darted towards me a perfectly murderous glance. I advanced toward them, and Felicia half rose.

"Capitaine Rotherby," she said, "oh, I am very glad to see you! This man here who sits by my side — he does not speak one word of English. Listen, I beg. Go and find some one in the café — you know whom I mean, I will not mention his name. Go and find him, and bring him here. Tell him that Bartot is here and is terrifying me, that he threatens all the time. Please bring him."

"I will go at once," I answered.

I bowed and turned away. Of Bartot I took no notice, though he rose at once and seemed about to address me. I hurried into the café, but it was a slack hour and there were no signs of Louis.

"Can you tell me where to find Louis?" I asked one of the waiters.

The man glanced at the clock and shrugged his shoulders.

"Perhaps in his office," he said, "but Monsieur Louis often goes out for an hour about this time."

"Where is his office?" I asked.

The man led me into the service room and turned to the left. He knocked at a closed door, and I heard a sleepy voice say —

"Come in!"

I entered, and found Louis in a tiny little sitting-room, curled up on a sofa. In his hand was a pocket-book and a pencil. He appeared to have been making memoranda. He sprang to his feet as I entered.

"Monsieur!" he exclaimed, putting away the pocket-book and rising to his feet.

"Sorry to disturb you, Louis," I said. "Miss Delora is in the little smoking-room, and Bartot is there, — just arrived, I suppose, from Paris. He is terrifying her. She sent me to fetch you."

I saw Louis' lips curl into something which I can only describe as a snarl. After that moment I never even partially trusted him again. He looked like a wild animal, one of those who creep through the hidden places and love to spring upon their prey unseen!

"So!" he muttered. "I come, monsieur. I come."

He followed me out and into the restaurant. As he passed along his features composed themselves. He bent courteously toward me. He even opened the door of the little smoking-room and insisted that I should precede him. I stood on one side then while he went up to the pair. I heard Felicia give a little murmur of relief. Bartot turned round fiercely. The two faced one another, and it seemed to me that unutterable things passed between them. They were like wild animals, indeed, — Louis silent, composed, serene, yet with a jaguar-like glare in his eyes, his body poised, as though to spring or defend himself, as circumstances might dictate. Bartot, who had risen to his feet, was like a clumsy but powerful beast, showing his fierce primitivism through the disguise of clothes and his falsely human form. To me those few seconds were absolutely thrilling! There was another man in the room, who continued writing as though nothing were happening. A couple of strangers passed through on their way to the bar, and seemed to see nothing except the meeting of Louis — the *maître d'hôtel* — with a possible client. Felicia had let fall her veil, so that her terror was no longer written in her face. She had separated herself now from Bartot, and with an involuntary movement I came

over to her side. Then the tension was suddenly broken.
It was Louis who showed his teeth, but it was with the
razor-edge of civility.

"Monsieur Bartot is very welcome," he said, speaking
in French. "Monsieur Bartot has promised so often to
make this visit, and has always disappointed us."

Bartot was no match for this sort of thing. His few
muttered words at first were scarcely coherent. Louis
bent towards him, always with the same attitude of polite
attention.

"If there is anything I can do," he said softly. "Monsieur has already, without doubt, selected his rooms. It
will give us great pleasure to see him in the café this
evening."

Bartot commenced to talk, but his voice was almost
inaudible, it was so thick with passion.

"I come to know what it means! It is not for pleasure
that I come to this villainous country! I come to know
what the game is! I will be told! Mademoiselle here —
she tells me that her uncle has been lost, and now that he
is ill. She will not let me see him!'"

Louis shrugged his shoulders.

"Alas!" he said. "That, I know, is quite impossible.
Monsieur Delora was taken ill on the voyage over. This
gentleman," he added, turning to me, "will bear me out
when I say this. He is now in bed, and a doctor is with
him. I am sorry, but it would not be possible to have
him disturbed."

"Then I wait!" Bartot declared, folding his arms.
"I wait till monsieur recovers!"

"Why not?" Louis asked. "It is what we most desire.
We will do our best to make monsieur comfortable here."

I felt Felicia's fingers press my arm. I glanced towards

her, and she made a motion toward the door. We moved off, unnoticed, and I rang the bell for the lift.

"Oh! Capitaine Rotherby," she exclaimed, "once more you have come to my help! I was so frightened at that man! He did speak to me so angrily, and he did not believe anything I told him. Indeed, it is true that my uncle is ill. You do not disbelieve that, do you, Capitaine Rotherby?"

The lift arrived a little opportunely for me. Then it stopped at the fifth floor.

"We must walk softly," she said. "My uncle is asleep, and the doctor says that he must not be wakened."

"You are going to have dinner with me?" I asked.

"I think so," she answered. "Yes, I think so! Let us go somewhere a long way off. Take me somewhere quiet, Capitaine Rotherby, where I shall not see any one I know."

"I will," I promised her. "Put on a high-necked gown and a hat. I will take you where there is plenty of music but few people. We will get a quiet table and talk. Indeed," I continued, "there are several things which I want to say to you, Miss Delora."

"And I," she murmured. "It will be delightful. But step gently, monsieur. He must not be awakened."

She pointed to that closed door, and I looked steadfastly into her eyes. It was not possible that she was acting. I was convinced that she believed that her uncle was really in the next room.

"I call for you here," I whispered, "at half-past seven."

"I shall be ready," she answered, "quite ready. You must not be late or I shall be impatient. Oh!" she added, with a little impulsive gesture," I am beginning to hate this place. I begin to long to escape from it forever. I look forward so much to going away, — the further the better, Capitaine Rotherby! I shall be ready when you come. Good-bye!"

CHAPTER XVII

A VERY SPECIAL DINNER

AT seven o'clock that evening I passed through the café on my way to the American bar. There was already a good sprinkling of early diners there, and Louis was busy as usual. Directly he saw me, however, he came forward with his usual suave bow.

"The table in the left-hand corner," he said, "is engaged for monsieur. I have also taken the liberty of commanding a little dinner."

"But I am not dining here, Louis!" I protested.

Louis' expression was one of honest surprise.

"Monsieur is serious?" he inquired. "It is only a short time ago that I was talking with Mademoiselle Delora, and she told me that she was dining with you here."

"I am dining with Miss Delora," I answered, "but I certainly did not understand that it was to be here."

Louis smiled.

"Perhaps," he remarked, "mademoiselle had, for the moment, the idea of going away for dinner. If so, believe me, she has changed her mind. Monsieur will see when he calls for her."

I passed on thoughtfully. There was something about this which I scarcely understood. It seemed almost as though Louis had but to direct, and every one obeyed. Was I, too, becoming one of his myrmidons? Was I, too, to dine at his café because he had spoken the word?

I made my way to number 157 precisely at half-past seven. Felicia was waiting for me, and for a moment I forgot to ask any questions, — forgot everything except the pleasure of looking at her. She wore a black lace gown, — beautifully cut, and modelled to perfection to reveal the delicate outline of her figure, — a rope of pearls, and a large hat and veil, arranged as only those can arrange them who have learnt how to dress in Paris. She looked at me a little anxiously.

"You like me?" she asked. "I will do?"

"You are charming," I answered. "You take my breath away. Indeed, mademoiselle, I have never dined with any one so charming."

She dropped me a little curtsey. Then her face clouded over.

"There is something I have to ask," she said, looking at me ruefully. "Do you mind if we dine downstairs?"

"Louis has already told me that it is your wish," I answered.

She picked up the train of her gown. I fancied that she turned away in order that I should not see her face.

"He was so disappointed," she murmured, "and he has been so kind, I did not like to disappoint him."

"How is your uncle?" I asked.

"I have not yet been allowed to see him," she answered, "but they tell me that he is better. If he has a good night to-night, to-morrow morning I may go to him."

"I certainly hope that he will have a good night!" I remarked. "Shall we go down?"

"If you are ready," she answered. "There, you shall carry my purse and handkerchief while I put on my gloves. To put them on is foolish, is it not, when one does **not** leave the place? Still, one must do these things."

"Your purse is heavy," I remarked, swinging it on my finger.

"I carry always with me much money," she answered. "It is my uncle's idea. Some day, I tell him, one of us will be robbed. He has always one or two hundred pounds in his pocket. I have there fifty or sixty pounds. It is foolish, you think?"

"I do," I answered. "It rather seems like asking people to rob you."

"Ah, well, they do not know!" she answered, stepping into the lift. "I am hungry, Capitaine Rotherby. I have eaten so little to-day."

"Louis has chosen the dinner himself," I remarked, "so we shall probably find it everything that it should be."

We found our way to the table which had been reserved for us, escorted by one of Louis' subordinates. Louis himself was busy in the distance, arranging the seating of a small dinner-party. He came up to us directly, however. The waiter was serving us with caviare.

"I hope you will enjoy very much your dinner," he said, bowing. "I have taken special pains with everything. Two dinners to-night I have ordered with my own lips from the chef. One is yours, and the other the dinner of our friend Monsieur Bartot."

He pointed to a table a little distance away, where Monsieur Bartot was already dining. His back was towards us — broad and ugly, with its rolls of fat flesh around the neck, almost concealing the low collar.

"Some day," I remarked, "our friend Monsieur Bartot will suffer from apoplexy."

"It would not be surprising," Louis answered. "He is looking very flushed to-night. The chef has prepared for

him a wonderful dinner. They say that he is never satisfied. We shall see to-night."

I looked away with a little gesture of disgust. Louis was
summoned elsewhere, a fact for which I was duly grateful.

"Tell me, Miss Delora," I said, "how long have you
known Louis?"

"Oh! for a very long time," she answered, a little
evasively. "He is wonderful, they all say. There is no
one quite like him. A rich man has built a great restaurant
in New York, and he offered him his own price if he would
go and manage it. But Monsieur Louis said 'No!' He
loves the Continent. He loves London. He will not go
so far away."

"Monsieur Louis has perhaps, too, other ties here," I
remarked dryly.

She looked at me across the table meaningly.

"Ah!" she said, "Louis — he does interest himself in
many things. He and my uncle always have had much to
say to one another. What it is all about I do not know,
but I heard my uncle say once that Louis very soon would
be as rich as he himself."

"Tell me how long you thought of staying in London?"
I asked.

"It is not sure," she answered. "My uncle's business
may be settled in a few hours, or it may take him weeks."

"The selling of his coffee?" I asked dryly.

"But certainly!" she answered.

"And from here you go to where?" I asked.

"Back to Paris," she answered, "and then, **alas, to**
South America, It is to be buried!"

"You have lived long in Paris?" I asked.

"Since I came there first to boarding-school," she answered. "A little child I was, with my hair in pigtails and

frocks to my knees. I have learned to think, somehow, that Paris is my home. What I have heard of South America I do not love. I wish very much that my uncle would stay here."

"There is no chance of that, I suppose?" I asked.

"I think not," she answered. "In South America he is a very important man. They speak of him one day as President."

"Had you any idea," I asked, "that he had enemies over here?"

She shook her head.

"It is not that," she said. "We will not talk of it just now. It is not that he has enemies, but he has very, very important business to arrange, and there are some who do not think as he thinks about it. Shall we talk about something else, Capitaine Rotherby? Tell me about your friends or relations, and where you live? I would like so much to know everything."

"I am afraid there is not much to tell," I answered. "You see I am what is called over here a younger son. I have a brother who owns the house in which I was born, and all that sort of thing, and I have had to go out into the world and look for my fortune. So far," I continued, "I can't say that I have been very successful."

"You are poor, then?" she asked timidly.

"I am not rich," I answered. "Still, on the whole, I suppose for a bachelor I am comfortably off. Then my brother has no sons, and his health is always delicate. I do not count on that, of course, but I might have to succeed him."

"Tell me his name?" she asked.

"Lord Welmington," I answered, — "the Earl of Welmington he is called."

THERE WAS THE SOUND OF A HEAVY FALL CLOSE AT HAND. I SPRANG TO
MY FEET. "BY JOVE, IT'S BARTOT!" I EXCLAIMED.

Page 135

"And you would be that," she asked naïvely, "if he died?"

"I should," I answered, "but I should be very sorry to think that there was any chance of it. I am going to find something to do very soon, probably at one of the embassies on the Continent. The army at home, with no chance of a war, is dull work."

"You play games and shoot, of course," she asked, "like all your countrymen?"

"I am afraid I do," I admitted. "I have wasted a good deal of time the last few years. I have made up my mind definitely now, though, that I will get something to do. Ralph — that's my brother — wants me to stand for Parliament for the division of Norfolk, where we live, and has offered to pay all my expenses, but I am afraid I do not fancy myself as a politician."

"I would come and hear you speak," she murmured.

"Thank you," I answered, "but I have other accomplishments at which I shine more. I would rather —"

I broke off in the middle of my sentence, attracted by a sudden little exclamation from my companion. There was the sound of a heavy fall close at hand. I sprang to my feet.

"By Jove, it's Bartot!" I exclaimed.

The man was leaning half across the table, his arms stretched out in an unnatural fashion, — the wine which he had overturned streaming on to the floor. His face was flushed and blotchy. His eyes were closed. He was groaning quite audibly, and gasping.

"*Empoisonné!*" he muttered. "*Empoisonné!*"

"Poisoned?" I repeated. "What does the fellow mean?"

I stopped short. A sudden realization of what he did

mean assailed me! He was desperately ill, there was no doubt about that. The word which he had uttered seemed likely to be his last for some time to come. They formed a sort of stretcher and carried him from the room. Felicia was sitting back in her chair, white to the lips. I was feeling a little queer myself. I called Louis, who had been superintending the man's removal.

"Louis," I whispered in his ear, "there were two dinners which you prepared yourself to-night!"

Louis smiled very quietly.

"You need have no anxiety, monsieur," he assured me, — "no anxiety at all!"

CHAPTER XVIII

CONTRASTS

WE sat out in the foyer and took our coffee. I did not suggest a visit to any place of entertainment, as I knew it was better for Felicia to retire early, in order that I might pass through the sitting-room to her uncle's room, unheard. The orchestra was playing delightful music; the rooms were thronged with a gay and fashionable crowd. Nevertheless, my companion's spirits, which had been high enough during dinner, now seemed to fail her. More than once during the momentary silence I saw the absent look come into her eyes, — saw her shiver as though she were recalling the little tragedy of a few minutes ago. I had hitherto avoided mentioning it, but I tried now to make light of the matter.

"I spoke to Louis coming out," I remarked. "The man Bartot has only had a slight stroke. With a neck like that, I wonder he has not had it before."

She found no consolation in my words. She only shook her head sadly.

"You do not understand," she said. "It is part of the game. So it goes on, Capitaine Rotherby," she said, looking at me with her sad eyes. "So it will go on to the end."

"Come," I said, "you must not get morbid."

"Morbid," she repeated. "It is not that. It is because I know."

"Do you believe, then," I asked, "that Bartot was poisoned?"

She looked at me as though in surprise. Her eyes were like the eyes of a child.

"I know it!" she answered simply. "There is not any question about it at all."

I listened to the music for several moments in silence. Once or twice I stole a glance at her. Notwithstanding a certain perfection of outline, and a toilette which removed her wholly from any suggestion of immaturity, there was yet something childish in the pale, drawn face, — in the eyes with their look of fear. My heart was full of sympathy for her. Such adventures as this one into which I seemed to have stumbled were well enough for men. She, at any rate, was wholly out of place in her present position! I had wild dreams at that moment. The wine and the music, and the absolute trustfulness with which she seemed, for the moment, to have committed herself to my keeping, fired my blood. I had thoughts of taking her hand in mine, of bidding her leave the hotel that night, that minute, with me, — of taking her away into the country, into some quiet place where we could be married, and where none of these things which terrified her could throw their shadows across her life! Yet barely had the thought come to me before I realized how impossible it all was. I, too, was an adventurer! If I were not actually in the power of these men, it was to them that I owed my liberty! My own spirits began to fall. It was a queer maze this into which I had been drawn.

The music changed its note. Even as we sat there its languorous, passionate rhythm passed away, to be succeeded by the quicker, cleaner notes of some old martial music. It came to me like a cold douche. I remembered that I had been — was still — a soldier. I remembered that my word was pledged to certain undertakings, and that after all I was fighting on her side. The momentary depression passed away. I found myself able to talk more lightly, until something of the old gayety came back to her also.

"Tell me," she said, as at last we rose to vacate our places, — "you spoke the other day of going down into the country."

"I am not leaving London just yet," I said decidedly.

If I had indeed made some great sacrifice, I should have been rewarded by the brilliant look which she flashed up at me. Her eyes for a moment were absolutely the color of violets. I heard people whisper as we passed by. We said very little more to one another. I left her at the lift, and she gave me both her hands with a little impulsive gesture which I had already learned to look for. Then one of those inexplicable moods seemed to take possession of her. As the lift shot away from me I saw that her eyes were full of tears.

I made my way back to the café. It was now almost deserted. All but one or two very late diners had gone, and the tables were being prepared for supper. Louis, however, was still there, sitting at the desk by the side of the cashier, and apparently making calculations. He came forward when he saw me enter, and we met by chance just as one of the under-managers of the hotel passed by.

"What can I do for you this evening, Captain Rotherby?" he asked, with his usual bow. "A table for supper, perhaps?"

"I want some coffee," I asked. "I want you to see that it is strong, and well made."

Louis turned and gave an order to a waiter. I sat down, and he stood by my side.

"Mademoiselle has gone to her room?" he asked.

"Five minutes ago," I answered.

"In an hour," he said, "it will be safe for monsieur to go to Mr. Delora's room. You need not pass through the sitting-room at all. There is a door into the bedroom connecting with the corridor. If mademoiselle hears anything, she will think that it is the doctor."

"I shall be quite ready," I answered. "There are only one or two things I want to ask you. One is this, what explanation is to be given of my occupying that room, if there is a row?"

"There will not be a row," Louis answered coolly. "If monsieur is hurt, I shall see to it that he is conveyed to his own apartment. If any one who attacks him, or tries to search the apartment, should be hurt by monsieur, I shall see, too, that they are removed quietly. These things are easy enough. The service through the night is almost abandoned. Monsieur may not know it, but on the floor on which he sleeps there is not a single servant."

"Supposing I ring my bell?" I asked.

"If it were answered at all," Louis said, "it would be by the lift man."

"On the whole," I remarked, "it seems to me that the residential side of the hotel is admirably suited to the nocturnal adjustment of small differences!"

Louis smiled.

"There has never been any trouble, sir," he said. "You see," he added, pointing to the clock, "it is now ten o'clock. In one hour monsieur should be there. I have ordered whiskey and soda to be put in the room."

"Shall I see anything of you, Louis?" I asked.

"It is not possible, monsieur," he answered. "I must be here until half-past twelve or one o'clock to attend to my supper guests."

I leaned back in my chair and laughed silently. It seemed to me a strange thing to speak so calmly of the service of the restaurant, while upstairs I was to lie quiet, my senses strained all the time, and the chances of life and death dependent, perhaps, on the quickness of my right arm, or some chance inspiration. I saw the usual throng come strolling in — I myself had often been one of them — actresses who had not time to make a toilette for the restaurant proper, actors, managers, agents, performers from all the hundreds of pleasure houses which London boasts, Americans who had not troubled to dress, Frenchwomen who objected to the order prohibiting their appearance in hats elsewhere, — a heterogeneous, light-hearted crowd, not afraid to laugh, to make jokes, certain to outstay their time, supping frugally or *au prince*, according to the caprice of the moment. And upstairs I saw myself waiting in a darkened room for what? I felt a thrill of something which I had felt just before the final assault upon Ladysmith, when we had drunk our last whiskey and soda, thrown away our cigarettes, and it had been possible to wonder, for a moment, whether ever again our lips would hold another. Only this was a very different matter. I might be ending my days, for all I knew, on behalf of a gang of swindlers!

"Louis," I said, "it would make me much more comfortable if you could be a little more candid. You might tell me in plain words what these men want from Delora. How am I to know that he is not the thief, and these others are seeking only their own?"

Louis was silent for a moment. He glanced carelessly

around the room to assure himself that there were no listeners.

"I can tell you no more, sir," he said, "for if I told you more, I should tell you lies. I will only remind you that you owe us a debt which I am asking you to pay, and that it is the uncle of mademoiselle whose place you are taking."

"I am not in the least convinced," I said, "that I am aiding the uncle of mademoiselle in allowing myself to be attacked in his place."

"As for that," Louis answered, "you shall be assured to-morrow, and, if you will, there is another adventure still to be undertaken. You shall go to see Mr. Delora, and be thanked with his own lips."

"There is some sense in that, Louis," I allowed, lighting another cigarette, "but I warn you I shall make him tell me the truth."

Louis smiled inscrutably.

"Why not, monsieur?" he said.

"Tell me this, at any rate, Louis," I asked. "What is it that you hope for from this evening? You believe that some one will break in with the idea of robbing or else murdering Mr. Delora. They will find me there instead. What is it you hope, — that they will kill me, or that I shall kill them, or what?"

"That is a very reasonable question," Louis admitted. "I will answer it. In the first place, I would have them know that they have not all the wits on their side, and if they plot, we, too, can counterplot. In the second place, I wish you to see the man or the men face to face who make this attempt, and be prepared, if necessary, to recognize them hereafter. And in the third place, there is one man to whom, if he should himself make the at-

tempt, I should be very glad indeed if harm came
of it."

"Thank you, Louis," I said, "I am not proposing to
do murder if I can help it."

"One must defend one's self," Louis said.

"Naturally," I answered, "up to a certain point. You
have nothing more to tell me, then?"

"Nothing, sir," Louis answered calmly. "I wish you
once more *bonne fortune!*"

I nodded, and left the café. Of the hall-porter I made
an inquiry as to the man who had had a fit in the café
earlier in the evening.

"The doctor has been to see him twice, sir," the man
told me. "It was a sort of apoplectic stroke, brought on
by something which he had eaten."

"Will he recover?" I asked.

"The doctor says it is serious," the man answered,
"but that with careful nursing he will pull round. We
have just sent a telegram to a lady in Paris to come
over."

I smiled as I rang the bell for the lift. So I might see
my lady of the turquoises again.

CHAPTER XIX

ARRIVED in my room, I changed my dress-coat for a smoking-jacket, and my patent shoes for loose slippers. Then I suddenly discovered that I had no cigarettes. I glanced at the clock. It was only half-past ten. I had still half an hour to spare.

I locked up my room and descended by the lift to the entrance hall. My friend the hall-porter was standing behind his counter, doing nothing.

"I wish you would send a boy into the café," I said, "and ask Louis to send me a box of my cigarettes."

"With pleasure, sir," the man answered. "By the bye," he added, "Louis is not there himself, but I suppose any of the others would know the sort you smoke, sir?"

"Not there?" I answered, glancing at the clock. "Ah! I suppose it is a little early for him."

"He will not be there at all this evening," the porter answered. "The second *maître d'hôtel* was here a few minutes ago, and told me so himself."

"Not there at all!" I repeated. "Do you mean to say that Louis has a night off?"

"Certainly, sir," the man answered. "He has just gone out in his morning clothes."

For a moment I was so surprised that I said nothing. Only a few minutes ago Louis had gone out of his way to tell me that he would be on duty that night in the café. All the time it was obviously a lie! He would not have deceived me without a reason. What was it? I walked to the door and back again. The hall-porter watched me a little curiously.

"Did you wish for Monsieur Louis particularly," he said, "or shall I send to Antoine for the cigarettes?"

I pulled myself together.

"Send to Antoine, by all means," I answered. "He knows what I want."

I took up an evening paper and glanced at the news. Somehow or other I was conscious, although I had had no exercise, of feeling unusually sleepy. When the boy returned with the cigarettes I thrust the box into my pocket, unopened. Then I went to the smoking-room on my way upstairs and drank a stiff brandy and soda. Of one of the junior waiters whom I met I asked a question.

"Do you know if Monsieur Louis will be here to-night?" I asked.

"No, sir!" he answered. "He has just left."

"Very well," I answered. "You need not mention my inquiry."

I gave the boy half-a-crown, and ascended once more to my room. I was feeling a little more awake, but, incomprehensible though it might seem, I began to have a curious idea concerning the coffee with which Louis had served me. I even remembered — or thought that I remembered — some curious taste about it. Yet what object could Louis have in drugging me just as I was on the point of entering into an enterprise on his behalf?

I had a spirit-lamp in my room, and I made myself

rapidly a cup of strong tea. Even after I had drunk it, I still felt the remains of the drowsy feeling hanging around me. It was now ten minutes to eleven, and I opened my wardrobe to find the only weapon with which I proposed to arm myself, — a heavily loaded Malacca cane, which had more than once done me good service. To my surprise it was not in its accustomed corner. I was perfectly certain that I had seen it since my return from Paris, and I proceeded to make a thoroughly methodical search. I left scarcely an inch of space in my rooms undisturbed. At last I was forced to come to the conclusion that the stick had gone. Either the valet or some one else must have borrowed it.

It was eleven o'clock by the time I had concluded my search, and there was no time for me to make any further inquiries. I locked up my rooms and descended to the fifth floor. The corridor was empty, and with the key which Louis had given me I opened the door of Mr. Delora's bedroom without difficulty. The room was in darkness, but the electric-light knob was against the wall. I turned it on quickly. There was neither any one in the room, nor any evidence of it having been recently occupied. Not satisfied with my first inspection, I looked into the wardrobe and lifted the curtains of the bed. Very soon I was assured that there was no one in hiding. I sat down on the edge of the bed and began to consider how to pass the time for the next hour or so. The whiskey and soda set out upon the table attracted my attention. I went over to it, struck by a sudden thought! First I poured out a little of the whiskey. It smelt harmless enough. I tried it upon my tongue. There was no distinctive flavor. Then I looked at the soda-water syphon. The top was screwed up tightly enough, and it easily came undone with the application of a little force. I examined the screw. I felt certain at once, for some reason or other, that it had been tampered with recently. I poured a little of the soda-water into a glass. It was quite flat, and when I tasted it it had a peculiar flavor. Something seemed to have been added to it which destroyed altogether its buoyancy. I screwed on the top again and whistled softly to myself. The whiskey and soda had been placed there by Louis. He had even gone so far as to call my particular attention to it. The coffee which I had drunk a little before had also been prepared by Louis. He was evidently taking no chances! It was his intention that I should be asleep when the intruder, whoever he might be, should enter the room. After all, it seemed that I was in for something a little more complicated in the way of adventures than I had imagined. I examined the lock of the door by which I had entered. It worked easily, and there was also a bolt on the inside. The door was by its side which led into the sitting-room. I also examined it, and I saw with satisfaction that there was at the top a narrow glass transept, which I carefully opened. The sitting-room was in darkness, so Felicia had evidently retired for the night. I sat down to wait!

The time dragged on slowly enough, as it might well have done under the circumstances. I was waiting for something, — I had not the least idea what, or in what form it would arrive. I heard the quarters chime one after the other until one o'clock. Then at last I heard the sound of a key in the outer door of the suite. I had already poured half the syphon of soda and a fair quantity of the whiskey out of the window. I now threw myself upon the bed, closed my eyes, and did my best to simulate a heavy sleep. The person who entered the apartments came up the little outer passage until he reached the door leading into my room. I heard that softly opened. Then there was a pause, broken only by my heavy breathing. Some one was in the room, and it was some one who had learned the art of absolute noiselessness. I heard no foot-steps, — not even a man's breathing. Suddenly there was the click of the electric light, and although I still heard nothing, I felt that some one had approached a little way towards the bed. I dared not open my eyes, but in a rest-less movement, which I felt I might safely make, I raised my hand to shield me, and caught a momentary glimpse of the person who was standing between me and the door. As I expected, it was Louis! He held the soda-water syphon in his hand, as though measuring its contents. I believe that he afterwards came and stood over me. I dared not open my eyes again, for I was none too good an actor, and I feared that he might not be deceived. The quantity of whiskey and soda, however, which I had apparently drunk, must have satisfied him, for he only stayed altogether about a minute in the room. Then he passed out into the sitting-room, closing the door behind him, and without noticing the open transept. I lay quite still, expecting that before long he would return. There were no signs of his coming, however, though through the transept I could see that the light in the sitting-room had been turned on. I rose softly from the bed and bolted both doors. If Louis were to make up his mind to return, it was better, after all, for him to discover that I had been deceiving him than to have him come upon me unawares!

From the top of a chair I was easily able to see through the transept into the sitting-room. At my first glance I thought that it was empty. Then, however, I saw Louis come in from the outer hall, as though from the door of Felicia's room. He came into the centre of the sitting-room and stood there waiting. He was in dark morning clothes, and there was no sign of that charming expression which his patrons found so attractive. His brows were contracted. His mouth seemed screwed together. His peculiar-colored eyes shone like gimlets. He seemed to be waiting impatiently — waiting for what? Once he moved a little, and glanced expectantly toward the open door of the sitting-room. For the first time a horrible fear gripped me. I could scarcely stand in my place. With both hands I held the cornice. My heart began to thump against my ribs. If it should be true! Then all of a sudden a little cry came to my lips, which Heaven knows how I stifled! My eyes were suddenly hot. There was a mist before them. I could see nothing, nothing save Felicia, who had entered the room in a dressing-jacket, with her hair still down her back. It was nothing to me, at that moment, that her eyes were round with fear, that she came as one comes who obeys the call of her master. I was so furious with anger that I had hard work to battle with the impulse which prompted me to throw open the door and confront them both.

"Louis, is this wise?" she murmured.

"There are times," he answered softly, "when one has to dare everything! Listen, Felicia."

"Yes?" she murmured.

"In a short time you will hear a soft knocking on the outside door. Take no notice. I shall open it. It will be some one to see your uncle. We shall talk in this sitting-room. I hope that nothing will happen, but if you hear the sound of blows or voices take no notice. Remain in your room till everything is quiet. Presently, if all is well,

I shall knock three times on your door. I may need your help."

"Very well," she answered. "And if you do not knock?"

He handed her a slip of paper.

"You have a telephone in your room," he said. "Ring up the number you will find there, and simply repeat the words which I have written."

"Is that all?" she asked.

"That is all."

"Louis," she said, — then she pointed in my direction, — "may I not go in just for one minute?"

"No!" he answered. "It is not wise."

"It seems unkind," she said, "to keep away from him all this time if he is ill."

"I did not know that you had so much affection for him!" Louis remarked.

"Why not?" she answered. "He was always kind to me, in his way."

There was a moment's pause. Then she spoke again, and her voice had in it a note of sharp inquiry.

"Louis, whose stick is that?" she demanded.

I raised myself a little higher. Upon the table, close to where Louis was standing, was a thick Malacca cane which I recognized at once.

"Mine!" Louis answered shortly.

"Are you sure?" she asked.

"Whose did you suppose that it was?" he demanded.

"Capitaine Rotherby was carrying one just like it," she declared. "I noticed it in the railway carriage."

"They are common enough," Louis answered. "This one, at any rate, is mine. Hush!"

They both, for a moment, seemed to be listening intently. Then Louis pointed to the door.

"Go back to your room," he said, in a low whisper. "Go back at once, and turn your key."

She stole away. When she was no longer in the room I could see more clearly, — I could take account of other things! Distinctly I could hear now the soft knocking upon the outer door!

CHAPTER XX

Louis disappeared from the room for the moment. I heard the outer door softly opened and closed. Then he came back into the sitting-room, followed by the man who had stood by our side at Charing Cross Station. The latter looked around the room quickly, and seemed disappointed to find it empty.

"I understood that Mr. Delora was here," he said.

"Mr. Delora is in his bedroom," Louis answered. "He is here, and perfectly willing to see you. But it is against the doctor's orders, and my instructions were that I was to warn you not to excite him. You must speak slowly, and you may have to repeat anything which you wish him to understand."

"Who are you?" the newcomer asked.

"I am Mr. Delora's servant," Louis answered.

The newcomer looked a little puzzled.

"Surely I have seen you before somewhere!" he exclaimed.

"It is very possible," Louis answered. "I am also a waiter in the café below, but I come from South America, and Mr. Delora, when he is over, is always kind to me. I spend most of my time, now that he is ill, up here looking after him."

The newcomer shook his head thoughtfully.

"What is your name?" he asked.

"Louis," was the quiet answer.

"Then, my friend Louis," the newcomer said, "understand me plainly. I am not here to be bamboozled, or to give you an opportunity for exercising any ability you may possess in the art of lying. I am here to see Delora, and if he is here, see him I will and must! If he is not here, well, it will come later. There is no roof nor any walls in London which will enclose that man and keep him from me!"

"Mr. Delora has no desire to hide himself from any one," Louis answered calmly.

"That is a statement which I may be permitted to doubt!" the visitor answered. "Is that the door of his sleeping chamber? If so, I am going in!"

He pointed to the door, through the transept of which I was looking into the sitting-room. Louis moved on one side.

"That is Mr. Delora's room," he said softly. "Perhaps you had better let me be sure that he is awake."

"You need not trouble," the other answered. "If he is asleep I shall wake him. If he is awake he will know very well that there is no escaping me."

He turned away from Louis. His hand was already outstretched toward the handle of my door. Then I saw Louis snatch the Malacca cane from its place and swing it behind his body. He was already poised for the blow — a blow which would have killed any man breathing — when I sprang to the ground and flung open the door.

"Look out!" I cried.

The newcomer sprang on one side. Louis, disturbed by my cry, lost his nerve, and the blow fell upon a small side table, smashing it through, and sending splinters flying into the air. Both men looked at me in the blankest of amazement. I came out into the sitting-room.

"You coward!" I said to Louis.

He shrank back against the wall. He still held the stick in his hand, but he showed not a sign of fight. The other man stood with clenched fists, as though about to spring upon him, but I stepped between them.

"In the first place," I said to the newcomer, "you had better look into that room. You will see that Mr. Delora is not there. I can assure you, from my own knowledge, that he has never been there. When you have finished, come back and tell me what you want with him."

Louis was still staring at me in amazement. The idea that I had discovered his attempt to make a cat's-paw of me was dawning upon him slowly, but knowing nothing of the transept, he could not account for my unexpected appearance. For once, at any rate, he had lost his nerve. I could see that he was shaking with fear.

"Come, Louis," I said, "put my stick down and talk like a man, if you can."

The stick fell from his fingers. He had scarcely strength enough left to hold it. Then the man who had been examining Delora's room came back and stepped past Louis up to me.

"I do not know why you are here, sir," he said. "You may be mixed up in this affair or you may not be. But if you are, let me warn you that you are on the wrong side. You saw his attempt?" he added, pointing to Louis. "I am going to wring the life out of him. He deserves it."

"No!" I answered, holding him back. "We will have no violence here. Louis has a little account to settle with me yet."

"He has a more serious one with me," the other muttered.

"Settle it when and where you will," I said, "but not

here. As for me, I have no longer any interest in or concern with any of you. I came into this thing by accident, and to-night I go out of it. You, sir, must leave the hotel at once. I do not know your name or anything about you. It is not my concern. If you have anything to say to Louis, choose another time."

He looked at me curiously. I could see that with every nerve in his body he was longing to spring upon Louis.

"You seem to be a masterful person, sir," he said. "Why should I obey you?"

"Because I saved your life, for one thing," I answered, "and because I will allow no violence in this room, for another. And if you need a third reason," I added, "because I have the advantage of you in strength. You need not be afraid of my further interference," I continued. "I shall leave London to-morrow, and I hope that I may never see one of you again. Now will you go?"

"Yes, I will go!" he said. "Let me tell you this, sir," he added, as he neared the door. "Your decision is a wise one. If you knew whose cause you had been aiding, whose tool you had very nearly become, I think that your manner would be a little more apologetic."

"I have your word, sir, that you will leave the hotel?" I asked.

"At once," the other answered.

We heard him close the outer door and depart. Then I turned to Louis.

"Louis," I said, "so this is your adventure! This is the way you proposed to make use of me! You got me into that room and drugged me. I was to lie there while you murdered that man with my weapon. Then you would creep away, and in the morning there was I and the dead man! I was to be the tool, — the girl there the lure. It was well worked out, Louis, but it was a coward's plan and a coward's trick!"

I reached out my hand and took him by the collar. I felt as though I were grasping some unclean insect, from whom the sting might shoot out at any moment.

"Have you anything to say?" I asked.

"You do not understand," he said, in a low tone. "I did not mean to put this thing upon you. I meant, perhaps, to disable that man who has just left. If you knew his history and mine, you would not wonder at it. But I meant to see that he was safely removed."

"Then why did you bring me down into that room," I asked, "under a false pretence? Why did you use that murderous cane of mine for your crime? Why did you insist upon it that I should be seen dining with the girl — God knows who she is! — who is in that room?"

"I can explain everything," Louis said. "I am confused! I cannot help it — you came so unexpectedly!"

"Unexpectedly indeed," I answered, "because I poured your whiskey and soda out of the window, and because I took an antidote to your coffee!"

"You speak of things which I do not understand," Louis declared.

"Oh! tell me no more lies!" I exclaimed. "Listen! You see I have you by the collar, and I have my cane. Now I am going to beat you till every bone in your body aches, till you will not be able to crawl about, until you tell me the real history of these things. For every lie — if I know it to be a lie — I shall strike you. Tell me who that man Delora is? Tell me who the girl is, posing as his niece, who meets you here after midnight? Tell me the name of that man who has just left us? Tell me how you are all bound together, and what your quarrel is? And tell me where Delora is now?"

"I have no strength," he gasped. "You are too rough. Let me sit down quietly. I must think."

"No!" I answered. "Speak! Speak now!"

I raised the stick as though to strike him. Then I saw a sudden change in his face. I looked toward the door. Almost as I did so I heard the faint flutter of moving draperies. Felicia stood there looking in upon us, her hands uplifted, her face full of terror.

"It is Capitaine Rotherby!" she cried. "Tell me, then, what has happened? Capitaine Rotherby!"

She came a little toward us, but I think that she read in my face something of what I was feeling, for she stopped suddenly and her lips quivered.

"What has happened?" she demanded. "Will neither of you tell me? Is my uncle worse? Has any one — any one tried to do him an injury?"

"Nothing is the matter," I answered, "except that we have come to an end of this tissue of lies and plots and counterplots. There is no uncle of yours in that room, nor ever has been. The man who was to have been murdered here has gone. And for the rest, I saw you here with Louis and I heard your conversation less than an hour ago."

"You saw us?" she gasped.

"From the transept there," I answered, pointing towards it. "I was brought into that room to personate your uncle, to receive an attack which was meant for him — a very clever scheme! I was drugged, and was to have lain there to cover this fellow's crime. But there, I don't suppose that I need tell you any of these things!" I added brutally.

She looked at me with horror.

"You do not believe —" she gasped.

"Oh! I believe nothing," I answered, — "nothing at all! Every word I have been told by both of you is a lie! Your lives are lies! God knows why I should ever have believed otherwise!" I said, looking at her.

"Let me go," Louis pleaded, "and you shall hear the truth."

"I shall be more likely to feel the knife you have in your pocket," I answered contemptuously, for I had seen his left hand struggling downward for the last few moments. "Oh! I'll let you go! I have no interest in any of you, — no interest in your cursed conspiracy, whatever it may be! Keep your story. I don't care to hear it. Lie there and talk to your accomplice!"

I sent him reeling aross the room till he fell in the corner. Then I walked out, closing the sitting-room door behind me, — out into the corridor and up the stairs into my own room. Then I locked and bolted my own door and looked at my watch. It was a quarter to three. I took a Bradshaw from my bookcase, packed a few clothes myself, set an alarm clock for seven o'clock in the morning, and turned into bed. I told myself that I would not think. I told myself that there was no such person in the world as Felicia, that she had never lived, that she was only part of this nightmare from which I was freeing myself! I told myself that I would go to sleep, and I stayed awake until daylight. All the time there was only one thought in my brain!

CHAPTER XXI

A CHANGE OF PLANS

AT a few minutes past nine on the following morning, I was standing outside the front door of the Court watching the piling of my luggage on to a four-wheel cab. The hall-porter stood by my side, superintending the efforts of his myrmidons.

"You had better send my letters on," I told him. "I am going down into Norfolk for several weeks, — perhaps longer."

"Very good, sir," he answered. "By the bye," he added, turning away, "this morning's letters have just arrived. There was one for you, I think."

He handed it to me, and I tore it open as I stepped on to the pavement. It was written from Feltham Court, Norfolk, and dated the previous day.

MY DEAR AUSTEN,

I send you a hurried line in case you should be thinking of coming down here. I have decided to come up to London for a few weeks, and have lent the Court to Lady Mary, with the exception of the shooting, which is reserved for you. If you are in town, do look me up at Claridge's.

Ever yours,

RALPH.

I was on the point of having the cab unloaded and reconsidering my plans. Suddenly, however, like an inspiration there flashed into my mind the thought that it would not, perhaps, be such a very bad thing if, under the circumstances, I kept my altered plans to myself. So I stuffed the letter into my pocket and stepped into the four-wheeler.

"You understand, Ashley?" I said. "Send everything on to Feltham Court, — cards, letters, or anything."

"Perfectly, sir," the man answered. "I hope you will have a pleasant time, sir."

"Tell the cabman Liverpool Street," I ordered, and got in.

We rolled out of the courtyard, and I drove all the way to Liverpool Street as though to catch my train. Arrived there, however, I deposited my luggage in the cloak-room and drove back to Claridge's in a hansom. I found that my brother was installed in a suite of rooms there, and his servant, who came into the sitting-room to me at once, told me that he believed they were up for at least a month.

"His Lordship has nearly finished dressing, sir," he added. "He will be in, in a few minutes."

I took up the morning paper, but found nothing of interest there. Then my brother came in, leaning heavily on two sticks, and moving slowly. He was not more than ten years older than I was, but the shock of his accident and subsequent sufferings had aged him terribly. His hair had gone prematurely gray, and his face was deeply lined. I stepped forward and took him by the hand.

"My dear Ralph," I said, "this is really first-class. The last time I saw you, you scarcely expected to be out of your bath-chair in six months."

"I am getting on, Austen," he answered, "thanks! I am getting on. I will sit in that easy-chair for a few minutes. Thanks! Then we will have some breakfast."

"I was starting for Feltham this morning," I told him, "when I got your letter."

"When did you get back from Paris?" he asked.

"Three or four days ago," I answered.

He raised his eyebrows.

"I know that I ought to have come at once," I said, "but there were several things in London. I found it hard to get away."

"Well?" he said.

"I met Tapilow face to face at a little French café," I told him. "They tell me that he will recover, but he is maimed and scarred for life."

My brother showed no excitement — scarcely, even, any interest in my information. His face, however, had darkened.

"I am glad that you did not kill him outright," he said. "Tell me, are you likely to get into any trouble for this?"

"No!" I assured him. "The affair happened in a very dubious sort of place. I don't think I shall hear anything more about it unless from Tapilow himself."

Ralph nodded.

"We will close the chapter," he said.

"You have no news —"

"None!" he interrupted me, shortly. "We will close the chapter."

So I spoke to him no more on his own affairs. His servant brought in the letters and papers, poked the fire, and announced that breakfast was ready.

"You will have something, Austen?" he asked.

"I have only had a continental breakfast," I answered. "I dare say I can manage to eat something."

"I have a letter from Dicky," he remarked, later on. "Asks me to be civil, if I can, to some people who have been remarkably kind to him out in Brazil. They have an estate there."

I nodded.

"Dicky doing all right?" I asked.

"Seems to be," Ralph answered.

Dicky was our younger brother, and rather a wanderer.

"What is the name of the people who are coming over?" I asked.

"Some odd name," Ralph answered, — "Delora, I think."

Ralph had drawn the *Times* towards him, and he did not notice my start. I sat looking at him in blank amazement.

"Ralph!" I said presently.

My brother looked up.

"Have you got Dicky's letter on you?" I asked.

He passed it over to me. I skimmed through the first part until I came to the sentence which interested me.

I have been out staying at an awfully fine estate here, right on the Pampas. It belongs to some people called Delora. One of the brothers is just off to Europe, on some Government business, and will be in London for a few days with his niece, I expect. He is going to stay at the Milan Hotel, and it would be awfully good of you if you would look him up, or drop him a line. They really have been very kind to me out here.

I pushed the letter back to Ralph.

"Have you done anything yet," I asked, "about this?"

Ralph shook his head.

"I thought you would not mind calling for me," he remarked. "I would like to be civil to any one who has done anything for Dicky. If he shoots, you might take him down to the Court. Mary's there, of course, but that would not matter. There is the whole of the bachelor wing at your disposal."

I nodded.

"I will look after it for you," I said. "You can leave it in my hands. It is rather an odd thing, but I believe that I have met this man in Paris."

My brother was not much interested. I was glad of the excuse to bury myself in the pages of the *Daily Telegraph*. Here at last, then, was something definite. The man Delora was not a fraud. He was everything that he professed to be — a wealthy man, without a doubt. I suddenly began to see things differently. What a coward I had been to think of running away! After all, there might be some explanation, even, of that meeting between the girl and Louis.

We finished our breakfast, and my brother hobbled over to the window. For several minutes he remained there, looking out upon the street with the aimless air of a man who scarcely knows what to do with his day.

"What are you thinking of doing, Austen?" he asked me.

"I had no plans," I answered. "Some part of the day I thought I would look up these people — the Deloras."

Ralph nodded and turned to his servant.

"Goreham," he said, "I will have the motor in an hour. Come and dine with me, will you, Austen?" he said, turning to me. "I don't suppose you will go down to Feltham for a day or two."

"I will come, with pleasure," I answered. "Where are you going to motor to?"

Ralph answered a little vaguely. He had some calls to make, and he was not altogether sure. I left him in a few minutes and descended to the street. I turned westward and walked for some little distance, when suddenly 1 was attracted by the sight of a familiar figure issuing from the door of a large, gray stone house. We came face to face upon the pavement. It was the man whose life I had probably saved only a few hours ago.

He lifted his hat, and his dark eyes sought mine interrogatively.

"You were not, by chance, on the way to call upon me?" he asked.

I shook my head.

"Not only," I answered, "was I ignorant of where you lived, but I do not even know your name."

"Both matters," he remarked quietly, "are unimportant."

I glanced at the house from which he had issued.

"It would seem," I remarked, "that you have diplomatic connections."

"Why not?" he answered. "Indeed," he continued thoughtfully, "I do not see, Captain Rotherby, why my name should remain a secret to you."

He drew a card from his pocket, and handed it to me. I read it with ill-concealed curiosity.

MR. ALFONSE LAMARTINE

Brazilian Legation.

12, Porchester Square.

"You are a South American?" I asked quickly.

"By birth," he answered. "I have lived chiefly in Paris, and here in London."

"You knew Mr. Delora at Brazil, then?" I asked.

"I know the family quite well," he answered. "They are very influential people. I have told you my name,

Captain Rotherby," he continued, "because I see no reason why we two should not be frank with one another. I am of necessity interested in the movements and doings of Mr. Delora and his niece. You," he continued, "appear to have been drawn a little way into the mesh of intrigue by which they are surrounded."

I drew my arm through his. We were walking now side by side.

"Look here," I said, "you were quite right in what you said. There is no reason why we should have secrets from one another. Tell me about these people, and why on earth they have any connections at all with persons of the class of Louis and those others."

My companion spread out his hand. He stopped short on the pavement, and gesticulated violently.

"It is you who ask me these things!" he exclaimed. "Yet it is from you I hoped to obtain information. I know nothing, — absolutely nothing! Simply my instructions were to meet Mr. Delora on his arrival in London, to show him every possible civility, and to assist him in any purpose where my help would be useful. I go to meet him — he has disappeared! I haunt his rooms — he has not returned! His niece knows nothing. I try to force my way into his rooms, and my life is attempted!"

"Wait a moment," I said. "You spoke of instructions. From whom do you receive them?"

"From my government," he answered a little shortly. "Mr. Delora has some private business of importance here in England, in which they are interested."

"Do you know anything of his niece?" I asked.

" Nothing whatever," the young man answered, "except that she seems a very charming young lady, and will, I believe, inherit a great fortune."

"Do you know of any enemies that he might have?"
I asked. "For instance, is this business of his connected
with any affairs which might bring him into touch with
such people as Louis and his associates?"

"I will be frank with you," the young man said. "I
do not know what his business was. Neither, curiously
enough, does my chief. My instructions simply were to
meet him, and to see him day by day. You yourself can
judge how well I have succeeded!"

"Have you been to the police?" I asked.

"I have not," Lamartine answered. "We have written
out to Brazil explaining the circumstances, and asking for
a cablegram in reply. By the bye," he continued, a little
diffidently, "did it strike you last night that Miss Delora
must have been associated with that blackguard Louis in
his little attempt upon me?"

"I do not believe anything of the sort!" I answered
shortly.

The young man smiled cynically.

"It is perhaps natural," he answered.

"You are not seriously suggesting," I asked, "that a
young lady in the position of Miss Delora would descend
to scheming with a head-waiter?"

"Captain Rotherby," my companion said, "I do not
know anything. I do not understand anything. I only
know that the Delora business has puzzled me, — has
puzzled my chief. We have important communications
for Mr. Delora, and he cannot be found."

"It is not possible," I declared, "for a man to disappear
in London."

"A man may disappear anywhere," Lamartine said
dryly, "when such people as Louis are interested in him!
However, we do no good by comparing notes when we

neither of us know anything. If I should gain any information of Mr. Delora's whereabouts — "

I gave him my card quickly.

"We will exchange our news," I assured him. "It is a promise."

He bowed, and left me with a little farewell wave of the hand.

CHAPTER XXII

A FORMAL CALL

I CHANGED my mind about calling at the Milan that morning, but toward five o'clock in the afternoon I presented myself there, and gave the hall-porter my card to send up to Miss Delora. He received me with some surprise, but I explained that I had been obliged to postpone my visit into the country.

"Miss Delora has asked twice about you this morning, sir," he announced. "I gave her your country address."

"Quite right," I answered. "By the bye, is Mr. Delora visible yet?"

"Not yet, sir," the man answered. "Rather a curious thing about his return, sir," he added. "Not a soul has even seen him yet."

I nodded, but made no remark. Presently the boy who had taken my card up returned.

"Miss Delora would be glad if you would step upstairs, sir," he announced.

I followed him into the lift and up to number 157. Felicia was there alone. She rose from the couch as I entered, and waited until the door had closed behind the disappearing page. Then she held out her hands, and there was something in her eyes which I could not resist. I was suddenly ashamed of all my suspicions.

"So you have come back," she said softly. "That is very kind of you, Capitaine Rotherby. I have been lonely — very lonely, indeed."

"I have come back," I answered, taking her hands into mine and holding them for a moment.

"I am nervous all the time, and afraid," she continued, standing close by my side and looking up. "Only think of it, Capitaine Rotherby, — it is this journey to London to which I have been looking forward for so many, many years, and now that it has come I am miserable!"

"Your uncle — " I asked.

"They told me what was not true!" she exclaimed. "He is not back. I am here all alone. He does not come to me, and he will not let me go to him. But you will sit down, Capitaine Rotherby?" she added. "You are not in a hurry? You are not going away again?"

"Not just yet, at any rate," I admitted. "Do you know that after all this is a very small world! I have come to pay you a formal call on behalf of my brother who is an invalid."

Her eyes grew round with surprise.

"But I do not understand!" she said.

I told her of my brother's letter from South America. She listened with interest which seemed mingled with anxiety.

"It is very strange," she said, when I had finished, — "very delightful, too, of course!" she added hurriedly. "Tell me, is it my uncle Maurice or my uncle Ferdinand of whom your brother spoke most in his letter?"

"He did not mention the Christian names of either," I told her. "He simply said that one of the Mr. Deloras and his niece were coming to London, and he begged us to do all we could to make their visit pleasant. Do you know," I continued, "that as I came along I had an idea?"

"Yes?" she exclaimed.

"Why should n't you come down into the country," I said, "to my aunt's? She will send you a telegram at once if I tell her to, and we could all stay together down at Feltham, — my brother's house in Norfolk. You are out of place here. You are not enjoying yourself, and you are worried to death. Beside which," I added more slowly, "you are mixed up with people with whom you should have nothing whatever to do."

"If only I could!" she murmured. "If only I could!"

"Why not?" I said. "Mr. Delora comes here with an introduction which precludes my criticising his friends or his connections, however strange they may be, but it is very certain that you ought not to be left here alone to rely upon the advice of a head-waiter, to be practically at the beck and call of men of whose existence you should be unconscious. I want you to make up your mind and come away with me."

A little flush of color stole into her cheeks, and her eyes danced with excitement.

"I do no good here!" she exclaimed. "Why not? You, too, Capitaine Rotherby, — you would come?"

"I would take you there," I answered, "and I would do my best, my very best, to keep you entertained."

"I shall ask!" she exclaimed. "To-night I shall ask."

"Ask whom?" I inquired. "Louis?"

She shook her head.

"My uncle," she answered.

"You will not see him!" I exclaimed.

"He will telephone," she answered. "He has promised."

I reached over towards her and took her hands into mine.

"Felicia," I said boldly, "I am your friend. The

letter I have told you of should prove that. I am only anxious for your good. Tell me what reason your uncle can have for behaving in this extraordinary way, for allowing himself to be associated even for a moment with such people as Louis and his friends?"

Everything that it had made me so happy to see in her face died away. She was once more wan and anxious.

"I cannot tell you," she said, — "I cannot, because I dare not! I have promised! Only remember this. My uncle has lived in Paris for so many years —"

"But I thought that he had just come from South America!" I interrupted.

"Yes, but before that," she explained breathlessly, — "before that! He loves the mysterious. He likes to be associated with strange people, and I do believe, too," she continued, "that he has business just now which must be kept secret for the sake of other people. Oh, I know it must all seem so strange to you! Won't you believe, Capitaine Rotherby, that I am grateful for your kindness, and that I would tell you if I could?"

"I must," I answered, with a sigh. "I must believe what you tell me. Listen, then. I shall wait until you hear from your uncle."

"Have you come back to your rooms?" she asked timidly.

"I shall do so," I announced, "but I hope that it will be only for the night. To-morrow, if all goes well, we may be on our way to Norfolk."

There was a knock at the door. She started, and looked at me a little uneasily. Almost immediately the door was pushed open. It was Louis who entered, bearing a menu card. He addressed me with a little air of surprise. I was at once certain that he had known of my visit, and had come to see what it might mean.

"Monsieur has returned very soon," he remarked, bowing pleasantly.

"My journey was not a long one, Louis," I answered. "What have you brought that thing for?" I continued, pointing to the menu card. "Do you want an order for dinner? Miss Delora is dining elsewhere with me!"

My tone was purposely aggressive. Louis' manners, however, remained perfection.

"Miss Delora has engaged a table in the café," he said. "I have come myself to suggest a little dinner. I trust she will not disappoint us."

She looked at me pathetically. There was something which I could not understand in her face. Only I knew that whatever she might ask me I was prepared to grant.

"Will you not stay and dine here with me?" she said. "Louis will give us a very good dinner, and afterwards I shall have my message, and I shall know whether I may go or not."

The humor of the idea appealed to me. There was suddenly something fantastic, unbelievable, in the events of last night.

"With pleasure!" I answered.

Louis bowed, and for a moment or two seemed entirely engrossed in the few additions he was making to the menu he carried. Then he handed it to me with a little bow.

"There, monsieur," he said. "I think that you will find that excellent."

"I have no doubt that we shall, Louis," I answered. "I will only ask you to remember one thing."

"And that, monsieur?" he asked.

"I dine with mademoiselle," I said, "and our appetites are identical!"

Louis smiled. There were times when I suspected him of a sense of humor!

"Monsieur has not the thick neck of Bartot!" he murmured, as he withdrew.

CHAPTER XXIII

FELICIA

It seemed to me that Felicia that night was in her most charming mood. She wore a dress of some soft white material, and a large black hat, under which her face — a little paler even than usual — wore almost a pathetic aspect. Her fingers touched my arm as we entered the restaurant together. She seemed, in a way, to have lost some of her self-control, — the exclusiveness with which she had surrounded herself, — and to have become at once more natural and more girlish. I noticed that she chose a seat with her back to the room, and I understood her reason even before she told me.

"I think," she said, "that to-night it would be pleasant to forget that there is any one here who disturbs me. I think it would be pleasant to remember only that this great holiday of mine, which I have looked forward to so long, has really begun."

"You have looked forward to coming to London so much?" I asked.

"Yes!" she answered. "I have lived a very quiet life, Capitaine Rotherby. After the Sisters had finished with me — and I stayed at the school longer than any of the others — I went straight to the house of a friend of my uncle's, where I had only a *dame de compagnie*. My uncle — he was so long coming, and the life was very dull. But always he wrote to me, 'Some day I will take you to London!' Even when we were in Paris together he would tell me that."

"Tell me," I asked, "what is your uncle's Christian name?"

"I have three uncles," she said, after a moment's hesitation, — "Maurice, Ferdinand, and Nicholas. Nicholas lives all the time in South America. Maurice and Ferdinand are often in Paris."

"And the uncle with whom you are now?" I asked.

I seemed to have been unfortunate in my choice of a conversation. Her eyes had grown larger. The quivering of her lips was almost pitiful.

"I am a clumsy ass!" I interrupted quickly. "I am asking you questions which you do not wish to answer. A little later on, perhaps, you will tell me everything of your own accord. But to-night I shall ask you nothing. We will remember only that the holiday has begun."

She drew a little sigh of relief.

"You are so kind," she murmured, "so very kind. Indeed I do not want to think of these things, which I do not understand, and which only puzzle me all the time. We will let them alone, is it not so? We will let them alone and talk about foolish things. Or you shall tell me about London, and the country — tell me what we will do. Indeed, I may go down to your home in Norfolk."

"I think you will like it there," I said. "It is too stuffy for London these months. My brother's house is not far from the sea. There is a great park which stretches down to some marshes, and beyond that the sands."

"Can one bathe?" she asked breathlessly.

"Of course," I answered. "There is a private beach, and when we have people in the house at this time of the year we always have the motor-car ready to take them down and back. That is for those who bathe early.

Later on it is only a pleasant walk. Then you can learn games if you like, — golf and tennis, cricket and croquet."

"I should be so stupid," she said, with a little regretful sigh. "In France they did not teach me those things. I can play tennis a little, but oh! so badly; and in England," she continued, "you think so much of your games. Tell me, Capitaine Rotherby, will you think me very stupid in the country if I can do nothing but swim a little and play tennis very badly?"

"Rather not!" I answered. "There is the motor, you know. I could take you for some delightful drives. We should find plenty to do, I am sure, and I promise you that if only you will be as amiable as you are here I shall not find any fault."

"You will like to have me there?" she asked.

Her question came with the simplicity of a child. She laughed softly with pleasure when I leaned over the table and whispered to her, —

"Better than anything else in the world!"

"I am not sure, Capitaine Rotherby," she said, looking at me out of her great eyes, "whether you are behaving nicely."

"If I am not," I declared, "it is your fault! You should not look so charming."

She laughed softly.

"And you should not make such speeches to a poor little foreign girl," she said, "who knows so little of your London ways."

Louis stood suddenly before us. We felt his presence like a cold shadow. The laughter died away from her eyes, and I found it difficult enough to address him civilly.

"Monsieur is well served?" he asked. "Everything all right, eh?"

"Everything is very good, as usual, Louis," I answered. "The only thing that is amiss you cannot alter."

"For example?" he asked.

"The atmosphere," I answered. "It is no weather for London."

"Monsieur is right," he admitted. "He is thinking of departing for the country soon?"

"It depends a little upon mademoiselle," I answered.

Louis shook his head very slowly. He had the air of a man who discusses something with infinite regret.

"It would be very delightful indeed," he said, "if it were possible for mademoiselle to go into Norfolk to your brother's house. It would be very good for mademoiselle, but I am not sure — I fear that her uncle —"

"How the mischief did you know anything about it?" I asked in amazement.

Louis smiled — that subtle, half-concealed smile which seemed scarcely to part his lips.

"Why should not mademoiselle have told me?" he asked.

"But I have not!" she declared suddenly. "I have not seen Louis since you were here this afternoon, Capitaine Rotherby."

Louis extended his hands.

"It is true," he admitted. "It is not from mademoiselle that I had the news. But there, one cannot tell. Things may alter at any moment. It may be very pleasant for Monsieur Delora that his niece is able to accept this charming invitation."

"So you have been in communication with Mr. Delora, Louis?" I asked.

"Naturally," Louis answered. "He told me of mademoiselle's request. He told me that he had promised to reply at ten o'clock this evening."

"Perhaps you can tell us," I remarked, "what that reply will be?"

Louis' face remained absolutely expressionless. He only shook his head.

"Mr. Delora is his own master," he said. "It may suit him to be without mademoiselle, or it may not. Pardon, monsieur!"

Louis was gone, but he had left his shadow behind.

"He does not think," she murmured, "that I may come!"

"Felicia, — " I said.

"But I did not say that you might call me Felicia!" she interrupted.

"Then do say so," I begged.

"For this evening, then," she assented.

"For this evening, then, Felicia," I continued. "I do not wish to worry you by talking about certain things, but do you not think yourself that your uncle is very inconsiderate to leave you here alone on your first visit to London, — not to come near the place, or provide you with any means of amusement? Why should he hesitate to let you come to us?"

"We will not talk of it," she begged, a little nervously. "I must do as he wishes. We will hope that he says yes, will we not?"

"He must say yes!" I declared. "If he does n't I'll find out where he is, somehow, and go and talk to him!"

She shook her head.

"He is very much engaged," she said. "He would not

like you to find him out, nor would he have any time to talk to you."

"Selling his coffee?" I could not help saying.

"To-night, Capitaine Rotherby," she answered softly, "we do not talk of those things. Tell me what else we shall do down at your brother's house?"

"We shall go for long walks," I told her. "There are beautiful gardens there — a rose garden more than a hundred years old, and at the end of it a footpath which leads through a pine plantation and then down to the sea marshes. We can sit and watch the sea and talk, and when you find it dull we will fill the house with young people, and play games and dance — dance by moonlight, if you like. Or we can go fishing," I continued. "There is a small yacht there and a couple of sailing-boats."

She listened as though afraid of losing a single word.

"Tell me," I asked, "have you been lonely all your life, child?"

"All my life," she answered, and somehow or other her voice seemed to me full of tears, so that I was almost surprised to find her eyes dry. "Yes, I have always been lonely!" she murmured. "My uncle has been kind to me, but he has always some great scheme on hand, and Madame Müller — she would be kind if she knew how, I think, but she is as though she were made of wood. She has no sympathy, she does not understand."

"I wonder," I said reflectively, "what made your uncle bring you here."

"It was a promise," she said hurriedly, — "a promise of long ago. You yourself must know that. Your letter from your brother in South America said, 'Mr. Delora and his niece.'"

"It is true," I admitted. "But why he should want

to bring you and then neglect you like this — But I
forgot," I interrupted. "We must not talk so. Tell me,
you have been often to the theatre in Paris?"

"Very seldom," she answered, "and I love it so much.
Madame Müller and I go sometimes, but where we live
is some distance from Paris, and it is difficult to get home
afterwards, especially for us two alone. My uncle takes
us sometimes, but he is generally so occupied."

"He is often in Paris, then?" I asked.

She started a little.

"Yes!" she said hurriedly. "He is often there, of
course. But please do not forget, — to-night we do not
talk about my uncle. We talk about ourselves. May I
ask you something?"

"Certainly!" I answered.

"If my uncle says 'No!' — that I may not come — do
you go away altogether, then, to-morrow?"

"No," I answered, "I do not! I shall not leave you
alone here. So long as you stay, I shall remain in London."

She drew a little breath, and with a quick, impetuous
movement her hand stole across the table and pressed
mine.

"It is so good of you!" she murmured.

"I am afraid that it is selfishness, Felicia," I answered.
"I should not care to go away and leave you here. I am
beginning to find," I added, "that the pleasures in life
which do not include you count for very little."

"You will turn my head," she declared, with a delightful little laugh.

"It is the truth," I assured her.

"I am quite sure now," she murmured, "that my great
holiday has commenced!"

CHAPTER XXIV

FELICIA laid down the receiver and looked at me. There was scarcely any need for words. Her disappointment was written into her white face.

"You are not to come!" I said.

"I am not — to come," she repeated. "After all, my holiday is not yet."

"Will you tell me," I asked, "where I can find your uncle?"

She shook her head.

"You must not ask me such a thing," she declared.

"Remember," I said, "that I have really called to make his acquaintance as a matter of courtesy on behalf of my brother. What excuse do you give me for his absence? Tell me what it is that you are supposed to say in such a case?"

"Simply that he is away for a few days, engaged in the most important business," she answered. "He will rejoin me here directly it is settled."

"And in the meantime," I said thoughtfully, "you are left in a strange hotel without friends, without a chaperon, absolutely unprotected, and with only a head-waiter in your confidence. Felicia, there is something very wrong here. I am not sure," I continued, "that it is not my duty to run away with you."

She clasped her hands.

"Delightful!" she murmured. "But I must n't think of it," she added, with a sudden gravity, "nor must you talk to me like that. What my uncle says is best to be done. He knows and understands. If he has had to leave me here alone, it is because it is necessary."

"You have a great deal of faith in him," I remarked.

"He has always been kind to me," she answered, "and I know that the business upon which he is engaged just now is hazardous and difficult. There are men who do not wish it to go through, and they watch for him. If they knew his whereabouts they would try to stop him."

"Felicia, do you know what that business is?" I asked.

"I have some idea of it," she answered.

Her answer puzzled me. If Felicia really had any idea as to the nature of it, and was content to play the part she was playing, it certainly could not be anything of an illicit nature. Yet everything else which had come under my notice pointed to Delora's being associated with a criminal undertaking. I paced the room, deep in thought. Felicia all the time was watching me anxiously.

"You are not going to leave me?" she asked very softly.

I came to a standstill before her.

"No, Felicia," I said, "I am not going to leave you! But I want to tell you this. I am going to try and find out for myself the things which you will not tell me. No, you must not try to stop me!" I said, anticipating the words which indeed had trembled upon her lips. "It must be either that or farewell, Felicia. I cannot remain here and do absolutely nothing. I want to find your uncle, and to have some sort of an explanation from him, and I mean to do it."

She shook her head.

"There are others who are trying to find him," she said, "but I do not think that they will succeed. The young man who was here the other night, for instance."

"If I fail, I fail," I answered. "At any rate, I shall be doing something. I must go back to my brother's to-night, Felicia, because I have promised to stay with him. In a day or two I shall return to my rooms here, and I shall do my best to find out the meaning of your uncle's mysterious movements. It may seem impertinent to you to interfere in anybody else's concerns. I cannot help it. It is for your sake. The present position is impossible!"

"You are not staying here to-night?" she asked.

"To-night, no!" I answered. "I will let you know directly I return."

"There is one thing else, Capitaine Rotherby. Could you promise it to me, I wonder?"

"I will try," I answered.

"Do not quarrel any more, if you can help it," she begged, "with Louis!"

Her question forced a laugh from my lips. Quarrel with Louis, indeed! What more could I do in that direction? Then I frowned, in temporary annoyance. I hated to hear her speak of him as a person to be considered.

"Louis is a venomous little person," I said, "but I certainly should not quarrel with him more than I can help. I am, unfortunately, in his debt, or I should have dealt with him before now."

I glanced at the clock and jumped up. It was very much later than I had thought. She gave me her hands a little wistfully.

"I do not like to think of you here alone," I said. "I wish that I could persuade you to engage a maid."

She shook her head.

"My uncle would not allow it," she said simply. "He says that servants are always prying into one's concerns. Good night, Capitaine Rotherby! Thank you so much for taking me out this evening. After all, I cannot help feeling that it has been rather like the beginning of this holiday."

I held her hands tightly in mine.

"When it really begins," I answered, "I shall try and make it a little more interesting!"

I declined a taxicab and turned to walk back to my brother's hotel. Certainly in the problem of these two people who had come so curiously into my life there was very much to give me matter for thought. I believed in the girl, and trusted her. More than that I did not dare to ask myself! I should have believed in her, even if her uncle were proved to be a criminal of the most dangerous type. But none the less I could not help realizing that her present position was a singularly unfortunate one. To be alone in a big hotel, without maid or chaperon, herself caught up in this web of mystery which Louis and those others seemed to have woven around her, was in itself undesirable and unnatural. Whatever was transpiring, I was quite certain that her share in it was a passive one. She had been told to be silent, and she was silent. Nothing would ever make me believe that she was a party to any wrong-doing. And yet the more I thought of Delora the less I trusted him. At Charing Cross Station, for instance, his had not been the anxiety of a man intrusted with a difficult mission. His agitation had been due to fear, — fear abject and absolute. I had seen the symptoms more than once in my life, and there was no mistaking them. I told myself that no man could be so shaken who was engaged in honest dealings. Even now he was in hiding, — it could not be called anything else, — and the one person with whom I had come in touch who was searching for him was, without a doubt, on the side of law and justice, with at least some settled position behind him. Delora's deportment was more the deportment of a fugitive from justice than of a man in the confidence of his government.

Walking a little carelessly, I took a turn too far northward, and found myself in one of the streets leading out of Shaftesbury Avenue. I was on the point of taking a passage which would lead me more in my proper direction, when my attention was attracted by a large motor-car standing outside one of the small foreign restaurants which abound in this district. I was always interested in cars, but I noticed this one more particularly from the fact of its utter incompatibility with its surroundings. It was one of the handsomest cars I had ever seen, — a sixty to eighty horse-power Daimler, — fitted up inside with the utmost luxury. The panels were plain, and the chauffeur, who sat motionless in his place, wore dark livery and was apparently a foreigner. I slackened my pace to glance for a moment at the non-skidding device on the back tire, and as I passed on I saw the door of the little restaurant open, and a tall *commissionnaire* hurried out. He held open the door of the car and stood at attention. Two men issued from the restaurant and crossed the pavement. I turned deliberately round to watch them — vulgar curiosity, perhaps, but a curiosity which I never regretted. The first man — tall and powerful — wore the splendid dress and black silk cap of a Chinese of high rank. The man who followed him was Delora. I knew him in a second, although he wore a white silk scarf around his neck, conceal-

ing the lower part of his face, and a silk hat pushed down
almost over his eyes. I saw his little nervous glance up
and down the street, I saw him push past the *commissionnaire* as though in a hurry to gain the semi-obscurity of
the car. I stopped short upon the pavement, motionless
for one brief and fatal moment. Then I turned back
and hastened to the side of the car. I knocked at the
window.

"Delora," I said, "I must speak to you."

The car had begun to move. I wrenched at the handle,
but I found it held on the inside with a grip which even I
could not move. I looked into the broad, expressionless
face of the Chinaman, who, leaning forward, completely
shielded the person of the man with whom I sought to
speak.

"One moment," I called out. "I must speak with
Mr. Delora. I have a message for him."

The car was going faster now. I tried to jump on to the
step, but the first time I missed it. Then the window was
suddenly let down. The Chinaman's arm flashed out and
struck me on the chest, so that I was forced to relinquish
my grasp of the handle. I reeled back, preserving my
balance only by a desperate effort. Before I could start in
pursuit, the car had turned into the more crowded thoroughfare, and when I reached the spot where it had disappeared
a few seconds later, it was lost amongst the stream of
vehicles.

I went back to the restaurant. It was like a hundred
others of its class — stuffy, smelly, reminiscent of the
poorer business quarters of a foreign city. A waiter in a
greasy dress-suit flicked some crumbs from a vacant table
and motioned me to sit down. I ordered a Fin Champagne,
and put half-a-crown into his hand.

"Tell me," I said, "five minutes ago a Chinaman and another man were here."

The man laid the half-crown down on the table. His manner had undergone a complete change.

"Perhaps so, sir," he answered. "We have been busy to-night. I noticed nobody."

I called the proprietor to me — a little pale-faced man with a black moustache, who had been hovering in the background. He hastened to my side, smiling and bowing. This time I did not ask him a direct question.

"I am interested in the restaurants of this quarter," I said. "Some one has told me that your dinner is marvellous !"

He smiled a little suspiciously. The word was perhaps unfortunate !

"I am bringing some friends to try it very soon," I said.

The waiter brought my Fin Champagne. I drank it and ordered a cigar.

"You have all sorts of people here," I remarked. "I noticed a Chinaman — he was very much like the Chinese ambassador, by the bye — leaving as I came in."

The proprietor extended his hands.

"We have people of every class, monsieur," he assured me. "One comes and tells his friends, and they come, and so on. I believe that there was a Chinese gentleman here to-night. One does not notice. We were busy."

I paid my bill and departed. The *commissionnaire* pushed open the door, whistle in hand. He looked at me a little curiously. Without doubt he had watched my attempt to speak to Delora. I drew a half-sovereign from my pocket.

"Tell me," I said, "do you want to earn that ?"

He was a German, with a large pasty face and a yellow

moustache. His eyes were small, and they seemed to contract with greed as they looked upon the coin.

"Sir!" he answered, with a bow.

"Who was the Chinese gentleman with the splendid motor-car?" I asked.

The man spread out his hands.

"Who can tell?" he said. "He dined here to-night in a private room."

A private room! Well, that was something, at any rate!

"You do not know his name or where he comes from?" I asked.

The man shook his head, glancing nervously towards the interior of the restaurant.

"The other gentleman?" I asked.

"I do not know his name, sir," the man declared with emphasis. "He has been here once or twice, but always alone."

I put the half-sovereign in my pocket and drew out a sovereign. The man stretched out an eager hand which he suddenly dropped. He pointed down the street. The swing door of the restaurant remained closed, but over the soiled white curtain I also could see the face of the proprietor peering out.

"It is the second turn to the left," the man said to me.

"And if you want that sovereign made into five," I said carelessly, "my name is Captain Rotherby, and I am going from here to Claridge's Hotel."

I walked down the street and left him looking after me. At the corner I glanced around. The proprietor and the *commissionaire* were talking together on the pavement.

CHAPTER XXV

PRIVATE AND DIPLOMATIC

THE following evening I dined alone with my brother, who was, for him, in an unusually cheerful frame of mind. He talked with more interest of life and his share in it than he had done — to me, at any rate — since the tragedy which had deprived him of a home. Toward the end of dinner I asked him a question.

"Ralph," I said, "how could I meet the Chinese ambassador here?"

He stared at me for a moment.

"Why, at any of the diplomatic receptions, I suppose," he said, seeing that I was in earnest. "He is rather a pal of Freddy's. Why don't you ring up and ask him?"

"I will, the moment after dinner," I answered.

"Why this sudden interest in Orientalism?" Ralph asked curiously.

"Curiously enough, it is apropos of these Deloras," I answered. "I called to-day, but only found the girl in. The man I saw later with a Chinaman whom I believe to be the ambassador."

"What is the girl like?" my brother asked.

"Charming!" I answered. "I am writing Aunt Mary to invite her down to Feltham. The difficulty seems to be to get hold of Delora."

"So you've written Aunt Mary, eh?" Ralph remarked, looking up at me. "Austen, I believe you're gone on the girl!"

"I believe I am," I admitted equably. "So would you be if you saw her."

Ralph half closed his eyes for a moment. It was a clumsy speech of mine!

"Seriously, Austen," he continued, a few moments later, "have you ever thought of marrying?"

"Equally seriously, Ralph," I answered, "not until I met Felicia Delora."

"Felicia Delora!" my brother repeated. "It's a pretty name, at any rate. I suppose I must go and see her myself."

"Wait for a day or two, Ralph," I begged. "She is a little upset just now. Her uncle seems to be neglecting her for some precious scheme of his."

"I wonder if, by any chance, you are in earnest, Austen?" my brother asked.

"I should not be surprised," I admitted.

"It's an interesting subject, you know," Ralph continued gravely. "Considering my accident, and other things which we need not allude to, I think we may take it for granted that there's no chance of my ever having an heir. It's our duty to look ahead a little, you know, Austen. There isn't any manner of doubt that some time between now and the next ten years you will have to take up my place. I only hope you won't make such a hash of it."

"Don't talk rubbish, Ralph!" I answered.

"It isn't rubbish," he said firmly. "You go and talk to my doctor if you don't believe me. However, I hadn't meant to say anything about this to-night. Your mentioning the girl put it into my head. I want you, of course, to know that I am not forgetful of my responsibilities. Your two thousand a year may do you very well as a bachelor, but you are heir apparent to the title now, and if you should think of marrying, the Fakenham estates are yours, and the house. They bring in between six and seven thousand a year, I think, — never less."

"It's very good of you, Ralph, —" I began.

"It's nothing of the sort," he answered. "It's your rightful position. The Fakenham estates have been held by the heir apparent for generations. Tell me a little about this Miss Delora."

"I'll bring her to see you presently, Ralph," I answered.

"You are in earnest, then?" he remarked, with a smile.

"I believe so," I answered.

He looked at me once more, searchingly.

"There is something on your mind, Austen," he said, — "something bothering you. I believe it is about these Deloras, too. Is there something about them which you can't understand, eh?"

"There is, Ralph," I admitted. "You saw what Dicky said. They are people of consequence in their own country, at any rate, yet over here the man seems to behave like a hunted criminal."

"Dicky also said," Ralph remarked, "that the man was intrusted with some business over here for his government. Nasty underhand lot, those republics of the Southern Hemisphere. I dare say he is driven to be a bit mysterious to carry the thing through."

"I shall know more about it soon, I hope," I answered. "I'll go and ring Freddy up, if you don't mind, now."

Ralph nodded.

"I'm off to my room, at any rate, old chap," he said. "Groves is going abroad for a month's holiday, and he has brought some papers for me to look through. See you some time to-morrow."

I made my way into the little sitting-room which belonged to the suite of rooms my brother had placed at my disposal. There I rang up Lord Frederic Maynard, my first cousin, and a junior member of the government. The butler told me that Lord Frederic was dining, but would doubtless speak to me for a moment. In a minute or two I heard his familiar voice.

"Freddy," I said, "I want to meet the Chinese ambassador."

"Eleven till one to-night here," he answered. "What the devil do you want with him?"

"Do you mean that he is coming to your house to-night?" I asked.

"Exactly," Freddy answered. "We've a political reception, semi-diplomatic. I saw our old friend only yesterday, and he reminded me that he was coming."

"You're a brick, Freddy!" I answered. "I'll be round."

"You have not answered my question," he reminded me.

"I'll tell you later," I answered, and rang off.

I was at Maynard House very soon after eleven, and, after chatting for a little while with my hostess, I hung around near the entrance, watching the arrivals. About midnight His Excellency the Chinese ambassador was announced, and I felt a little thrill of exultation. I was right! The tall, powerful-looking man whom I saw bowing over my cousin's hand was indeed the person whom I had seen with Delora a few hours ago. I ran Freddy to ground, and presently I found myself also bowing before His Excellency. He regarded me through his horn-rimmed spectacles with a benign and pleasant expression. I had been in the East, and I talked for a few moments upon the subjects which I thought would interest him.

"Your Excellency, I dare say, is well acquainted with London," I remarked, apropos of something he said.

"I know your great city only indifferently," he answered. "I am always anxious to take the opportunity of seeing more of it."

"Last evening, for instance," I remarked, "Your Excellency was, I think, exploring a very interesting neighborhood."

"Last evening," he repeated. "Let me think. No, not last evening, Captain Rotherby! I was giving a little dinner at my own house."

I looked at him for a moment in silence. There was nothing to be learned from his expression.

"I thought," I said, "that I saw your Excellency in a street near Shaftesbury Avenue, leaving a small foreign restaurant, — the Café Universel. Your Excellency was with a man named Delora."

Very slowly the ambassador shook his head.

"Not me!" he said. "Not me! I did dine with the younger members of the Legation in Langham Place. What name did you say?"

"A man named Delora," I repeated.

Once more the ambassador shook his head, slowly and thoughtfully.

"Delora!" he repeated. "The name is unknown to me. There are many others of my race in London now," he continued. "The costume, perhaps, makes one seem like another to those who look and pass by."

I bowed very low. It was the most magnificently told lie to which I had ever listened in my life! His Excellency smiled at me graciously as I made my adieux, and passed on. Despite my disappointment, I felt that I was now becoming profoundly interested in my quest. The evidence, too, was all in favor of Delora. It seemed, indeed, as though this undertaking in which he was involved might, after all, be connected with other things than crime!

CHAPTER XXVI

It was past one o'clock in the morning when I returned to the hotel, yet the porter who admitted me pointed toward the figure of a man who stood waiting in the dimly lit hall.

"There is a person here who has been waiting to see you for some hours, sir," he said. "His name is Fritz."

"To see me?" I repeated.

The man came a step forward and saluted. I recognized him at once. It was the *commissionnaire* at the Café Universel.

"It is quite right," I told the porter. "You had better come up to my rooms," I added, turning to Fritz.

I led the way to the lift and on to my sitting-room. There I turned up the electric lights and threw myself into an easy-chair.

"Well, Fritz," said I, "I hope that you have brought me some news."

"I have lost my job, sir," the man answered, a little sullenly.

"How much was it worth to you?" I asked.

"It was worth nearly two pounds a week with tips," he declared, speaking with a strong foreign accent.

"Then I take you into my service at two pounds ten a week from to-night," I said. "The engagement will not be a long one, but you may find it lucrative."

The man fingered his hat and looked at me stolidly.

"I am not a valet, sir," he replied.

"If you were I should not employ you," I answered. "You can make yourself very useful to me in another direction, if you care to."

"I am very willing, sir," the man declared, — "very willing indeed. I have a wife and children, and I cannot afford to be out of employment."

"Come, then," I said. "The long and short of it is this. I want to discover the whereabouts of the man who was with the Chinaman at your restaurant last evening."

The man looked at me with something like surprise in his face.

"You do not know that?" he said.

"I do not," I admitted. "Your business will be to find out."

"And what do I get," the man asked, "if I do discover the staying place of that gentleman?"

"A ten-pound note," I answered, "down on the nail."

A slow smile suffused Fritz's face.

"I will tell you now," he said. "You have the ten pounds, so?"

"I have it ready," I answered, rising to my feet. "Come on, Fritz, you are a brave fellow, and I promise you it shall not end at ten pounds."

"You are serious?" Fritz persisted. "This is not a joke?"

"Not in the least," I assured him. "Why should you think so?"

The smile on the man's face broadened.

"Because," he said, "that gentleman — he is staying here, in this very hotel."

For a moment I was silent. The thing seemed impossible!

"How on earth do you know that, Fritz?" I asked.

"I will tell you," Fritz answered. "There was a night, not long ago, when he did come to the restaurant with the Chinese gentleman. They talked for a long time, and then I was sent for into the private room where they were taking dinner. The gentleman he wrote a note and he gave it to me. He said, 'You will take a hansom cab and you will drive to Claridge's Hotel. You will give this to the cashier, and he will hand you a small parcel which you will bring here.' I told him that I could not leave my post, but he had already seen the proprietor. So I came to this very hotel with that note, and I did take back to the restaurant a small parcel wrapped in brown paper."

"Fritz," I said, "sit down in that easy-chair and help yourself to whiskey and soda. I am sorry that I have not beer, but you must do the best you can with our own national drink. Take a cigar, too. Make yourself quite comfortable. I am going downstairs to the reception office. If I find that what you have told me is true, there will be two five-pound notes in my hand for you when I come back."

"So!" Fritz declared, accepting my hospitality with calm satisfaction.

I descended into the hall of the hotel and made my way to the reception office. The one clerk on duty was reading a novel, which he promptly laid aside at my approach. It occurred to me that my task, perhaps, might not prove so easy, as Delora would scarcely be staying here under his own name.

"I wanted to ask you," I said, "if you have a gentleman here named Delora."

The man shook his head.

"There is no one of that name in the hotel, sir," he answered.

"I scarcely expected that there would be," I remarked. "The fact is, the gentleman whom I want to find, and whom I know is or was staying here, is using another name which I have not heard. You know who I am?"

"Certainly, Captain Rotherby!" the man replied. "You are Lord Welmington's brother."

"You will understand, then," I said, "that if I ask questions which seem to you impertinent, I do so because the matter is important, and not from any idle curiosity."

"Quite so, sir," the man answered. "I shall be pleased to tell you anything I can."

"This gentleman of whom I am in search, then," I answered, "he would have arrived probably last Wednesday evening from the Continent. I do not know what name he would give, but it would probably not be the name of Delora. He is rather tall, pale, thin, and of distinctly foreign appearance. He has black eyes, black imperial, and looks like a South American, which, by the bye, I think he is. Does that description help you to recognize him?"

"I think so, sir," the man answered. "Do you happen to know whether, by any chance, he would be a friend of the Chinese ambassador?"

"I should think it very likely," I answered. "He is staying here, then?"

"He was staying here until a few hours ago, sir," the man answered. "He came in about ten o'clock and went at once to his rooms, sent for his bill, and left the hotel in a great hurry. I remember the circumstance particularly, because he had said nothing about his going, and from the manner of his return and his hasty departure it is quite clear that he had not expected to leave so soon himself."

I was a little staggered. It seemed hard luck to have so nearly succeeded in my search, only to have failed at the last moment. It was maddening, too, to think that for all these hours I had been in the same hotel as the man whom I so greatly desired to find!

"Tell me, did he leave any address?" I asked.

"None whatever, sir," the man answered. "Our junior clerk here asked him where he would wish letters to be forwarded, and he replied that there would not be any. I think he said that he was leaving for abroad almost at once, but would call before he sailed in case there were any letters or messages for him."

"Tell me under what name he stayed here?" I asked.

"Mr. Vanderpoel," the man told me.

"He was quite alone, I suppose?" I asked.

"Absolutely," the man answered. "He had a few callers at different times, but he spent most of his time in his rooms. If you are particularly anxious to discover his whereabouts," the clerk continued, "the night porter who would have started him off is still on duty."

"I should like very much to speak to him," I said.

The clerk touched a bell, and the porter came in from outside.

"You remember Mr. Vanderpoel leaving this evening?" the clerk asked.

"Certainly, sir," the man answered. "He went at about eleven o'clock."

"Did he go in a cab?" the clerk asked.

"In a four-wheeler, sir," the porter answered.

"Do you remember what address he gave?"

The porter looked dubious for a moment.

"I don't absolutely remember, sir," he said, "but I know that it was one of the big railway stations."

The clerk turned to me.

"Is there anything else you would like to ask?" he inquired.

I shook my head.

"No, thanks!" I answered. "I am afraid there is nothing more to be learned."

The porter went back to his duties, and I bade the clerk good night. Up in my room Fritz was waiting anxiously.

"You were right and wrong," I announced. "Mr. Delora has been staying here and left to-night."

"He has gone!" Fritz exclaimed.

"He left at eleven o'clock," I answered. "He saw me, and I suppose he knew that I was looking for him. Here's half your money, anyhow," I continued, giving him a five-pound note. "The next thing to do is to find out where he has gone to. I think you could help here, Fritz."

"What must I do?" the man asked.

"First of all," I said, "go to the big railway hotels and try and find out from one of the porters — you Germans all stick together — whether any one arrived in a four-wheel cab at between eleven and twelve this evening, whose description coincides with that of Mr. Delora. I reckon that will take you most of to-morrow. When you have finished come to me at the Milan Court, and let me know how you have got on."

"So!" the man remarked, rising from his seat. "To-morrow morning I will do that. They will tell me, these fellows. I know many of them."

"Good night, Fritz, then!" I said. "Good luck!"

CHAPTER XXVII

EARLY on the following morning I moved back to my rooms in the Milan Court. Curiously enough I entered the building with a sense of depression for which I could not account. I went first to my own rooms and glanced at my letters. There was nothing there of importance. In other words, there was nothing from Felicia. I descended to the fifth floor and knocked at the door of her room. As I stood there waiting I was absolutely certain that somehow or other a change had occurred in the situation, that the freeness of my intercourse with Felicia was about to be interfered with. I was not in the least surprised when the door was at last cautiously opened, and a woman who was a perfect stranger to me stood on the threshold, with the handle of the door still in her hand.

"I should like to see Miss Delora," I said. "My name is Captain Rotherby."

The woman shook her head. She was apparently French, and of the middle-class. She was dressed in black, her eyes and eyebrows were black, she had even the shadow of a moustache upon her upper lip. To me her appearance was singularly forbidding.

"Miss Delora cannot see you," she answered, with a strong foreign accent.

"Will you be so good as to inquire if that is so?" I answered. "I have an appointment with Miss Delora for this morning, and a motor-car waiting to take her out."

"Miss Delora cannot receive you," answered the woman, almost as though she had not heard, and closed the door in my face.

There was nothing left for me but to go down and interview my friend the hall-porter. I commenced my inquiries with the usual question.

"Any news of Mr. Delora, Ashley?" I asked.

"None at all, sir," the man replied. "A companion has arrived for Miss Delora."

"So I have discovered for myself," I answered. "Do you know anything about her, Ashley?"

The man shook his head.

"She arrived here yesterday afternoon," he said, "with a trunk. She went straight up to Miss Delora's room, and I have not seen them apart since."

"Do they come down to the café?" I asked.

"So far, sir," the man answered, "they have had everything served in their sitting-room."

I went back to my room and rang up number 157. The voice which answered me was the voice of the woman who had denied me admission to the room.

"I wish to speak to Miss Delora," I said.

"Miss Delora is engaged," was the abrupt answer.

"Nonsense!" I answered. "I insist upon speaking to her. Tell her that it is Captain Rotherby, and she will come to the telephone."

There was a little whirr, but no answer. The person at the other end had rung off. By this time I was getting angry. In five minutes time I rang up again. The same voice answered me.

"Look here," I said, "if you do not let me speak to Miss Delora, I shall ring up every five minutes during the day!"

"Monsieur can do as he pleases," was the answer. "I shall lay the receiver upon the table. It will not be possible to get connected."

"Do, if you like," I answered, "but how about when Mr. Delora rings you up?"

The woman muttered something which I did not catch. A moment afterwards, however, her voice grew clear.

"That is not your business," she said sharply.

I tried to continue the conversation, but in vain. Nothing came from the other end but silence. I busied myself for a time glancing at a few unimportant letters, and afterwards descended to lunch in the café. I fancied, for a moment, that Louis' self-possession was less perfect than usual. He certainly showed some surprise when he saw me, and he came to my table with a little less alacrity.

"Louis," I said, "I shall order my lunch from some one else, not from you."

"Monsieur has lost confidence?" he asked.

"Not in your judgment, Louis," I answered.

Louis looked me straight in the eyes. It was not a practice which he often indulged in.

"Captain Rotherby," he said, "you should be on our side. It would not be necessary then to interfere with any of your plans."

He looked at me meaningly, and I understood.

"It is you, Louis, I presume, whom I have to thank for the lady upstairs?" I remarked.

Louis shrugged his shoulders.

"Why do you seek the man Delora?" he asked. "What concern is it of yours? If you persist, the consequences are inevitable."

"If you will take the trouble to convince me, Louis, — " I said.

Louis interrupted me; it was unlike him. His little gesture showed that he was very nearly angry.

"Monsieur," he said, "sometimes you fail to realize that at a word from us the hand of the gendarme is upon your shoulder. We would make use of your aid gladly, but it must be on our terms — not yours."

"State them, Louis," I said.

"We will tell you the truth," Louis answered slowly. "You shall understand the whole business. You shall understand why Delora is forced to lie hidden here in London, what it is that he is aiming at. When you know everything, you can be an ally if you will. On the other hand, if you disapprove, you swear upon your honor as a gentleman — an English gentleman — that no word of the knowledge which you have gained shall pass your lips!"

"Louis," I said, "I will have my lunch and think about this."

Louis departed with his customary smile and bow. I ordered something cold from the sideboard within sight, and a bottle of wine which was opened before me. There scarcely remained any doubt in my mind now but that some part of Delora's business, at any rate, in this country, was criminal. Louis' manner, his emphatic stipulation, made it a matter of certainty. Again I found myself confronted by the torturing thought that if this were so Felicia could scarcely be altogether innocent. Once when Louis passed me I stopped him.

"Louis," I said, "let me ask you this. Presuming things remain as they are, and I act independently, do you intend to prevent my seeing Miss Delora?"

"It is nothing to do with me," Louis lied. "It is the wish of her uncle."

"Thank you!" I answered. "I wanted to know."

I finished my luncheon. Louis saw me preparing to depart and came up to me. My table was set in a somewhat obscure corner, and we were practically alone.

"I will ask you a question, Louis," I said. "There is no reason why you should not answer it. There are laws from a legal point of view, and laws from a moral point. From the former, I realize that I am, at this moment, a criminal — possibly, as you say, in your power. Let that pass. What I want you to tell me is this, — the undertaking in which Mr. Delora is now engaged, is it from a legal point of view a criminal one, or is it merely a matter needing secrecy from other reasons?"

Louis stood thoughtfully silent for some few moments.

"Monsieur," he said at last, "I will not hide the truth from you. According to the law in this country Mr. Delora is engaged in a conspiracy."

"Political?" I asked.

"No!" Louis answered. "A conspiracy which is to make him and all others who are concerned in it wealthy for life."

"But the Deloras are already rich," I remarked.

"Our friend," Louis said, "has speculated. He has lost large sums. Besides, he loves adventures. What shall you answer, Captain Rotherby?"

"It is war, Louis," I said. "You should know that. If I have to pay the penalty for taking the law into my hands over the man Tapilow, I am ready to answer at any time. As for you and Delora, and the others of you, whoever they may be, it will be war with you also, if you will. I intend, for the sake of the little girl upstairs, to solve all this mystery, to take her away from it if I can."

Louis' eyes had narrowed. The look in his face was almost enough to make one afraid.

"It is a pity," he said. "Even if you had chosen to remain neutral —"

"I should not do that unless I could see as much of Miss Delora as I chose," I interrupted.

"If that were arranged," Louis said slowly, — "mind, I make no promises, — but I say if that were arranged, would it be understood between us that you stopped your search for Mr. Delora, and abandoned all your inquiries?"

"No, Louis," I answered, "unless I were convinced that Miss Delora herself was implicated in these things. Then you could all go to the devil for anything I cared!"

"Your interest," Louis murmured, "is in the young lady, then?"

"Absolutely and entirely," I answered. "Notwithstanding what you have told me, and what I have surmised, the fact that you stood by me in Paris would be sufficient to make me shrug my shoulders and pass on. I am no policeman, and I would leave the work of exposing Delora to those whose business it is. But you see I have an idea of my own, Louis. I believe that Miss Delora is innocent of any knowledge of wrong-doing. That I remain here is for her sake. If I try to discover what is going on, it is also for her sake!"

"Monsieur has sentiment," Louis remarked, showing his teeth.

"Too much by far, Louis," I answered. "Never mind, we all have our weak spots. Some day or other somebody may even put their finger upon yours, Louis."

He smiled.

"Why not, monsieur?" he said.

CHAPTER XXVIII

CHECK

In my rooms a surprise awaited me. Felicia was there, walking nervously up and down my little sitting-room. She stopped short as I entered and came swiftly towards me. In the joy of seeing her so unexpectedly I would have taken her into my arms, but she shrank back.

"Felicia!" I exclaimed. "How did you come here?"

"Madame Müller went down for lunch," Felicia answered. "I said that I had a headache, and stole up here on the chance of seeing you."

"They are making a prisoner of you!" I exclaimed.

"It is your fault," she answered.

I looked at her in surprise. Her face was stained with tears. Her voice shook with nervousness.

"You have been making secret inquiries about my uncle," she said. "You have been seen talking to those who wish him ill."

"How do you know this, Felicia?" I asked calmly.

"Oh, I know!" she answered. "They have told me."

"Who?" I asked. "Who has told you?"

"Never mind," she answered, wringing her hands. "I know. It is enough. Capitaine Rotherby, I have come to ask you something."

"Please go on," I said.

"I want you to go away. I do not wish you to interest yourself any more in me or in any of us."

"Do you mean that, Felicia?" I asked.

"I mean it," she answered. "My uncle has a great mission to carry out here. You are making it more difficult for him."

"Felicia," I said, "I do not trust your uncle. I do not believe in his great mission. I think that you yourself are deceived."

She held her head up. Her eyes flashed angrily.

"As to that," she said, "I am the best judge. If my uncle is an adventurer, I am his niece. I am one with him. Please understand that. It seems to me that you are working against him, thinking that you are helping me. That is a mistake."

"Felicia," I said, "give me a little more of your confidence, and the rest will be easy."

"What is it that you wish to know?" she asked.

"For one thing," I answered, "tell me when your uncle left South America and when he arrived in Paris?"

"He had been in Paris ten days when you saw us first," she said, after a moment's hesitation.

"And are you sure that he came to you from South America?" I demanded.

"Certainly!" she answered.

"To me," I said slowly, "he seems to have the manners of a Parisian. Two months ago I lunched at Henry's with some old friends. Can you tell me, Felicia, that he was not in Paris then?"

"Of course not!" she answered, shivering a little.

"Then he has a wonderful double," I declared.

"What is this that is in your mind about him?" she asked.

"I believe," I answered, "that he is personating some one, or rather I have believed it. I believe that he is personating some one else, and is afraid of being recognized by those who know."

"Will it satisfy you," she said slowly, "if I tell you, upon my honor, Capitaine Rotherby, that he is indeed my uncle?"

"I should believe you, Felicia," I answered. "I should then feel disposed to give the whole affair up as insoluble."

"That is just what I want you to do," she said. "Now, listen. I tell you this upon my honor. He is my uncle, and his name is truly Delora!"

"Then why does he leave you here alone and skulk about from hiding-place to hiding-place like a criminal?" I asked.

"It is not your business to ask those questions," she answered. "I have told you the truth. Will you do as I ask or not?"

I hesitated for a moment. She was driving me back into a corner!

"Felicia," I said, "I must do as you ask me. If you tell me to go away, I will go away; but do you think it is quite kind to leave me so mystified? For instance," I added slowly, "on the night when that beast Louis planned to knock that young Brazilian on the head, and leave me to bear the brunt of it; he was up here talking to you, alone, as though you were equals."

"It is my uncle who makes use of Louis," she said.

"I'm hanged if I can see how he can make use of a fellow like that if his business is an honest one," I answered.

"It is not for you to understand," she answered. "You are not a policeman. You are not concerned in these things."

"I am concerned in you!" I answered passionately. "Felicia, you drive me almost wild when you talk like this.

You know very well that it is not curiosity which has made me set my teeth, and swear that I will discover the truth of these things. It is because I see you implicated in them, because I believe in you, Felicia, because I love you!"

She was in my arms for one long, delicious moment. Then she tore herself away.

"You mean it, Austen?" she whispered.

"I mean it!" I answered solemnly. "Felicia, I think you know that I mean it!"

"Then you must be patient," she said, "for just a little time. You must wait until my uncle has finished his business. It will take a very short time now. Then you may come and call again, and remind us of your brother. You will understand everything then, and I believe that you will be still willing to ask us down to your country home."

"And if I am, Felicia?" I asked.

"We shall come," she murmured. "You know that. Good-bye, Austen! I must fly. If Madame Müller finds that I have left the room I shall be a prisoner for a week."

I opened the door. Even then I would have kept her, if only for a moment; but just as I bent down we heard the sound of footsteps outside, and she hurried away. I sat down and lit a cigarette. So it was over, then, my little attempt at espionage! My word was pledged. I could do no more.

I walked round to Claridge's later in the evening and saw my brother.

"Ralph," I said, "if your offer of the shooting is still good, I think I will take a few men down to Feltham."

"Do, Austen," he answered. "Old Heggs will be ever

so pleased. It seems a shame not to have a gun upon the place. I shall come down myself later on. What about those people, the Deloras?"

"The uncle is away," I answered, "and the girl cannot very well come by herself. Perhaps we may see something of them later on."

Ralph looked at me a little curiously, but he made no remark.

"You won't be lonely up here alone?" I asked.

He shook his head.

"I have plenty to do," he answered. "I shall probably be down myself before the end of the month. Whom shall you ask?"

I made a list of a few of the men whom I knew, and who I believed were still in town, but when I sat down to write to them I felt curiously reluctant to commit myself to staying at Feltham. Even if I were not to interfere, even if I were to stand aside while the game was being played, I could not believe that the scheming of Louis and the acquiescence of Felicia went for the same thing, and I had an uncomfortable but a very persistent conviction to the effect that she was being deceived. Everything from her point of view seemed reasonable enough. What she had told me, even, seemed almost to preclude the fear of any wrong-doing. Yet I could not escape from the conviction of it. Some way or other there was trouble brewing, either between Delora and Louis, or Delora and the arbiters of right and wrong. In the end I wrote to no one. I determined to go down alone, to shoot zealously from early in the morning till late at night, but to have no house-party at Feltham, — to invite a few of the neighbors, and to be free myself to depart for London any time, at a moment's notice. It would come! somehow or other I felt sure of it. I should receive a summons from her, and I must be prepared at any moment to come to her aid.

I went into the club after I had left Claridge's, and stayed playing bridge till unusually late. It was early in the morning when I reached the Milan, and the hotel had that dimly lit, somewhat sepulchral appearance which seems to possess a large building at that hour in the morning. As I stood for a moment inside the main doors, four men stepped out of the lift on my right, carrying a long wooden chest. They slunk away into the shadows on tiptoe. I watched them curiously.

"What is that?" I asked the reception clerk who was on duty.

He shrugged his shoulders.

"It was a man who died here the day before yesterday," he whispered in my ear.

"Died here?" I repeated. "Why are they taking his coffin down at such an hour?"

"It is always done," the man assured me. "In hotels such as this, where all is life and gayety, our clients do not care to be reminded of such an ugly thing as death. Half the people on that floor would have left if they had known that the dead body of a man has been lying there. We keep these things very secret. The coffin has been taken to the undertaker's. The funeral will be from there."

"Who is the man?" I asked. "Had he been ill long?"

The clerk shook his head.

"He was a Frenchman," he said; "Bartot was his name. He had an apoplectic stroke in the café one day last week, and since then complications set in."

I turned away with a little shiver. It was not pleasant to reflect upon — this man's death!

CHAPTER XXIX

BEFORE I was up the next morning I was informed that Fritz was waiting outside the door of my room. I had him shown in, and he stood respectfully by my bedside.

"Sir," he said, "I have once more discovered Mr. Delora."

"Fritz," I answered, "you are a genius! Tell me where he is?"

"He is at a small private hotel in Bloomsbury," Fritz declared. "It is really a boarding-house, frequented by Australians and Colonials. The number is 17, and the street is Montague Street."

I sat up in bed.

"This is very interesting," I said.

Fritz coughed.

"I trusted that you would find it so, sir," he admitted.

I thought for several moments. Then I sprang out of bed.

"Fritz," I said, "our engagement comes to an end this morning. I am going to pay you for two months' service."

I went to my drawer and counted out some notes, which Fritz pocketed with a smile of contentment.

"I am obliged to give up my interest in this affair," I said, "so I cannot find any more work for you. But that money will enable you to take a little holiday, and I have no doubt that you will soon succeed in obtaining another situation."

Fritz made me a magnificent bow.

"I am greatly obliged to you, sir," he announced. "I shall take another situation at once. Holidays — they will come later in life. At my age, and with a family, one must work. But your generosity, sir," he wound up, with another bow, "I shall never forget."

I dressed, and walked to the address which Fritz had given me. As I stood on the doorstep, with the bell handle still in my hand, the door was suddenly opened. It was Delora himself who appeared! He shrank away from me as though I were something poisonous. I laid my hand on his shoulder, firmly determined that this time there should be no escape.

"Mr. Delora," I said, "I want a few words with you. Can I have them now?"

"I am busy!" he answered. "At any other time!"

"No other time will do," I answered. "It is only a few words I need say, but those few words must be spoken."

He led the way reluctantly into a sitting-room. There were red plush chairs set at regular intervals against the wall, and a table in the middle covered by papers — mostly out of date. Delora closed the door and turned toward me sternly.

"Captain Rotherby," he said, "I am quite aware that there are certain people in London who are very much interested in me and my doings. Their interests and mine clash, and it is only natural that they should plot against me. But where the devil you come in I cannot tell! Tell me what you mean by playing the spy upon me? What business is it of yours?"

"You misunderstand the situation, sir," I answered. "More than ten days ago you left me in charge of your niece at Charing Cross, while you drove on, according to your own statement, to the Milan Hotel. You never went to that hotel. You never, apparently, meant to. You have never been near it since. You have left your niece in the centre of what seems to be a very nest of intrigue. I have the right to ask you for an explanation of these things. This morning I have a special right, because to-day I have promised to go away into the country, and to take no further interest in your doings."

"Let us suppose," Delora said dryly, "that it is already to-morrow morning."

"No!" I answered. "There is something which I mean to say to you. You need not be alarmed. The few words I have to say to you are not questions. I do not want to understand your secrets,— to penetrate the mystery which surrounds you and your doings. I will not ask you a single question. I will not even ask you why you left your niece in such a fit of terror, and have never yet dared to show your face at the Milan."

"A child would understand these things!" Delora exclaimed. "The Milan Hotel is one of the most public spots in London. It is open to any one who cares to cross the threshold. It is the last place in the world likely to be a suitable home for a man like myself, who is in touch with great affairs."

"Then why did you choose to go there?" I asked.

"It was not my choice at all," Delora answered. "Besides, it was not until I arrived in London that I understood exactly the nature of the intrigues against me."

"At least," I protested, "you should never have brought your niece with you. Frankly, your concerns don't interest me a snap of the fingers. It is of your niece only that I think. You have no right to leave her alone in such anxiety!"

"Nor can I see, sir," Delora answered, "that you have any better right to reproach me with it. Still, if it will shorten this discussion, I admit that if I had known how much trouble there was ahead of me I should not have brought her. I simply disliked having to disappoint her. It was a long-standing promise."

"Let that go," I answered. "I have told you that I have handed in my commission. I have nothing more to do with you or your schemes, whatever they may be. But I came here to find you and to tell you this one thing. Felicia says that you are her uncle, she scouts the idea of your being an impostor, she speaks of you as tenderly and affectionately as a girl well could. That is all very well. Yet, in the face of it, I am here to impress this upon you. I love your niece, Mr. Delora, — some day or other I mean to make her my wife, — and I will not have her dragged into anything which is either disreputable or against the law."

"Has my niece encouraged you?" Delora asked calmly.

"Not in the least," I answered. "She has been kind enough to give me to understand that she cares a little, and there the matter ends. Nothing more could be said between us in this state of uncertainty. But I came here for this one purpose. I came to tell you that if by any chance Felicia should be mistaken, if you play her false in any way, if you seek to embroil her in your schemes, or to do anything by means of which she could suffer, I shall first of all shake the life out of your body, and then I shall go to Scotland Yard and tell them how much I know."

"About Mr. Tapilow, also?" Delora asked, with a sneer.

"Do you think I am afraid to take the punishment for

my own follies?" I asked indignantly. "If I believed that, I would go and give myself up to-morrow. Louis can give me away if he will, or you. I don't care a snap of the fingers. But what I want you to understand is this. Felicia is, I presume, your niece. I should have been inclined to have doubted it, but I cannot disbelieve her own word. I think myself that it is brutal to have brought such a child here and to have left her alone —"

"She is not alone," Delora interrupted stiffly. "She has a companion."

"Who arrived yesterday," I continued. "She has spent some very bad days alone, I can promise you that."

"I have telephoned," Delora said, "twice a day — sometimes oftener."

I laughed ironically.

"For your own sake or hers, I wonder," I said. "Anyhow, we can leave that alone. What I want you to understand is this, that if there is indeed anything illegal or criminal in your secret doings over here, you must take care that Felicia is safely provided for if things should go against you. She is not to be left there to be the butt of a great criminal action. If I find that you or any of your friends are making use of her in any way whatever, I swear that you shall suffer for it!"

Delora smiled at me grimly. He seemed in his few dry words to have revealed something of his stronger and less nervous self.

"You terrify me!" he said. "Yet I think that we must go on pretty well as we are, even if my niece has been fortunate enough to enlist your sympathies on her behalf. Never mind who I am, or what my business is in this country, young man. It is not your affair. You should have enough to think about yourself in this country of easy extradition. My niece can look after herself. So can I. We do not need your aid, or welcome your interference."

"You insinuate," I declared indignantly, "that your niece is one of your helpers! I do not believe it!"

"Helpers in what?" he asked, with upraised eyebrows.

"God knows!" I exclaimed, a little impatiently. "What you do, or what you try to do, is not my business. Felicia is. That is why I have warned you."

"Am I to have the honor, then?" Delora asked, with a curl of his thin lips, —

"You are," I interrupted, "if you call it an honor, although to tell you frankly, as things are at present, I am not inclined to go about begging too many different people's permission. If it were not that my brother Dicky has just written over from Brazil to ask me to be civil to you and your niece, you would n't have left this place so easily."

"Your brother!" Delora said, looking at me uneasily. "Say that again."

"Certainly!" I answered. "My brother Dicky, who is now out in Brazil, and who has written to me about you. You met him there, of course?" I added. "He stayed with you at — let me see, what is the name of your place?" I asked suddenly.

"Menita," Delora answered, without hesitation. "Now you mention it, of course I remember him! If he has written you to be civil to us, you can do it best by minding your own business. In a fortnight's time I shall be free to entertain or to be entertained. At present I am on a secret mission, and I do not wish my work to be interfered with."

I moved toward the door.

"I have said all that I wish to say," I remarked. "If I hear nothing from you I shall come back to London in fourteen days."

"You will find me with my niece," Delora said, "and we shall be happy to see you."

I left him there, feeling somehow or other that I had not had the best of our interview. Yet my position from the first was hopeless. There was nothing for me to do but to keep my word to Felicia and let things drift.

I drove to the club on my way to the station, where I had arranged for my baggage to be sent. As I crossed Pall Mall I met Lamartine. He was standing on the pavement, on the point of entering a motor-car on which was piled some luggage.

"So you, too, are leaving London," I remarked, stopping for a moment.

He looked at me curiously.

"I am going to Paris," he said.

"A pleasure trip?" I asked.

He shook his head.

"Not entirely," he said. "Only this morning I made a somewhat surprising discovery."

"Concerning our friend?" I asked.

"Concerning our friend," Lamartine echoed.

He seemed dubious, for a moment, whether to take me into his confidence.

"You have not found Delora yet?" I asked.

"Not yet," he answered. "And you?"

"I have seen him," I admitted.

"Are you disposed to tell me where?" Lamartine asked softly.

I shook my head.

"I have finished with the affair," I told him. "I finish

as I began, — absolutely bewildered! I know nothing and understand nothing. I am going down into the country to shoot pheasants."

Lamartine smiled.

"I," he remarked, entering the car, "am going after bigger game!"

CHAPTER XXX

TO NEWCASTLE BY ROAD

I FOUND several of my brother's friends staying at Feltham, who were also well known to me, and my aunt, who was playing hostess, had several women staying with her. We spent the time very much after the fashion of an ordinary house-party during the first week of October. We shot until four o'clock, came home and played bridge until dinner-time, bridge or billiards after dinner, varied by a dance one night and some amateur theatricals. On the fifth day a singular thing happened to me.

The whole of the house-party were invited to shoot with my uncle, Lord Horington, who lived about forty miles from us. We left in two motor-cars soon after breakfast-time, and for the last few miles of the way we struck the great north road. It was just after we had entered it that we came upon a huge travelling car, covered with dust, and with portmanteaus strapped upon the roof, hung up by the side of the road. Our chauffeur slowed down to find out if we could be of any use, and as the reply was scarcely intelligible, we came to a full stop. He dismounted to speak to the other chauffeur, and I looked curiously at the two men who were leaning back in the luxurious seats inside the car. For a moment I could not believe my eyes! Then I opened the door of my own car and stepped quickly into the road. The two men who were sitting there, and by whom I was as yet unobserved, were Delora and the Chinese ambassador!

I walked at once up to the window of their car and knocked at it. Delora leaned forward and recognized me at once. His face, for a moment, seemed dark with anger. He let down the sash.

"What does this mean?" he asked. "Have you forgotten our bargain?"

I laughed a little shortly.

"My dear sir," I said, "it is not I who have come to see you, but you to see me. I am within a few miles of my own estate, on my way to shoot at a friend's."

He stared at me for a moment incredulously.

"Do you mean to tell me," he said, in a low tone, "that you have not followed us from London?"

"Why I have not been in London, or near it, for five days," I told him. "I slept last night within thirty miles from here, and, as I told you before, am on my way to shoot with my uncle at the present moment."

"I know nothing of the geography of your country," Delora said shortly. "What you say may be correct. His Excellency and I are having a few days' holiday."

"May I hope to have the pleasure of seeing you at Feltham?" I inquired.

"I am afraid not," Delora answered. "If we had known that we should have been so near, we might have arranged to pay you a visit. As it is, we are in a hurry to get on."

"How far north did you think of going?" I asked.

"We have not decided," Delora answered. "Remember our bargain, and ask no questions."

"But this is a holiday trip," I reminded him. "Surely I may be permitted to advise you about the picturesque spots in my own country!"

"You can tell me, at any rate, what it is that has happened to our car," Delora answered. "Neither His Excellency nor I know anything about such matters."

I walked round and talked to the two chauffeurs. The accident, it seemed, was a trivial one, and with the help of a special spanner, with which we were supplied, was already rectified. I returned and explained matters to Delora.

"Have you come far this morning?" I asked.

"Not far," Delora answered. "We are taking it easy."

I looked at his tired face, at the car thick with dust, at the Chinese ambassador already nodding in his corner, and I smiled to myself. It was very certain to me that they had run from London without stopping, and I felt an intense curiosity as to their destination. However, I said no more to them. I made my adieux to Delora, and bowed profoundly to the Chinese ambassador, who opened his eyes in time solemnly to return my farewell. The chauffeur was already in his place, and I stopped to speak to him. I saw Delora spring forward and whistle down the speaking-tube, but my question was already asked.

"How far north are you going?" I asked.

"To Newcastle, sir," the man answered.

He turned then to answer the whistle, and I re-entered my own car. We started first, but they passed us in a few minutes travelling at a great rate, and with a cloud of dust behind them. Delora threw an evil glance at me from his place. For once I had stolen a march upon him. They had both been too ignorant of their route to keep their final destination concealed from the chauffeur, and they certainly had not expected to meet any one on the way with whom he would be likely to talk! But why to Newcastle? I asked myself that question so often during the morning that my shooting became purely a mechanical

thing.   Newcastle, — the Tyne, coals, and shipbuilding!
I could think of nothing else in connection with the
place.

Late that evening I sat with a whiskey and soda and
final cigar in the smoking-room.   The evening papers
had just arrived, brought by motor-bicycle from Norwich.
I found nothing to interest me in them, but, glancing down
the columns, my attention was attracted by some mention
of Brazil.   I looked to see what the paragraph might be.
It concerned some new battleships, and was headed, —

LARGEST BATTLESHIPS IN THE WORLD!

It is not generally known, that there will be launched
from the works of Messrs. Halliday & Co. on the Tyne, within
the next three or four weeks, two of the most powerful battleships of the " Dreadnought " type, which have yet been built.

There followed some specifications, in which I was not
particularly interested, an account of their armament, and
a final remark, —

One is tempted to ask how a country, in the financial position
of Brazil, can possibly reconcile it with her ideas of national
economy, to spend something like three millions in battleships,
which there does not seem to be the slightest chance of her
ever being called upon to use!

Somehow or other this paragraph fascinated me.   I
read it over and over again.   I could see no connection between it and the visit of Delora to Newcastle, especially
accompanied as he was by the Chinese ambassador.   Yet
the more I thought of it, the more I felt convinced that in
some way the two were connected.   I put down the paper
at last, and called out of the room to a motoring friend.

"How far is it to Newcastle from here, Jacky?"

Jacky Dalton, a fair-haired young giant, one of the keenest sportsmen whom I had ever met, and whose mind and soul was now entirely dominated by the craze for motoring, told me with only a few moments' hesitation.

"Between two hundred and two hundred and twenty miles, Austen," he said, "and a magnificent road. With my new Napier, I reckon that I could get there in six hours, or less at night, with this moon."

I walked to the window. Across the park the outline of the trees and even the bracken stood out with extraordinary distinctness in the brilliant moonlight. There was not a breath of air, although every window in the house was open. We were having a few days of record heat.

"Jove, what a gorgeous run it would be to-night!" Dalton said, with a little sigh, looking out over my shoulder. "Empty roads, as light as day, and a breeze like midsummer! You don't want to go, do you, Austen?"

"Will you take me?" I asked.

"Like a shot!" he answered. "I only wish you were in earnest!"

"But I am," I declared. "If you don't mind missing the day's shooting to-morrow I'd love to run up there. It's impossible to sleep with this heat."

"It's a great idea," Dalton declared enthusiastically. "I'd love a day off from shooting."

I turned to a younger cousin of mine, who had just come in from the billiard-room.

"Dick," I said, "will you run things to-morrow if I go off motoring with Dalton?"

"Of course I will," he answered. "It's only home shooting, anyway. I'd rather like a day off because of the cricket match in the afternoon."

"Jacky, I'm your man!" I declared.

"We'll have Ferris in at once," he declared. "Bet you what you like he's ready to start in a quarter of an hour. I always have her kept ready tuned right up."

I rang the bell and sent for Jacky's chauffeur. He appeared after a few minutes' delay, — a short, hard-faced young man, who before Jacky had engaged him had driven a racing car.

"Ferris," his master said, "we want to start for Newcastle in half an hour."

"To-night, sir?" the man asked.

"Certainly," Dalton answered. "I shall drive some of the way myself. Everything is in order, I suppose?"

"Everything, sir," the man answered. "You can start in ten minutes if you wish."

"Any trouble about petrol?" I asked.

"We carry enough for the whole journey, sir," the man answered. "I'll have the car round at the front, sir, in a few minutes."

"Let's go up and change our clothes," Dalton said. "Remember we are going to travel, Austen, especially up the north road. You will want some thickish tweeds and an overcoat, although it seems so stifling here."

I nodded.

"Right, Jacky!" I answered. "I'll be down in a quarter of an hour, or twenty minutes at the most."

In less than half an hour we were off. It was only when the great car swung from the avenue into the country lane that Jacky, who was driving, turned toward me.

"By the bye," he asked, "what the devil are we going to Newcastle for?"

I laughed.

"We are going to look at those new battleships, Jacky," I answered.

He stared at me.

"Are you in earnest?"

"Partly," I answered. "Let's say we are going for the ride. It's worth it."

Dalton drew a long breath. We were rushing now through the silent night, with a delicious wind, strong and cool, blowing in our faces.

"By Jove, it is!" he assented.

CHAPTER XXXI

AN INTERESTING DAY

IT was a little after seven o'clock the next morning when we turned into the courtyard of the County Hotel in Newcastle. Immediately in front of us was the car in which we had seen Delora on the previous afternoon. The chauffeur was at work upon it, and although he looked up at our entrance, he paid no particular attention to us.

I blew through the whistle to Ferris.

"Back out of the yard at once," I said, "and go to another hotel."

Dalton looked at me in surprise.

"Forgive my ordering your chauffeur about," I said, as we glided backwards into the street. "That's the car we've come up after, and I don't want the people who travelled in it to know that we are on their heels."

Dalton whistled softly.

"So we are on a chase, are we?" he asked. "You might tell me about it, Austen."

"I can't," I answered. "It's altogether too indefinite. I shouldn't tell you anything which would sound like common sense except this, — that I am exceedingly curious, for several reasons, to know what those two men who came up in that car have to do in Newcastle."

"Who are they?" Dalton asked.

"One is a rich Brazilian named Delora, and the other the Chinese ambassador," I answered.

The names seemed to convey nothing to my companion, who merely nodded. We had now arrived at the other hotel, and the prospects of breakfast were already claiming our attention. We sat down in the coffee-room and attacked our bacon and eggs and coffee with zest.

"How long do you want to stay here?" Dalton asked.

"I am not quite sure," I answered. "Look here, Jacky," I continued, "supposing I wanted to stay all day and to go back to-night, so that we got home to breakfast to-morrow morning, would that be too long for you?"

"That would do me splendidly," Dalton declared. "I have never been in this part of the world, and I should like to look round. We must be back for to-morrow morning, you know, because all those fellows are coming to shoot from Horington's."

I nodded.

"We will make that the latest," I said.

Jacky left me, a few minutes later, to visit the local garage. Without any clear idea as to what was best to be done, I still felt that I was justified in making a few inquiries as to the cause of Delora's presence in Newcastle with that particular companion. I went to the telephone, therefore, and rang up the County Hotel. I asked to speak to the manager, who came at once to the instrument.

"I understand," I said, "that the Chinese ambassador has just arrived at your hotel. Would you be so kind as to ask him whether he would consent to be interviewed as to the reasons of his visit?"

I waited several minutes for a reply. When it came it was at least emphatic. The visit of the ambassador, the manager told me, was entirely a private one. He was simply on a motor tour with a friend, and they had called at Newcastle as it was an interesting city which the ambassador had never seen. He declined most firmly to have anything to do with any interviewer.

The reply being exactly what I had expected, I was not in the least disappointed.

"Perhaps," I said to the manager, "you can tell me how long he is staying."

"I have no idea, sir," the manager answered. "They have just ordered a carriage to make a call in the town."

I thanked him, and left the hotel at once on foot. When I arrived near the County Hotel a four-wheel cab was drawn up at the entrance. From a safe distance I stood watching it, and in a few minutes I saw the ambassador and Delora come swiftly out of the hotel and step inside. I waited till they had driven off, and then crossed the road to where the hall-porter was still standing on the pavement. I put five shillings into his hand.

"I am a reporter," I said. "Can you tell me where the ambassador has gone to?"

He smiled, and touched his hat.

"They are going to the offices of Messrs. Halliday & Co., the great shipbuilders, in Corporation Street," he answered.

I thanked him, and walked slowly away. I found plenty of material for thought, but it seemed to me that there was nothing more which I could do. Nevertheless, I walked along towards the address which the porter had given me, and found, as I had expected, that the cab was standing empty outside. Opposite was a small public-house. I went in, ordered a whiskey and soda, and lit a cigarette. Then I sat down facing the window. Half an hour passed, and then an hour. It was one o'clock before the two men reappeared. They were accompanied by a third person, whom I judged to be a member of the firm, and who entered the cab with them. On the pavement they were accosted by a young man in spectacles, who took off his hat and said a few words to the ambassador. The latter, however, shaking his head, stepped into the cab. The young man pushed forward once more, but the cab drove off. As soon as it had turned the corner I hurried out and addressed him.

"His Excellency does not care to be spoken to," I remarked.

The reporter — his profession was quite obvious — shook his head.

"I only wanted a word or two," he said, "but he would not have anything to say to me."

"I wonder if he is going to look over any of the ships that are building," I remarked.

"There is nothing much in the yards," the young man said, "except the two Brazilian battleships. I don't think that Hallidays are allowed to show any one over them unless they have a special permit from the Brazilian Government."

I nodded.

"Fine ships, are n't they?" I asked.

"The finest that have ever left the Tyne," the young man answered enthusiastically. "What a little country like Brazil can possibly want with the most powerful warships in the world no one can guess. Are you on a London paper?" he asked me.

I nodded.

"I have followed them all the way down here," I said, "but they have not a word to say. By the bye," I added, "did you know that the gentleman with the Chinese ambassador was a very prominent Brazilian?"

The reporter whistled softly.

"I wonder what that means!" he said. "It sounds interesting, somehow."

"Come and have a drink," I said.

He accepted at once.

"What paper are you on?" he asked, as we crossed the street.

"To be honest with you," I replied, "I am not on a paper at all. I am not even a reporter. I am interested in the visit of these two men to Newcastle for more serious reasons."

The young man looked at me thoughtfully. He slipped his arm through mine as though he intended never to let me go. Evidently he scented a story.

"I suppose," he said, "you mean that you are a detective?"

"No!" I answered, "scarcely that. I can only tell you that it is my business to watch the movements of those two men."

I could see from his manner that he believed me to be a government spy, or something of the sort. We ordered our drinks and then turned, as though by common consent, once more to the window. A motor-car was drawn up in front of the place, and an elderly man was descending hurriedly.

"Hullo!" the reporter exclaimed. "That's Mr. Halliday, the head of the firm! They must have telephoned for him. He never comes down except on a Thursday. Let's watch and see what happens."

The shipbuilder entered his offices, and was gone for about a quarter of an hour. When he reappeared he was followed by two clerks, one of whom was carrying a great padlocked portfolio under each arm, and the other a huge roll of plans. They entered the motor-car and drove off.

"Come on," I said, finishing my drink hurriedly, "they are off to the County Hotel."

We took a hansom at the corner of the street, and, sure enough, when we arrived at the hotel Mr. Halliday's motor-car was waiting outside. We went at once into the office, where my companion was quite at home.

"Who's with the Chinaman?" he asked the manager, who greeted him cordially.

"A whole crowd," he answered. "First of all, Dickinson — Halliday's manager — came back with him, and the old man himself has just arrived with a couple of clerks."

"What's the game, do you suppose?" the reporter asked.

The hotel manager shrugged his shoulders.

"We're hoping it means orders," he said. "We can do with them. Hallidays could put on another twelve hundred men and not be crowded, and China's about the most likely customer they could get hold of just now."

"Which sitting-room are they in?" my friend asked.

"Number 12," the manager answered. "I can't do anything for you, though, Charlie," he added. "I'd do anything I could, but they have given special orders that no one is to interrupt them, and they decline to be interviewed by or communicate with any strangers."

"I shall see the thing out, nevertheless," my friend announced

"And I," I answered. "Let's have lunch together. Is there a smart boy in the place who could let us know directly any one leaves the sitting-room?"

The manager smiled.

"Mr. Sinclair knows all about that, sir," he said, pointing to my friend. "I have nothing to say about it, of course."

Sinclair left the room for a minute or two. When he came back he nodded confidentially.

"I have a boy watching the door," he said. "The moment any one leaves we shall hear of it."

We went into the restaurant and ordered lunch. In about half an hour a small boy came hastily in and addressed Sinclair.

"They have ordered luncheon up in the sitting-room, sir," he said. "I thought I'd better let you know."

"For how many?" Sinclair asked quickly.

"For four, sir," he answered. "I fancy the two clerks are coming out. The door opened once, and they had their hats on."

"Run along," Sinclair said, "and let us know again directly anything happens."

The boy returned almost at once.

"The clerks have left," he said. "The other four are going to lunch together."

"Did the clerks take the plans with them?" I asked.

"Not all," the boy answered. "They left two port-folios behind."

We finished our luncheon and returned to the bar. It was more than two hours before anything else happened. Then the boy entered a little hurriedly.

"Mr. Halliday has telephoned for his car, and is just leaving, sir," he said. "The two gentlemen from London have just ordered theirs, and I believe it looks as though Mr. Dickinson were going with them. He has telephoned for a bag from his house."

I shook hands with my friend the reporter, and we parted company. I left the hotel quickly and returned to the King's Arms, where we were staying. I was lucky enough to find Jack just finishing lunch.

"I say, old man," I exclaimed, "I wish you'd start for home at once!"

"Right away!" he answered. "We'll ring for Ferris."

The chauffeur came in and received his orders. We got into our coats and walked out toward the front door. Suddenly I drew Jacky back and stood behind a pillar. A great touring car had turned the corner and was passing down the street. In it were three men, — the Chinese ambassador, Delora, and the man who had left the offices of Messrs. Halliday with them.

"Is that the road to London?" I asked the porter.

"It is the way into the main road, sir," he answered, — "two hundred and sixty-five miles."

They swung round the corner and disappeared. Our own car was just drawing up. I turned to Jacky.

"We'd better wait a few minutes," I said, "and tell your man not to overtake that car!"

Jacky looked at me in surprise. He was by no means a curious person, but he was obviously puzzled.

"What a mysterious person you have become, Austen!" he said. "What's it all about?"

"You will know some day," I answered, as we made ourselves comfortable, — "perhaps before many hours are past!"

CHAPTER XXXII

A PROPOSAL

WE arrived at Feltham at a few minutes past ten o'clock, having seen nothing of the car which had left Newcastle a few minutes before ours. Several times we asked on the road and heard news of it, but we could find no sign of it having stopped even for a moment. Apparently it had been driven, without pause for rest or refreshment, at top speed, and we learned that two summonses would probably be issued against its owners. Jacky, who was delighted with the whole expedition, sat with his watch in his hands for the last few miles, and made elaborate calculations as to our average speed, the distance we had traversed, and other matters interesting to the owner of a powerful car.

We were greeted, when we arrived, with all sorts of inquiries as to our expedition, but we declined to say a word until we had dined. We had scarcely commenced our meal before the butler came hurrying in.

"His Lordship is ringing up from London, sir," he said. "He wishes to speak to you particularly. The telephone is through into the library."

I made my way there and took up the receiver without any special interest. Ralph was fidgety these days, and I had no doubt that he had something to say to me about the shooting. His first words, however, riveted my attention.

"Is that you, Austen?" he asked.

"I am here," I answered. "How are you, Ralph?"

"I am all right," he said. "Rather better than usual, in fact. Where on earth have you been to all day? I have rung up four times."

"I have been motoring with Jacky," I told him. "We have been for rather a long run. Have you been wanting me?"

"Yes!" he answered. "I have had a very curious cable from Dicky which I can't understand. I am sorry to bother you, but I think you had better come up to town by the first train in the morning. It's something to do with these Deloras."

"The devil it is!" I exclaimed. "I'll come, Ralph. I shall motor to Norwich, and catch the eight o'clock. Could you give me an idea of what it is?"

"I think I'd rather not over the telephone," Ralph declared, after a moment's hesitation.

"Don't be an idiot!" I answered. "I am really very much interested."

"It's a queer business," Ralph said, "but it will keep until to-morrow. I shall send the car for you to Liverpool Street, and you had better come straight to me."

"Dicky is all right, I hope?" I asked.

"Dicky's all right," Ralph answered. "What sort of sport are you having there?"

"Very fair," I answered. "Heggs sends you the figures every day, I suppose?"

"Yes!" Ralph answered. "You seem to have done very well at the birds. Till to-morrow, Austen!"

"Till to-morrow," I replied. "Good night, old chap!"

"Good night!"

I put down the receiver and went back to my dinner more than ever puzzled. Ralph's summons, I felt, absolved me from any promise I might have made to Delora, and I was looking eagerly forward to the morrow, when I should be once more in London. What puzzled me, however, more even than Dicky's message, was the extreme interest Ralph's tone seemed to denote. His voice sounded quite like his old self.

"Jacky," I said, as we finished dinner, "will you lend me your car to take me into Norwich to-morrow? I have to catch the eight o'clock train to town."

"I'll lend it you with pleasure," Jacky said, looking at me in amazement, "but what on earth's up?"

"Nothing," I answered. "Simply Ralph wants to see me. He isn't particularly communicative himself, but he is very anxious that I should go to town to-morrow. Somehow or other I have more confidence in your Napier than in either of our cars when it comes to catching a train at that time in the morning."

"I'll run you up to town, if you like," Jacky declared, in a burst of good-nature.

"It isn't necessary," I answered. "I shall get up quicker by train, and Ralph's going to meet me at Liverpool Street. Thanks, all the same!"

Jacky lit a cigar.

"I'll go out and tell Ferris myself," he said.

Once more Jacky's car did not fail me. Punctually at a quarter to eight we drove into Norwich Station yard. I breakfasted on the train, and reached Liverpool Street a few minutes after eleven. I found Ralph's big Panhard there, but Ralph himself had not come.

"His Lordship is expecting you at the hotel, sir," the chauffeur told me. "He would have come down himself, but he was expecting a caller."

In less than half an hour I was in my brother's sitting-room. Ralph greeted me cordially.

"Austen," he said, "I am not at all sure that I have not brought you up on rather a fool's errand, but you seemed rather mystified yourself about these Deloras. Here 's the cable from Dicky. What do you make of it? Must have cost him something, extravagant young beggar!"

He passed it across to me. I read it out aloud.

DELORA HERE PUZZLED NOT HEARING FROM BROTHER SHOULD BE IN LONDON IMPORTANT BUSINESS FEARS SOMETHING WRONG ALL CODED CABLES REMAIN UN-ANSWERED INQUIRE MILAN HOTEL IF POSSIBLE FIND DELORA BEG HIM CABLE AT ONCE IN CHALDEAN CODE.

I read the cable through three times.

"May I take this, Ralph?" I said. "I will go round to the Milan at once."

"Certainly," Ralph answered. "I will leave the matter entirely in your hands. It seems as though there were something queer about it."

"There is something queer going on, Ralph," I assured him. "I have found out as much as that myself. Exactly what it means I can't fathom. To tell you the truth, it has been taking a lot of my time lately, and I know very little more than when I started."

"It's the young lady, I suppose," Ralph remarked thoughtfully.

I nodded.

"I am not over keen about interfering in other people's concerns, Ralph," I said. "You know that. It's the girl, of course, and I am afraid, I am very much afraid, that there is something wrong."

"Anyhow," Ralph said, "it does n't follow that the girl 's in it."

"I am jolly certain she is n't!" I said. "What bothers me, of course, is that I hate to think of her being mixed up with anything shady. The Deloras may be great people in their own country, but I'll swear that our friend here is a wrong 'un."

"I suppose you are sure," Ralph said thoughtfully, "that he is Delora — that he is not an impostor, I mean?"

"I thought of that," I answered, "but you see there's the girl. She'd know her own uncle, would n't she? And she told me that she had seen him on and off for years. No, he is Delora right enough! One can't tell," I continued. "Perhaps the whole thing's crooked. Perhaps the Deloras who seem to Dicky such charming people in their own country are a different sort of people on this side. At any rate, I'm off, Ralph, with that cable. I'll look you up as soon as I have found out anything."

Ralph smiled.

"I don't believe," he said, "you are sorry to have an excuse for having another turn at this affair."

"Perhaps not," I answered.

"Take the car," Ralph called out after me. "You may find it useful."

I drove first to the small hotel where I had last seen Delora. Here, however, I was confronted with a certain difficulty. The name of Delora was quite unknown to the people. I described him carefully, however, to the landlady, and she appeared to recognize him.

"The gentleman you mean was, I think, a Mr. Henri-quois. He left us the day before yesterday."

"You know where he went to?" I asked.

She shook her head.

"He asked for a Continental time-table," she said, "but he gave no address, nor did he tell any one of his intentions. He was a gentleman that kept himself to himself," she remarked, looking at me a little curiously.

I thanked the woman and departed. Delora was scarcely likely to have left behind any reliable details of his intentions at such a place. I drove on to the Milan, and entered the Court with a curious little thrill of interest. The hall-porter welcomed me with a smile.

"Glad to see you back again, Captain Rotherby," he said. "Have you any luggage?"

"None," I answered. "I am not sure whether I shall be staying."

"This morning's letters are in your room, sir," he announced.

I nodded. I was not particularly interested in my letters! I drew Ashley a little on one side.

"Tell me," I said, "is Miss Delora still here?"

"She is still here, sir," Ashley announced.

"The companion also?" I asked.

"Yes, sir!" he answered. "I am not sure whether they are in, sir, but they are still staying here."

"And Mr. Delora?" I asked, — "has he ever turned up yet?"

"Not yet, sir. The young lady said that they were expecting him now every day."

"Telephone up and see if Miss Delora is in, Ashley," I asked.

He disappeared for a moment into his office.

"No answer, sir," he announced presently. "I believe that they are out."

Almost as he spoke I saw through the windows of the hair-dresser's shop a familiar figure entering the hotel.

I left Ashley hurriedly, and in a moment I was face to face with Felicia. She gave a little cry when she saw me, and it was a joy to me to realize that it was a cry of pleasure.

"Capitaine Rotherby!" she exclaimed. "You!"

She gave me her hands with an impetuous little movement. I held them tightly in mine.

"I want to speak to you at once," I said. "Where can we go?"

"Madame is out for an hour," she said. "We could go in the little smoking-room. But have you forgotten your promise?"

"Never mind about that, Felicia," I whispered. "Something has happened. I went first to see your uncle, but I could not find him. I must talk with you. Come!"

We walked together across the hall, through the end of the café, down which she threw one long, anxious glance, and entered the little smoking-room. It was empty except for one man writing letters. I led the way into the most remote corner, and wheeled out an easy-chair.

"Felicia," I said, "if I can get a special license, will you marry me to-morrow?"

CHAPTER XXXIII

FELICIA HESITATES

FELICIA looked at me for a moment with wide-open eyes. Then a little stream of color rushed into her cheeks, her lips slowly parted, and she laughed, not altogether without embarrassment.

"Capitaine Rotherby," she said, "you must not **say** such things — so suddenly!"

"Last time we met," I reminded her, "you called me Austen."

"Austen, then, if I must," she said. "You know very well that you should not be here. You are breaking a promise. It is very, very nice to see you," she continued. "Indeed, I do feel that. But I am afraid!"

"I have sufficient reasons for breaking my promise, dear," I said, taking her hand in mine. "I will explain them to you by and by. In the meantime, please answer my question."

"You are serious, then?" she asked, looking at me with wide-open eyes, and lips which quivered a little — whether with laughter or emotion I could not tell.

"I am serious," I answered. "You want taking care of, Felicia, and I am quite sure that I should be the best person in the world to do it."

Her eyes fell before mine. She seemed to be studying the point of her long patent shoe. As usual she was dressed delightfully, in a light fawn-colored tailor-made gown and a large black hat. Nevertheless she seemed to me to be thinner and frailer than when I had first seen her — too girlish, almost, for her fashionable clothes.

"Do you think that you would take care of me?" she said softly. "I am afraid I am a very ignorant little person. I do not know much about England or English ways, and every one says that things are so different here."

"There is one thing," I declared, "which is the same all the world over, and that is that when two people care for one another, the world becomes not such a very difficult place to live in, Felicia. I wonder if you could not try and care a little for me?"

"I do," she murmured, without looking up.

"Enough?" I asked.

She sighed. Suddenly she raised her eyes, and I saw things there which amazed me. They were no longer the eyes of a frightened child. I was thrilled with the passion which seemed somehow or other to have been born in their deep blue depths.

"Dear Austen," she said, "I think that I care quite enough. But listen. How can I say, 'Yes,' to you? Always my uncle has been kind, in his way. I know now that he is worried, harassed to death, afraid, even, of what may happen hour by hour. I could not leave him. He would think that I had lost faith, that I had gone over to his enemies."

"Felicia dear," I said, "I do not wish to be the enemy of any one who is your friend. Indeed, your uncle and his doings mean so little to me. If they are honest, I might be able to help him. If he is engaged in transactions of which he is ashamed, then it is time that you were taken away."

"I will never believe that," she declared.

"Felicia," I said, "I will tell you why I have broken my

promise and come to London. I believe I told you that I had a brother out in Brazil?"

"Yes!" she answered, — "Dicky, you called him."

"He wrote, you know, and said that he had been staying with the Deloras on their estate, and he begged that I should call upon your uncle here. Now I have had a cable from him. Felicia, there is something wrong. You shall read the cable for yourself."

I gave it to her. She read it word by word. Then she read it again, aloud, very softly to herself, and finally gave it back to me.

"I do not understand," she whispered. "I do not know why my uncle has not communicated with his brother."

"I am beginning to believe, Felicia," I said, "that I know more than you. I tell you frankly I believe that your uncle has kept silence because he is not honestly carrying out the business on which he was sent to England. Tell me exactly, will you? When did he arrive from America?"

She shook her head.

"Austen," she said, "you know there were some things which I promised to keep silent about, and this is one."

"At any rate," I said, half to myself, "he could not have been in Paris more than three weeks. I do not understand how in that three weeks he could have obtained such a hold upon you that you should come here and do his bidding blindly, although you must know that some of the things he does are extraordinary and mysterious."

She was obviously distressed.

"There is something," she said, "of course, which I am not telling you, — something which I promised to keep secret. But, Austen," she went on, laying her fingers upon my coat sleeve, "let me tell you this. I am getting more and more worried every day. I understand nothing. The explanations which I have had from my uncle grow more and more extraordinary. Why we are here, why he is still in hiding, why he lives in the shadow of such fear day by day, I cannot imagine. I am beginning to lose heart. Through the telephone last night I told him that I must see him. He has half promised that I shall, to-day or to-morrow. I shall tell him, Austen, that I must know more about the reasons for all this mystery, or I will go back to Madame Quintaine's. I wrote to her soon after I came here, when I was frightened, and she told me that she would gladly have me back. My uncles have always paid her a good deal of money," she went on, "for taking care of me."

I drew a long breath of relief.

"Felicia," I said, "you are talking like a dear, sensible little woman. But," I added, "you have not answered my question!"

She looked away, laughing.

"Of course you are not in earnest!" she exclaimed.

"Of course I am!" I persisted.

"You must know," she said softly, "that I could not do a thing like that. My uncle has always been so kind to me —"

"But you have only seen him three weeks," I interrupted. "Before that he was in Brazil!"

She was silent for several moments.

"Well," she said, "even if it were so, he could be very kind to me, could n't he, even if he was in Brazil and I was in Paris? You see, my father was the poor one of the family, who died without any money at all, yet I have always had everything in the world I want, and when I come of age they are going to give me a great sum of money. It is not that I think about," she went on, "but they write to me always, and they treat me as though I were their own daughter. Often they have said how they would love to have had me out in Brazil. I think that it is really their own kindness that they let me stay in Paris."

"Felicia," I said, "tell me really how much you do know of your uncle — the one who is with you now?"

She shook her head.

"No!" she said. "I cannot do that. I made a promise and I must keep it. But I will promise you this, if you like. If I find that it is not the truth which I have been told I will come to you if you want me."

I held her hands tightly in mine.

"You are beginning to have doubts, are you not?" I asked.

"Oh, I don't know!" she answered. "I don't know! There are times when I am frightened. Austen, I must go now."

I looked at the clock. It was almost two o'clock.

"We couldn't have lunch together, I suppose?" I asked.

She shook her head, laughing.

"I had lunch more than an hour ago," she said, "and I have to meet madame at a dress-maker's. I must go, really, Austen."

"Can't I see you again, dear?"

"I will come into this room, if I can, about five," she said. "Don't come out with me now. It is the luncheon time in the café, and I am afraid of Louis."

She flitted away, leaving behind a faint odor of violets shaken from the skirts she had lifted so daintily as she had hurried down the few steps. I watched her out of sight.

Then I opened the door myself and passed out into the café. . . .

Louis, for the first few minutes, was not visible, but one of the other *maîtres d'hôtel* procured for me a table in a somewhat retired corner of the room. My luncheon was already served before Louis appeared before me. For the second time his impassive countenance seemed to be disturbed.

"Back in London, Captain Rotherby," he remarked, with the ghost of his usual welcoming smile.

"Back again, Louis," I answered cheerfully.

Louis bent over my table.

"I thought," he said, "that an English gentleman never broke his promise!"

"Nor does he, Louis," I answered, "unless the circumstances under which it was given themselves change. I came up from the country this morning."

"Upon private business?" Louis asked.

"No!" I answered. "Upon the business in which you and Mr. Delora are both interested. Did you know, Louis, that I had a brother in Brazil?"

"What of it, monsieur?" Louis asked sharply.

For once I had the best of matters. Louis was evidently in a highly nervous state, from which I imagined that things connected with their undertaking, whatever it might be, had reached a critical stage. There were lines underneath his eyes, and he looked about him every now and then nervously.

"My brother," I remarked, "first wrote to me to be sure and look up Mr. Delora, and to be civil to him. I have done this to the best of my ability!"

Louis frowned.

"Go on," he said.

"Last night," I continued, speaking very deliberately, "my brother who is in London rang me up in Norfolk. He told me that he had just received a cable from Dicky concerning Mr. Delora. It was at his earnest request that I came to London this morning. By the bye, Louis," I added, "I think that I should like some *Riz Diane*."

Louis looked for a moment as though he were about to consign my innocent desire for *Riz Diane* to the bottommost depths. The effort with which he recovered himself was really magnificent. He drew a long breath, and bowed his acquiescence.

"By all means, monsieur!"

He called to a waiter, and was particular in his instructions as to my order. Then he turned back to me.

"Monsieur," he said, "you will tell me what was in that cable?"

"I think not, Louis," I answered. "You see I really cannot recognize you in this matter at all. I must find Mr. Delora at once. It is important."

"But if he cannot be found?" Louis asked quickly.

"Then I think that the best thing I can do," I continued, after a moment's pause, "is to call at the Brazilian embassy."

I had a feeling, the feeling for a moment that, notwithstanding the crowded room and Louis' attitude of polite attention, my life was in danger. There flashed something in his eyes indescribably venomous. I seemed to see there his intense and passionate desire to sweep me from the face of the earth.

"Of course," I continued, "if I can find Mr. Delora, that is what I would really prefer. There is a certain matter upon which I must have an explanation from him."

"Monsieur will not have finished his luncheon for twenty

minutes or so," Louis said calmly. "At the end of that time I will return."

"Always glad to have a chat with you, Louis," I declared.

"You will not leave," he asked, "before I come back?"

"Not if you return in a reasonable time," I answered.

Louis bowed and hurried off. I saw him disappear for a moment into the service room. When he came out into the restaurant he was once more discharging his duties, moving about amongst his clients, supervising, suggesting, bidding farewell to departing guests, and welcoming new arrivals. A very busy man, Louis, for the café was crowded that day. I wondered, as I saw him pass backwards and forwards, with that eternal and yet not displeasing smile upon his lips, what lay at the back of his head concerning me!

CHAPTER XXXIV

AN APPOINTMENT WITH DELORA

My *Riz Diane* duly arrived, but was served, I noticed, by a different waiter. It looked very tempting, and it was indeed a dish of which I was particularly fond, but I realized that it had been specially ordered by Louis, and with a sigh I pushed it on one side. I finished my luncheon with rolls and butter, and took care to procure my coffee before Louis returned.

"Well," I asked, as he stopped once more before me, "what is it to be? Are you going to give me Delora's address?"

"That is not the trouble, monsieur," Louis declared. "Mr. Delora is away from London."

"I think you will find that he is back again, Louis," I answered. "It was a very interesting trip to Newcastle, but it was soon over. He arrived in London with his illustrious companion last night."

This time I had really astonished Louis! He looked at me with a genuine expression of profound surprise.

"You are under the impression," he said slowly, "that Mr. Delora has been to Newcastle!"

"That is scarcely the way I look at it, Louis," I answered. "You see I was in Newcastle myself and saw him."

I fancy that Louis' manner toward me, from this time onward, acquired a new respect, but I recognized the fact that there was danger greater than ever before under his increasing suaveness.

"Captain Rotherby," he said, "you were not meant to be an idle man. You have gifts of which you should make use!"

"In the meantime," I said, "when can I see Mr. Delora?"

"This afternoon, if you like," Louis answered. "Here is his address."

He scribbled a few words down on a piece of paper and passed it to me. When I had received it I did not like it. It was an out-of-the-way street in Bermondsey, in a quarter of which I was absolutely ignorant except by repute.

"Couldn't we arrange, don't you think, Louis," I asked, "to have Mr. Delora come up here?"

"You could send down a note and ask him," Louis answered. "He is staying at that address under the name of Hoffmeyer."

"I will write him a letter," I decided, signing my bill.

"You will let me know the result?" Louis asked, looking at me anxiously.

"Certainly," I answered.

I rose to my feet, but Louis did not immediately stand aside.

"Captain Rotherby," he said, "there is one thing I should like to ask you. How did you know of Mr. Delora's projected visit to Newcastle?"

I smiled.

"Why should I give away my methods, Louis?" I said. "You know very well that the movements of Mr. Delora have become very interesting to me. You and I are on opposite sides. I certainly do not feel called upon to disclose my sources of information."

I passed out of the restaurant, and ascended to my own room.   There I drew a sheet of paper toward me and wrote.

DEAR SIR,

I trust you will recognize the fact that although I am writing to you from London, and from the Milan Hotel, I have not intentionally broken the compact I made with you.   The fact is, a somewhat singular thing has occurred.   My brother — Mr. Richard Rotherby — whom you will doubtless remember, and who speaks most gratefully of your hospitality in Brazil, has sent me a cable on behalf of your brother — Mr. Nicholas Delora.   It seems that you have not kept him acquainted with your doings here, and that you have failed to make use of a certain cipher that was agreed upon.   He is, therefore, exceedingly anxious to know of your doings, and has begged me to see you at once and report.   Will you, for that purpose, be good enough to grant me a five minutes' interview ?

Sincerely yours,

AUSTEN ROTHERBY.

I sealed this letter, and addressed it to the very obscure street in Bermondsey which Louis had designated.   Then I procured a messenger boy and sent it off, with instructions that the bearer must wait for an answer.   Afterwards there was little for me to do but wait.   I tried to see Felicia, but I only succeeded in having the door of her rooms practically slammed in my face by Madame Müller. I was too anxious for a reply to my letter to go round to the club, so I simply hung about the place, smoking and waiting.   When at last the messenger boy came back, however, it was only to report a certain amount of failure.   He had found the right address and delivered the note, but the gentleman was out, and not expected in till the evening.   After this, I went round to my club, leaving an order that any note or message was to be sent after me. I cut into a rubber of bridge, but I had scarcely finished my second game before a telegram was brought in for me, sent on from the Milan. I tore it open. It was from Delora.

Have received your note.   Will see you at this address ten o'clock this evening.

I thrust the telegram into my waistcoat pocket and finished the rubber. Soon afterwards I cut out and took a hansom round to Claridge's Hotel. I found my brother in and expecting to hear from me.

"Ralph," I said, "I can't bring you any news just now. If you must cable Dicky, you had better just cable that we are making inquiries. I have an appointment to see Delora at ten o'clock to-night."

"Where is he?" Ralph asked, with interest.

"The address he has sent me is some low street in Bermondsey," I answered. "It is absolutely impossible that he should have chosen such a place to stop in except as a hiding-place. I don't like the look of it, Ralph."

"Then don't go," Ralph said quickly. "There is no need for you to run into danger for nothing at all."

"I am not afraid of that," I answered. "What really bothers me is that I am up against a problem which seems insoluble. Frankly, I don't believe a snap of the fingers in Delora. No man, however secret or important his business might be, would descend to such subterfuges. The only point in his favor is that this dodging about may be all due to political reasons. I cannot understand his friendship with the Chinese ambassador."

"Can't you?" Ralph answered. "I have been thinking

over what you told me, Austen, and I fancy, perhaps, I can give you a hint. Do you know that at the present moment the two most powerful battleships in the world are being built on the Tyne for Brazil?"

"I know that," I admitted. "Go on."

"What does Brazil want with battleships of that class?" my brother continued. "Obviously they would be useless to her. She could not man them. It would be a severe strain to her finances even to put them into commission. I am of opinion that the order to build them was given as a speculation by a few shrewd men in the Brazilian Government who foresaw unsettled times ahead, and they are there to be disposed of to the highest European or Asiatic bidder!"

I saw Ralph's point at once.

"By Jove!" I exclaimed. "You think, then, that Delora is over here to arrange for the sale of them to some other Government — presumably to China?"

"Why not?" Ralph asked. "It is feasible, and to some extent it explains a good deal of what has seemed to you so mysterious. There could be no more possible purchaser of the battleships than China, except, perhaps, Russia, and transactions of that sort are always attended with a large amount of secrecy."

"Of course, if you are on the right track," I admitted, "everything is explained, and Delora is justified. There is just one thing which I do not understand, and that is why he should have associated with such a pack of thieves as the people at the Café des Deux Épingles, and why he should be forced to make an ally — I had almost said accomplice — of Louis."

"Well, you can't understand everything all at once," Ralph answered. "At the same time, if I were you, I would try and see if the hint I have given you fits in with the rest of the puzzle."

"I'll get the truth out of Delora to-night!" I declared. "And, Ralph!"

"Well?" he asked.

"I have asked Felicia Delora to marry me," I continued. Ralph looked at me for a moment, doubtfully.

"Would n't it have been better to have had this matter cleared up first?" he asked.

"I could n't help it," I answered. "The child is all alone, and it makes my heart ache to think what a poor little pawn she is in the game these men are playing. I'd like to take her right away from it, Ralph, but she is staunch. She fancies that she is indebted to her uncle, and she will obey his orders."

"You can't think any the worse of her for that," Ralph remarked.

"I don't," I answered, sighing, "but it makes the position a little difficult."

"Come and see me to-morrow morning," Ralph said, "and tell me exactly what passes between you and Delora. We must cable Dicky some time soon."

"I will," I promised, taking up my hat. "Good-day, Ralph!"

CHAPTER XXXV

A NARROW ESCAPE

I FELT that night an unusual desire to take all possible precautions before leaving the Milan for Bermondsey. I wrote a letter explaining my visit and my suspicions, and placed it in Ashley's hands.

"Look here, Ashley," I said, "I am going off on an errand which I don't feel quite comfortable about. Between you and me, it is connected with the disappearance of Miss Delora's uncle. I feel that it is likely, even probable, that I shall get into trouble, and I want you to promise me this. If I am not back here by half-past eleven, I want you to take this letter, which contains a full statement of everything, to Scotland Yard. Either take it yourself," I continued, "or send some one absolutely trustworthy with it."

The man looked a little serious.

"Very good, sir," he said. "I'll attend to it. At the same time, if I might make the suggestion, I should take a couple of plain-clothes policemen with me. It's a pretty low part where you are going, and one hears of queer doings, nowadays."

"I am bound to go, Ashley," I answered, "but I am not likely to come to much grief. I have a revolver in my pocket, and I have not studied boxing with Baxter for nothing. I don't fancy there's anything in Bermondsey going to hurt me."

"I hope not, sir," Ashley answered civilly. "At half-past eleven, if I do not hear from you, I shall go myself to Scotland Yard."

I nodded.

"And in the meantime," I said, "a taxicab, if you please."

I drove to the address given me on the paper. It was an odd, half-forgotten street, terminating in a *cul-de-sac*, and not far from the river. The few houses it contained were larger than the majority of those in the neighborhood, but were in a shocking state of repair. The one at which I eventually stopped had a timber yard adjoining, or rather attached to it. I left the taxicab outside, and made my somewhat uncertain way up to the front door. Only a few yards from me a great black dog was straining at his collar and barking furiously. I was somewhat relieved when the door was opened immediately at my knock.

"Is Mr. Hoffmeyer staying here?" I asked.

A little old man carrying a tallow candle stuck into a cheap candlestick nodded assent, and closed the door after me. I noticed, without any particular pleasure, that he also drew the bolts.

"What do you do that for?" I asked sharply. "I shall only be here a few minutes. It is not worth while locking up."

The man looked at me but said nothing. He seemed to show neither any desire nor any ability for speech. Only as I repeated my question he nodded slowly as one who barely understands.

"Mr. Hoffmeyer is in his room," he said. "He will be glad to see you."

I followed him along as miserable a passage as ever I

saw in my life. The walls were damp, and the paper hung down here and there in long, untidy patches. The ceiling was barely whitewashed; the stairs by which we passed were uncarpeted. The whole place had a most dejected and weary appearance. Then he showed me into a small sitting-room, in which one man sat writing at a table. He looked up as I entered. It was Delora.

"Well," he said, "so this is how you keep your promise!"

"Something has happened since then," I answered. "I have received a cable from my brother which we do not understand."

"A cable from your brother in Brazil?" he asked slowly.

"Yes!" I answered.

Delora turned slowly in his chair and rose to his feet. He was tall and gaunt. His face was lined. He had somehow or other the appearance of a man who is driven to bay. Yet there was something splendid about the way he nerved himself to listen to me with indifference.

"What does he say — your brother?"

"The cable is inspired by Nicholas Delora," I answered. "Listen, and I will read it to you."

I read it to him word by word. When I had finished he simply nodded.

"Is that all?" he asked.

"That is all," I answered. "You will see that what makes your brother anxious is that not only have you failed to keep your word so far as regards communicating with him, but you have not made use of a certain private code arranged between you."

"The business upon which I am engaged," Delora said calmly, "is of great importance, but I do not care to be rushing all the time to the telegraph office. Nicholas is a nervous person. In a case like this he should be content to wait. However, since he has sought the interference of outsiders, I will cable him to-morrow morning."

"Very well," I answered. "I can ask no more than that. I shall go myself to the cable office and send my brother a message."

"What shall you tell him?" Delora asked.

"I shall tell him that I have seen you," I answered, "that you are well, and that he will hear from you to-morrow morning."

"Why cable at all?" Delora asked. "Surely to-morrow morning will be soon enough?"

"From your point of view, yes!" I said. "But there is one other thing which I am going to do. I am going to say in my cable, that if the news he receives from you to-morrow morning is not satisfactory, I shall lay the matter before the Brazilian legation here, and I shall explain why!"

Delora's eyes were like points of fire. Nevertheless, his self-restraint was admirable. He contented himself, indeed, with a low bow.

"You will tell our friends there," he said slowly, "that you have seen me? That I am — you see I admit that — living practically in hiding, apart from my niece? You will also, perhaps, inform them of various other little episodes with which, owing to your unfortunate habit of looking into other people's business, you have become acquainted?"

"Naturally," I answered.

"I think not!" Delora said.

There was an instant's silence. I looked at Delora and wondered what he meant. He looked at me as a man looks at his enemy.

"May I ask how you intend to prevent me?" I inquired.

"Easily!" he answered, with a slight sneer. "There are four men in this house who will obey my bidding. There are also five modes of exit, two of which lead into the river."

"I congratulate you," I said, "upon the possession of such a unique lodging-house."

Delora sighed.

"I can assure you," he said, "that it is more expensive than the finest suite in the Milan. Still, what would you have? When one has friends who are too curious, one must receive them in a fitting lodging."

"You are a very brave man, Mr. Delora," I said.

"Indeed!" he answered dryly. "I should have thought that the bravery had lain in another direction!"

I shook my head.

"I," I said, "am, I fear, a coward. Even when to-night I started out to keep my appointment with you I had fears. I was so afraid," I continued, "that I even went so far as to insure my safety."

"To insure your safety!" he repeated softly, like a man who repeats words of whose significance he is not assured.

"I admit it," I answered. "It was cowardly, and, I am sure, unnecessary. But I did it."

His face darkened with anger.

"You have brought an escort with you, perhaps?" he said. "You have the police outside?"

I shook my head.

"Nothing so clumsy," I answered. "There is just my taxicab, which won't go away unless it is I who says to go, and a little note I left with the hall-porter of the Milan, to be opened in case I was not back in an hour and a half. You see," I continued, apologetically, "my nerve has been a little shaken lately, and I did not know the neighborhood."

"You are discretion itself," Delora said. "Some day I will remember this as a joke against you. Have you been reading Gaboriau, my young friend, or his English disciples? This is your own city — London — the most law-abiding place on God's earth."

"I know it," I answered, "and yet a place is so much what the people who live in it may make it. I must confess that your five exits, two on to the river, would have given me a little shiver if I had not known for certain that I had made my visit to you safe."

Delora tried to smile. As a matter of fact, I could see that the man was shaking with fury.

"You are a strange person, Captain Rotherby," he said. "If I had not seen you bear yourself as a man of courage I should have been tempted to congratulate your army upon its freedom from your active services. You have no more to say to me?"

"Nothing more," I answered.

"To-morrow morning at eleven o'clock," Delora said, "you will be arrested for the attempted murder of Stephen Tapilow."

"It is exceedingly kind of you," I answered, "to give me this warning. I will make my arrangements accordingly."

"One thing," Delora said, "would change the course of Fate."

"That one thing," I remarked, "being that I should not send this cablegram."

"Exactly!" Delora answered, "in which case you will find your banking account the richer by ten thousand pounds."

I looked at him steadfastly.

"What manner of a swindle is this," I asked, "in which you, Louis, poor Bartot, the Chinese ambassador, and Heaven knows how many more, are concerned?"

"You are an ignorant person to use such words!" Delora replied.

"Tell me, at least," I begged, "whether your niece is implicated in this?"

"Why do you ask?" Delora exclaimed.

"Because I want to marry her," I answered.

"Do nothing until the day after to-morrow, Captain Rotherby, and you shall marry her and have a dowry of fifty thousand pounds, besides what her Uncle Nicholas will leave her."

"You overwhelm me!" I answered, turning toward the door.

He made no movement to arrest my departure. Suddenly I turned towards him. Why should I not give him the benefit of this one chance!

"Delora," I said, "from the moment when you disappeared from Charing Cross I have had but one idea concerning you, and that is that you are engaged in some nefarious if not criminal undertaking. I believe so at this minute. On the other hand, there is, of course, the chance that you may be, as you say, engaged in carrying out some enterprise, political or otherwise, which necessitates these mysterious doings on your part. I have no wish to be your enemy, or to interfere in any legitimate operation. If you care to take me into your confidence you will not find me unreasonable."

Delora bowed. I caught the gleam of his white teeth underneath his black moustache. I knew that he had made up his mind to fight.

"Captain Rotherby," he said, "I am much obliged for your offer, but I am not in need of allies. Send your cable as soon as you will. You will only make a little mischief of which you will afterwards be ashamed."

I shrugged my shoulders and turned away. No one came to let me out, but I undid the bolts myself, and stepped into my taxicab with a little breath of relief. Somehow or other I felt as though I had escaped from a danger which I could not define, and yet which I had felt with every breath I had drawn in that damp, unwholesome-looking house!

CHAPTER XXXVI

AN ABORTIVE ATTEMPT

IMMEDIATELY I arrived at my brother's hotel I rang up the hall-porter of the Milan and informed him of my whereabouts. Afterwards Ralph and I between us concocted a cable to Dicky, for which I was thankful that I had not to pay. I had now taken Ralph into my entire confidence, and I found that he took very much the same view of Delora's behavior as I did. This is what we said, —

Have seen Delora. Behavior very mysterious. Is living apart from niece in secrecy. Seen several times with Chinese ambassador. Offered me large bribe refrain cabling you till Thursday. Fear something wrong.

"Do you think that you could give me a bed here to-night, Ralph?" I asked.

"By all means, old fellow," my brother answered. "To tell you the truth, I think you are better here than at the Milan. You can have the rooms you had the other night."

I had had a tiring day, and I dropped off to sleep almost as soon as my head touched the pillow. I was awakened by the sound of the telephone bell close to my head. I had no idea as to the time, but from the silence everywhere I judged that I had been asleep for several hours. I took up the receiver and held it to my ear.

"Hullo!" I exclaimed.

"Is that Captain Rotherby?" a familiar voice asked.

"Yes!" I said. "That's Ashley, isn't it?"

"Yes, sir!" the man answered. "I am on night duty here. Will you excuse my asking you, sir, if you have lent your room to any one?"

"Certainly not!" I replied. "Why?"

"It's a very odd thing, sir," he continued. "A person arrived here with a small bag a little time ago and presented your card, — said that you had given him permission to sleep in your room. I let him go up, but I didn't feel altogether comfortable about it, so I took the liberty of ringing up Claridge's to see if you were there. I thought that as you were here this evening, you would have told us if you had proposed lending it."

"You are quite right, Ashley," I declared. "I have lent the room to no one. You had better go and see who it is at once. Shall I come round?"

"I will ring you up again, sir," the man answered, "as soon as I have been upstairs."

"By the bye," I asked, "he didn't look like a Frenchman, did he?"

"I could not say so," Ashley replied. "I will ring you up in a few minutes. I shall go up and inquire into this myself."

I sat on the edge of the bed, waiting. In less than ten minutes the telephone bell rang again. Once more I heard Ashley's voice.

"I am ringing up from your sitting-room, sir," he said. "There is no one here at all, but the room has been opened. So far as I can see, nothing has been taken, but a bottle of chloroform has been dropped and broken upon the floor in your bedroom, and I have a strong idea that some one left the room by the other door as I entered the sitting-room."

"I 'll come along at once, Ashley," I said, — "that is, as soon as I can get dressed."

"I was wondering, sir," was the quiet reply, "whether I would advise you to do so. I did not like the look of the man who came, and I am afraid he was not up to any good here. He is somewhere in the hotel now."

"You say that nothing has been disturbed?" I asked.

"Nothing at all, sir. "It was n't for robbery he came!"

"I think I can guess what he wanted, Ashley," said I. "Perhaps you are right. I won't come round till the morning."

"If anything fresh happens, sir, I will let you know," the man said. "Good night, sir!"

"Good night, Ashley!" I answered.

I got back into bed, but I did not immediately fall off to sleep again. There was no doubt at all that my visitor had come at the instigation of Delora, and that his object had been to prevent my sending that cable, which was already on its way. I got up and saw that my door was securely fastened. I am ashamed to confess that at that moment I felt a tremor of fear! I no longer had the slightest doubt that Delora, if not an impostor, was engaged in some great criminal operation. And Felicia! I thought of the matter in every way. It was impossible that Delora could be an impostor pure and simple. Felicia was content to travel with him. She knew him for her uncle. He must be her uncle, unless she herself had deceived me! I felt my blood run cold at the thought. I flung it from me. I would have no more of it. Felicia, at least, was above suspicion! Delora had, perhaps, been led into this enterprise, whatever it might be, by Louis and his friends. At any rate, the morrow was likely to clear things up. I was the more convinced of that when I remembered that it was one day's grace only that Delora had begged of me. I went off to sleep again soon, and only woke when my brother's servant called me for my bath. At half-past ten, after a consultation with my brother, I drove to the Brazilian Embassy. I sent in my card, and asked to see Mr. Lamartine. He came to me in a few minutes.

"Captain Rotherby!" he exclaimed, holding out his hand. "You have some news?"

"I am not sure whether you will call it news," I answered. "I came to see you about this man Delora."

"Sit down," Lamartine said. "I only wish that you had given me all your confidence the other day."

"To tell you the truth, I am not sure whether I have any to give now," I answered. "There are just one or two facts which seem to me so peculiar that I decided to look you up."

"I am very glad indeed to see you, Captain Rotherby," Lamartine said. "Something is happening in connection with this person which I am afraid may lead to very serious trouble. I know now more than I did when I hung around you and Miss Delora at Charing Cross Station, and in the course of the day I hope to know more."

"I should have washed my hands of the whole affair," I told him, "before now, but from the fact that I have received a cable from my brother, who is in Rio, concerning these very people. He had first of all, in a letter, asked me to be civil and to look them up. His cable begged me, on behalf of an elder brother out there, to look after Delora, find out what he was doing, and report. I gathered that he was over here on some special mission, as to the progress of which he should have made reports to his brother in Brazil. He has not done so, nor has he used the private code agreed upon between those two."

"This is very interesting," Lamartine said, — "very interesting indeed!"

"I came to you," I said, "because, since the receipt of this cable, I have convinced myself that Delora is engaged in some sort of underground work the crisis of which must be very close at hand. I found him last night in a miserable, deserted sort of building down near the river in Bermondsey. He offered me ten thousand pounds not to reply to his brother's cable. I think that he would have done his best to have detained me there but for the fact that I had taken precautions before I started."

"Have you any idea," Lamartine asked, "what the nature of this underground business is?"

"I cannot imagine," I answered. "In some way it seems to me that it is connected with the Chinese ambassador, because I have seen them several times together. That, however, is only surmise. I can give you one more piece of information," I added, "and that is that the Chinese ambassador and Delora have recently visited Newcastle."

Lamartine smiled.

"I know everything except one thing," he said, "and that we shall both of us know before the day is out. Our friend Delora has played a great game. Even now I cannot tell you whether he has played to win or to lose. Since you have been so kind as to look me up, Captain Rotherby," he went on, "let us spend a little time together. Do me, for instance, the honor to lunch with me at the Milan at one o'clock."

"With Louis?" I asked grimly.

"I do not think that Louis will hurt us," Lamartine

answered. "There is just a chance, even, that we may not find him on duty to-day."

"I will lunch with you with pleasure," I said, "but there is one thing which I must do first."

Lamartine looked at me narrowly.

"You want to see Miss Delora?" he asked.

It was foolish to be offended. I admitted the fact.

"Well," he said, "it is natural. Miss Delora is a very charming young lady, and, so far as I know, she believes in her uncle. At the same time, I am not sure, Captain Rotherby, that the neighborhood of the Milan is very safe for you just now."

"At this hour of the morning," I said, "one should be able to protect one's self."

"It is true," Lamartine answered. "Tell me, Captain Rotherby, at what hour did you send that cable last night?"

"At midnight," I answered.

Lamartine glanced at the clock.

"Soon," he said, "we shall have an official cable here, and then things will be interesting. Shall we meet, then, at the Milan?"

"Precisely," I answered. "You don't feel inclined," I added, "to be a little more candid with me? My head has ached for a good many days over this business."

"A few hours longer won't hurt you," Lamartine answered, laughing. "I can promise you that it will be worth waiting for."

CHAPTER XXXVII

DELORA RETURNS

At a few minutes before twelve I entered the Milan by the Court entrance, and received at once some astonishing news. Ashley, who came out to meet me, drew me at once upon one side with a little gesture of apology.

"Mr. Delora has returned, sir," he said.

For the moment I had forgotten the sensation which Delora's non-arrival on that first evening had made, and which had always left behind it a flavor of mystery. I could see from Ashley's face that he was puzzled.

"Is Mr. Delora with his niece?" I asked.

"They have moved into Number 35, sir," Ashley told me. "Mr. Delora complained very much of his rooms, said they were too small, and threatened to move to Claridge's. Number 35 is the best suite we have."

I stood, for a moment, thinking. Ashley, meanwhile, had retreated to his place behind the counter. I approached him slowly.

"Ashley," I said, "ring up and tell Mr. Delora that I have called."

Ashley went at once to the telephone.

"Don't be surprised," I said, "if his reply isn't exactly polite. I don't think he is very well pleased with me just now."

I strolled away for a few minutes to look into the café, where the waiters were preparing for luncheon. There was no sign of Louis. When I returned, Ashley leaned forward to me from the other side of the desk.

"Mr. Delora wishes you to step up, sir," he said.

I was a little surprised, but I moved promptly to the lift.

"On the third floor, is n't it?" I asked.

"Exactly, sir," Ashley answered. "Shall I send a page with you?"

I shook my head.

"I can find it all right," I said.

My knock at the door was answered by a dark-faced valet. He ushered me into a large and very handsome sitting-room. Felicia and Delora were standing talking together near the mantelpiece. They both ceased at my entrance, but I had an instinctive feeling that I had been the subject of their conversation. Felicia greeted me timidly. There were signs of tears in her face, and I felt that by some means or other this man had been able to reassert his influence over her. Delora himself was a changed being. He was dressed with the almost painful exactness of the French man of fashion. His slight black imperial was trimmed to a point, his moustache upturned with a distinctly foreign air. He wore a wonderful pin in his carefully arranged tie, and a tiny piece of red ribbon in his button-hole. The manicurist whom I had met in the passage had evidently just left him, for as I entered he was regarding his nails thoughtfully. He did not offer me his hand. He stared at me instead with a certain restrained insolence.

"I should be glad to know, Captain Rotherby," he said calmly, "to what I owe this intrusion?"

"I am sorry that you look upon it in that light, sir," I answered. "My visit, as a matter of fact, was intended for your niece."

She took a step towards me, but Delora's outstretched arm barred her progress.

"My niece is very much honored," he answered, "but her friends and her acquaintances are mine. You were so good as to render me some service on our arrival at Charing Cross a few days ago, but you have since then presumed upon that service to an unwarrantable extent."

"I am sorry that you should think so," I answered.

"I did not know," Delora continued, "that the young men of your country had time enough to spare to devote themselves to other people's business in the way that you have done. I came to this country upon a peculiar and complicated mission, intrusted to me by my own government. The chief condition of success was that it should be performed in secrecy. You were only a chance acquaintance, and how on earth you should have had the impertinence to associate yourself with my doings I cannot imagine! But the fact remains that you made my task more difficult, and, in fact, at one time seriously endangered its success. Not only that," Delora continued, "but you have chosen to ally yourself with those whose object it has been to wreck my undertaking. Yet, with the full knowledge of these things, you have had the supreme impudence to force your company upon my niece, — even, I understand, to pay her your addresses!"

"The dowry of fifty thousand pounds," I began, —

He stretched out his hand with a commanding air.

"We will not allude to that, sir," he declared. "I was forced to make an attempt to bribe you, I admit, but it was under very difficult circumstances. As it is, I am only thankful that you declined my offer. I have arranged matters so that your cable shall do me no harm. It has precipitated matters by twenty-four hours, but that is no one's loss and my gain. When I heard your name sent up I could scarcely believe my ears, but since you are here, since you have ventured to pay this call, I wish to inform you, on behalf of my niece and myself, that we consider your further acquaintance undesirable in the extreme."

The man's deportment was magnificent. But for the fact that I had long ago lost all faith in him I should have felt, without the shadow of a doubt, that I had made a supreme fool of myself. But as it was, my faith was only shaken. The hideous possibility that I had made a mistake was there like a shadow, but I could not accept it as a certainty.

"Mr. Delora," I said, "from one point of view I am very glad to hear you speak like this. If I have been mistaken in supposing that your extraordinary behavior in London —"

"But what the devil has my extraordinary behavior got to do with you?" Delora demanded, with the first note of anger in his tone which he had shown.

"My interest was for your niece, sir," I answered.

"My niece does not require your protection or your interest," Delora answered. "It seems to me that you have chosen a queer way to return the hospitality which it was our pleasure to extend to your brother in Brazil. I have still a busy morning, sir, and I have seen you for this one reason only: to have you clearly understand that we — my niece and I — do not find your further acquaintance desirable."

She made another little movement towards me, and by doing so came into the light. I saw that her eyes were red with weeping, and notwithstanding an angry exclamation from Delora she held out her hands to me.

"Capitaine Rotherby," she said, "I believe, I do, indeed, that you have acted out of kindness to me. My uncle, as you see, is very angry. What he has said has not been

I RAISED HER FINGERS TO MY LIPS, AND SMILED INTO HER FACE.

Page 275

from my heart, but from his. Yet, as you know, I must obey!"

I raised her fingers to my lips, and I smiled into her face.

"Felicia," I said, "do not be afraid. This is not the end!"

Delora turned to the servant whom he had summoned.

"Show this gentleman out, François," he said coldly.

Lamartine was a few minutes late. He drove up in a large motor-car with an elderly gentleman, who remained inside, and with whom he talked for a few minutes earnestly before he joined me.

"You forgive me?" he asked, as he handed his hat and stick to an attendant. "The chief kept me talking. He brought me down here himself."

I nodded.

"It is of no consequence," I said. "I have some news for you."

"Nothing," Lamartine declared, passing his arm through mine, "will surprise me."

"Delora is here," I said, "with his niece!"

Lamartine stopped short.

"Under his own name?" he asked. "Do you mean that he has thrown off all disguise? That he is here as Maurice Delora?"

"I never knew his Christian name," I answered, "but he is here as Delora, right enough. He has taken the largest suite in the Court, and for the last quarter of an hour he has been dressing me down in great shape."

"He is magnificent!" Lamartine said softly. "If he can keep it up for twenty-four hours longer, he who has been a beggar practically for ten years will be worth a great fortune!"

"So that," I remarked, "was the stake!"

"A worthy one, is it not so, my friend?" Lamartine declared.

"Does he win?" I asked.

"Heaven knows!" Lamartine answered. "Even now I cannot tell you. Unless something turns up, I should say that it was very likely."

We entered the café. When Louis saw us arrive together he stood for a moment motionless upon the floor. His eyes seemed to question us with swift and fierce curiosity. Had we arrived together? Was this a chance meeting? How much was either in the other's confidence? These things and many others he seemed to ask. Then he came slowly towards us. A ray of sunshine, streaming through the glass roof of the courtyard and reflected through the window, lay across the floor of the café. As Louis passed over it I saw a change in the man. Always colorless, his white cheeks were graven now with deep, cobwebbed lines. His eyes seemed to have receded into his head. His manner lacked that touch of graceful and not unbecoming confidenc : which one had grown to admire.

"What can I do for you, messieurs?" he asked, with a little bow. "A table for two — yes? This way."

We followed him to a small table in the best part of the room.

"Monsieur had good sport in the country?" he asked me.

"Excellent, Louis!" I answered. "How are things in town?"

Louis shrugged his shoulders and glanced around.

"As one sees," he answered, "here we are fortunate.

Here we are always, always busy. We turn people away all the time, because we prefer to serve well our old customers."

"Louis," I said, "you are wonderful!"

"What will the gentlemen eat?" Louis asked.

I looked at Lamartine, and Lamartine looked at me. The same thought was in the minds of both of us. Curiously enough we felt a certain delicacy in letting Louis perceive our dilemma!

"Those cold grouse look excellent," Lamartine said to me, pointing to the sideboard.

"Cold grouse are very good," Louis assented. "I will have one specially prepared and sent up."

Lamartine shook his head.

"Bring over the dish there, and let us look at them, Louis," he said.

Louis obeyed him. There was no alternative. Lamartine, without hesitation, coolly took one of the birds on to his own plate.

"Our luncheon is arranged for, Louis," he said. "Let a waiter bring us a dish and carving-knife. I like to carve myself at the table."

"But certainly!" Louis assented, and, calling a waiter, he glided away. Lamartine and I exchanged glances.

"I fancy we are pretty safe with this bird," he remarked.

"Absolutely," I answered. "He never had the ghost of a chance to tamper with it. The question of drinks is a little difficult," I continued.

"And I am very thirsty," Lamartine said. "An unopened bottle of hock, eh?"

I shook my head.

"No good," I answered. "I am convinced that Louis has a cellar of his own. Did you notice the fellow, by the bye?" I went on. "He shows signs of the worry of this thing. Somehow or other I do not fancy that Louis will be in this place a week from to-day."

"That may be," Lamartine answered, "but I must drink!"

There was a bottle of whiskey upon the table next to us, from which its occupant had been helping himself. He rose now to go, and I seized the opportunity the moment he had left, and before the waiter could clear the table I had secured the bottle.

"We won't risk soda-water," I said. "Whiskey and water is good enough."

The one waiter whom I disliked — a creature of Louis', as I knew well — came hurrying forward and endeavored to possess himself of the bottle.

"Let me get you another bottle of whiskey, sir," he said.

I shook my head.

"This one will do, thank you," I said.

"Soda-water or Perrier, sir?" he asked.

"Neither, thank you," I answered.

The man moved away, and I saw him in a corner talking to Louis. Lamartine served the grouse, and leaned across the table to me.

"Captain Rotherby," he said, "I think I will tell you now why, notwithstanding the risk of Monsieur Louis, I asked you to lunch with me here at this restaurant. But look! See who comes!"

He laid his fingers upon my coat-sleeve. I turned my head. Felicia was sailing down the room, — Felicia exquisitely dressed as usual, walking with a soft rustle of lace, — delightful, alluring; and in her wake Delora himself, tall, well-groomed, aristocratic, looking around him with mild but slightly bored interest. Louis was piloting them to a table, the best in the place. We watched them seat themselves. Delora, through a horn-rimmed eyeglass, studied the menu. Felicia, drawing off her gloves, looked a little wearily out into the busy courtyard. So they were sitting when the thing happened which Lamartine, I believe, had expected, but which, for me, was the most wonderful thing that had yet come to pass amongst this tangle of strange circumstances!

CHAPTER XXXVIII

AT BAY

THE entrance of these two persons into the room, apart from its astonishing significance to us, seemed to excite a certain amount of interest amongst the ordinary throng. My lady of the turquoises wore a dark-blue closely fitting gown, which only a Paris tailor could have cut, a large and striking hat, and a great bunch of red roses in the front of her dress. But, after all, it was upon her companion, not upon her, that our regard was riveted. He was dressed with the neat exactitude of a Frenchman of fashion. He wore a red ribbon in his button-hole. His white hair and moustaches were perfectly arranged. He leaned heavily upon a stick, and he had the appearance of a man prematurely aged, as though by an illness or some great suffering. His tone, as he turned to his companion, was courteous enough but querulous.

"My dear," he said, "this place is full of draughts. We must find a table over there by the palm."

He pointed with his stick, and it was just at this moment that Louis, rounding the corner from a distant part of the room, came face to face with them. Once before during the last twenty-four hours I had been struck with the pallor of Louis' expression. This time he stood quite still in the middle of the floor, as though he had seen a ghost! He was close to a pillar, and I saw his hand suddenly go out to it as though in search of support. His breath was coming quickly. From where I sat I could see the little beads of sweat breaking out upon his forehead.

"Monsieur !" he exclaimed.

The newcomer turned to look at him. For a moment he seemed puzzled. It was as though some old memory were striving to reassert itself.

"My man," he said to Louis, "surely I know your face ? You have been here a long time, have n't you ?"

"Ten years, sir," Louis answered. "Permit me !"

He gave them a table not far away from mine. The memory of his face as he preceded them down the room never left me. I glanced instinctively towards Delora. His back was turned towards the entrance of the restaurant, and he had apparently seen nothing. Felicia, on the contrary, sat as though she were turned to stone. I saw her lean over and whisper to her companion. A little murmur of excitement broke from my companion's lips.

"This," he murmured, "is amazing ! The girl is a fool to bring him here. She must know that Louis is in it !"

"Who is the man ?" I asked.

Lamartine looked at me with a curious expression in his dark eyes.

"Do you mean to say that you cannot guess ?" he asked.

I shook my head.

"Only that he must be some relation to Delora," I declared. "There has been no time, though, for his brother to get across from South America."

Lamartine smiled.

"You are dull," he said. "But watch ! What is going to happen now, I wonder ?"

Delora had risen to his feet. He had the look of a man who has received a shock. He brushed past some people who were taking their places at a table without remark or apology. He passed my companion and myself without even, I believe, being conscious of our presence. He walked straight to the table where the two newcomers sat. I saw his hand fall upon the shoulder of the other man.

"Ferdinand!" he said.

The lady of the turquoises was leaning forward in her place as though to push Delora away. A few feet in the background Louis was hovering.

"Ferdinand," I heard Delora repeat, "what are you doing here? Who is this person? You know that you are not well enough to travel."

The older man looked at him with a slightly puzzled air. There was a certain vacuity in his expression, for which one found it hard to account.

"You!" he murmured, as though perplexed. "Why, this is not Paris, Maurice!"

Louis had glided a little nearer to the table. My lady of the turquoises half rose to her feet. Her blue eyes were fierce with anger. She looked as though she would have struck Delora.

"You shall not take him away!" she cried. "Don't have anything to say to them!" she added, bending downwards to her companion. "You are not safe with any one else except me!"

Delora turned towards her with an angry exclamation.

"Madame," he said, "this gentleman is my relation, and he is ill. He is certainly not in a condition to be travelling about the country with — with you!"

Her self-control was beginning to evaporate. She addressed him shrilly. People at the surrounding tables were beginning to observe this unusual conversation.

"What, then?" she cried. "Is he not safer with me

than you? How about Henri — Henri who came over here because we had been deceived, he and I, — poor Henri who died?"

"This," Delora muttered, "is your revenge, then!"

"It is my revenge, and I mean to have it," she answered. "This afternoon you will see."

Louis advanced and bowed to the man who still sat at the table, looking a little puzzled, and with his eyes still fixed upon Delora.

"Monsieur," he said, "shall I serve luncheon?"

There was an instant's pause. I fancied that I saw something pass between Louis and Delora. The latter turned away with a little shrug of the shoulders.

"Presently will be time," he said. "We will speak together, all three of us, before you leave."

The woman struck the table with the palm of her hand.

"There is nothing which you need say!" she exclaimed. "It is finished, this fine scheme of yours! See, he is here himself. This afternoon we go to warn those whom you would rob!"

Once more that look flashed between Louis and Delora, and this time there was borne in upon me the swift consciousness of what it might mean. Delora returned to his place opposite Felicia. I bent across the table to Lamartine.

"Lamartine," I said, "there was a man who came here once — a companion of that woman — Bartot. He came to make trouble with Louis, and he dined here once. He dined nowhere else on earth!"

Lamartine was suddenly grave.

"Would Louis dare!" he muttered.

"Why not?" I answered. "See, Louis is watching us even now!"

Lamartine half rose from his seat. I pushed him back.

"No!" I said. "It is not for you! It is I who will arrange this thing."

I left my place and walked towards the table where the two were sitting. I saw Delora lay down his knife and fork and watch me with fixed, intent gaze. I saw Louis' lips twist into a snarl. He glided to the table even as I did. I held out my hand to the woman.

"You have not forgotten me, I hope?" I asked. "I am very glad indeed to see you in London."

She gave me her hand, and smiled her most bewitching smile. I turned and stared at Louis. He had no alternative but to fall back a pace or two.

"Madame," I said, bending towards her, "it was here that Bartot came and dined. I have heard it whispered that it is not safe to eat here if you are not a friend of Louis'!"

For a moment she failed to grasp the significance of my words. Then the color died slowly out of her cheeks. Her face was like the face of an old woman. Fear had come suddenly, and she was haggard.

"You mean that he would dare, monsieur?" she said —

"It is easy," I answered. "A dozen or more of these waiters are his creatures. From what I have heard I gather that your visit here with this gentleman is for a purpose inimical to some scheme in which Delora and Louis are interested. I warn you that if it is so, you had better change your mind about lunching."

"We will go at once!" she answered. "You are very kind. I came to confront Louis and that other with me," she declared, nodding vigorously at her companion.

"I came because I would have them understand who it was that had ruined their plans, because they made use of me — of Bartot and me — and threw us aside like gloves that were finished with. But it was a foolish thing to do, monsieur. I see that, and I thank you now for your warning."

She gathered her things together for her departure, and leaned across towards her companion. What she said to him I do not know, for I returned to my place.

"They will not eat," I whispered to Lamartine. "Tell me, who is the man?"

"Hush!" Lamartine said. "Look there!"

Apparently angry words had been passing between Felicia and Delora. She had risen to her feet, notwithstanding his efforts to detain her, swept past my table with scarcely a glance, and made her way towards where the two latest arrivals were sitting. She stooped down towards the man, and talked to him earnestly for several moments. All the time he looked at her with the puzzled, half-vacant expression of a child who is confronted with something which it does not understand. Delora had risen to his feet, and stood nervously clutching the serviette in his hand. Louis hurried up to him, and they talked together for a moment.

"At all costs," I heard Louis say, "she must be fetched away. They will not remain here to eat. Rotherby has warned them. See how he is looking at her! It is not safe!"

Something more passed between them in a low tone. Delora glanced at his watch, and then at the clock. Finally he crossed the room to where his niece was standing, and laid his hand upon the man's shoulder.

"Ferdinand," he said, "I am glad to see that you are

better. Come up to my rooms for a few minutes. We must have a talk."

At the sound of his voice something seemed to come back to the face of the older man. He rose slowly to his feet. I could see his white fingers trembling, but I could see his eyes suddenly fill with a new and stronger light.

"You!" he exclaimed. "Yes, I am here to talk to you! It had better be at once! Lead the way!"

I saw Delora look towards the lady of the turquoises. Apparently he made some remark which I failed to overhear.

"This lady is my companion," I heard the other say. "She has been very kind to me — kinder, I am afraid, as a stranger, than others have been on whom I should have relied. She will accompany us. She does not leave me."

Then the four of them turned towards the door. Lamartine jogged my shoulder and I too rose. Behind, Louis was hovering, watching their departure with a nervous anxiety which he could not conceal. Lamartine and I went out close upon their heels.

"A new move, Louis?" I asked, as I passed.

"The last, monsieur," Louis answered, with a bow.

CHAPTER XXXIX

THE UNEXPECTED

THE entrance to the Milan Court was small and unimposing, compared with the entrance to the hotel proper. I reached it to find some confusion reigning. A tall, gray-bearded man was talking anxiously to the hall-porter. Felicia, standing a little apart, was looking around with an air of bewilderment. My lady of the turquoises was standing by the side of the lift, with her arm drawn through her companion's. Lamartine no sooner saw the face of the man who was in conversation with the hall-porter than he sprang forward.

"Your Excellency!" he exclaimed.

The ambassador turned quickly towards him.

"Where is Delora?" he asked.

"He was here but five seconds ago," Lamartine answered. "He must have left the door as you entered it!"

The man who was standing with my lady of the turquoises turned suddenly round.

"Delora!" he exclaimed. "That is my name! I am Ferdinand Delora! My brother Maurice was here a moment ago. You are Signor Vanhallon, are you not?" he continued. "You must remember me!"

The ambassador grasped him by the hand.

"My dear Delora," he said, "of course I do! What has been the meaning of all this mystery?"

Lamartine stepped quickly forward.

"Can't you see what it all means?" he exclaimed. "Ferdinand Delora here arrives in Paris on a secret mis-

sion to England. There, through some reason or through
some cause, — who knows? — he falls ill. There comes
to London Maurice Delora with some papers, playing
his part. Maurice Delora was here a moment ago. His
game is up and he is evidently gone. The one thing to be
feared is that we are too late!"

The ambassador turned swiftly to the new Delora, who
was looking from one to the other with the pained, half-
vacant expression of a child.

"Delora," he exclaimed, "how comes it that you have
let your brother intervene? Did you not understand how
secret your mission was to be? — how important?"

The man shook his head slowly.

"I am sorry," he said, "I have been ill. I know nothing. There was an accident in Paris. I have no papers
any longer. Maurice has them all."

My lady of the turquoises plunged into the conversation.

"But it has been a wicked conspiracy!" she cried.
"Monsieur here," she added, clutching his arm, "was
drugged and poisoned. Since then he has been like a
child. He was left to die, but I found him, I brought him
here. And meanwhile, that wicked brother has been
playing his part, — using even his name."

I went to Felicia.

"Felicia," I said, "it is you who can clear this up. The
time has come when you must speak."

Felicia was standing with her hands clasped to her
head, looking from one to the other of the speakers as
though she were trying in vain to follow the sense of what
they said. At my words she turned to me a little piteously.
She was beginning to understand, but she had not realized
the whole truth yet.

"The lady over there," she said, pointing to my lady of the turquoises, "has spoken the truth. Uncle Ferdinand was ill when he arrived in Paris. He stayed with us — that is, my uncle Maurice and I — in the Rue d'Hauteville. He seemed to get worse all the time, and he was worried because of some business in London which he could not attend to. Then it was arranged that my Uncle Maurice should take his place and come over here, only no one was to know that it was not Ferdinand himself. It was secret business for the Brazilian Government. I do not know what it was about, but it was very important."

"Your Uncle Maurice, then," I said, "was the uncle who lived in Paris — whom you knew best?"

She nodded.

"Yes! I have had to call him Ferdinand over here. It was hateful, but they all said that it was necessary."

A motor drew up outside. The Chinese ambassador stepped out with more haste than I had ever seen him use, and by his side a man in dark clothes and silk hat, who from the first I suspected to be a bank manager. The Brazilian minister welcomed them on the threshold.

"You are looking for Delora?" he exclaimed.

The Chinese ambassador looked around at the little circle. His face was emotionless, yet he spoke with a haste which was unusual.

"It is true that I seek him," he said. "This morning he has cashed a cheque for two hundred thousand pounds. I do not understand. There is a part of our bargain which he has not kept."

A gleam of intelligence flitted into the face of the newly discovered Delora. He stepped forward.

"It is in order," he said. "You have taken over from

my brother, who represents the Brazilian Government, two new battleships."

"That is so," His Excellency answered, "but I want the indemnity of your ambassador."

"I cannot give it you," the ambassador declared, "until I have received the money."

"Where is Delora?" some one asked.

We looked around. The same suspicion was in the minds of all of us. Delora had fled! I drew my arm through Felicia's, and led her to the lift.

"Dear," I said, "you must come upstairs with me."

She clung to me a little hysterically.

"What do they mean?" she said. "It is not true that my uncle has been working for the Government?"

"It is true enough," I answered. "The only point for doubt is what he has done with the money he received on their account. Your Uncle Ferdinand there was the person who was intrusted with the plans and commission. For some reason or other your Uncle Maurice has carried it through, and to tell you the truth, I believe he has gone off with the money. If you take my advice you will bring your Uncle Ferdinand upstairs, and the lady who is with him, if you like, and let the others fight it out."

She took my advice. The new Delora was exhausted, and without any complete comprehension of what had taken place. Felicia busied herself attending to him. Then a sudden idea struck me. I opened the door of the further bedchamber softly and stood face to face with Delora. There was a quick flash, and I looked into the muzzle of a revolver. Delora was apparently preparing for flight. He had changed his clothes, and a small handbag, ready packed, was upon the bed.

"So it's you, you d——d interfering Englishman!" he said. "There's no one I'd sooner send to perdition!"

I stood quite still. I could not exactly see what was best to be done, for the man's hand was steady, and I scarcely saw how I could escape if indeed he pressed the trigger.

"They are looking for you everywhere," I said. "The sound of that revolver would fill your room."

"Do you think I don't know it?" he answered. "Do you think you would not have had a bullet through your forehead before now if I was not sure of it?"

"Put your revolver down and talk sense!" I said. "I am interested in no one except your niece."

"It's a lie!" he answered. "It's through you I'm in this hole!"

"Well, here's a chance for you," I said. "They are all of them down at the Court entrance. Probably some of them are on their way up now. Turn to the left and take the other lift. Leave the hotel by the Embankment entrance."

"And walk into a trap!" he snarled.

"Upon my honor I know of none," I answered. "It is exactly as I have said."

I knew from his face that he had forgotten the other lift. He snatched up his hat and disappeared. I returned to the sitting-room, and, although I had made no promise, the consciousness of my escape kept me silent as to having seen him. Felicia was sitting on the sofa, talking to her uncle. My lady of the turquoises, with a triumphant smile upon her lips, was occupying the easy-chair.

Felicia rose at once and drew me to the window.

"Capitaine Rotherby," she said, "I fear that you will never forgive me nor believe me, — perhaps it does not matter so very much,— but you see I have seen no one but my Uncle Maurice since I was at school. He used to visit me there. He was always kind. My Uncle Ferdinand there came as a stranger. I knew nothing of him except that he was taken ill. How he met with his illness no one told me. Then my Uncle Maurice came to me one night and said that his brother had come to Europe on a wonderful secret mission, and that now he was too ill to go on with it, it must be carried through for the honor of the family. He meant to call himself Ferdinand Delora, and to come to England and do his best, and I was to come with him and hold my peace, and help him where it was possible. I begin to understand now that, somehow or other, this poor Ferdinand was ill-treated, and that my Uncle Maurice took his place, meaning to steal the money he received. But I did not know that. Indeed, I did not know it!" she said, sobbing.

I passed my arm around her waist.

"Felicia, dear," I said, "who would doubt it? Let them fight this matter out between them. It is nothing to do with us. You are here, and you remain!"

She came a little closer into my arms with a sigh of content. My lady of the turquoises laughed outright.

"You are *infidèle*, monsieur!" she exclaimed. "But there, the poor child is young, and she needs some one to look after her. Listen! What is that?"

We all heard it, — the sound of a shot in the corridor. I kept Felicia back for the moment, but the others were already outside. The waiter and the valet had rushed out of the service room. A chambermaid, with her apron over her head, ran screaming along the corridor. There in the middle Delora lay, flat on his back, with his hands thrown out and a smoking revolver by his side! . . .

I did then what might seem to be a callous thing. I left them all crowding around the body of the dead man. I let even Felicia be led back to her room by her companion. I took the lift downstairs, and I made my way into the café.

"Where is Louis?" I asked the first waiter I saw.

"He is away for a minute or two, sir," the man answered.

Almost as he spoke Louis entered from the further end of the restaurant. He did not see me, and I noticed that his fingers were arranging his tie, and that as he passed a mirror he glanced at his shirt-front. When I came face to face with him he was breathing fast as though he had been running.

"Louis," I said, "five flights of stairs are trying at our time of life!"

He looked at me blankly, and as one who does not comprehend.

"Five flights of stairs, monsieur!" he repeated.

I nodded.

"I myself came down by the lift," I said. "Louis, Delora is lying in the corridor outside his rooms with a bullet through his forehead. I am wondering whether he shot himself, or whether —"

"Or whether what?" Louis asked softly.

I shrugged my shoulders.

"After all," I said, "I suppose the truth will come out. Have you any idea, I wonder, where those two hundred thousand pounds are?"

"I, monsieur!" — Louis held out his hands. "Delora has had several hours to dispose of them. If he had taken my advice he would have been flying to the south coast in his motor by now. As to the money, well, it may be anywhere "

"It may, Louis!" I admitted.

"Delora was a bungler," Louis said slowly. "The game was in his hands. Even the reappearance of his brother was not serious. He was carrying out a perfectly legitimate transaction in which no one could interfere."

"Excepting," I remarked, "that he proposed to retain the proceeds of this sale of his."

"That would have been hard to prove if he had chosen to assert the contrary," Louis remarked. "Vanhallon would have had little enough to say if the money had passed into his hands."

"And the Chinese ambassador?" I remarked.

"His documents would have been good enough," Louis replied. "He has the ships. He has value for his money. There was no need for Delora to have despaired. His behavior during this last hour has been the behavior of a child. Monsieur will pardon me!"

Louis glided away, and I saw him smilingly escorting a party of late guests to their places. I stood where I was and watched him. To me, the man was something amazing! I firmly believed, even at that moment, that he had, safely hidden, part, if not the whole, of the proceeds of this gigantic scheme of fraud. I believed, too, that his had been the hand which had killed Delora. And there he was, within a few minutes of the time when the tragedy had happened, waiting upon his guests, consulted about the vintages of wines, suggesting dishes! Upstairs Delora lay, with a little blue mark upon his temple! It was the survival of the fittest, this, in crime as well as in the other things of life!

I retraced my steps upstairs. The Chinese ambassador, Vanhallon, and Lamartine were deep in conversation in the dead man's sitting-room. I was admitted to their confidence after a few minutes' hesitation. A draft for one hundred and sixty thousand pounds had been found upon the dead man, but notes to the value of forty thousand pounds were missing! They looked at me a little curiously as I entered, and Lamartine explained the situation to me.

"We were wondering about the young lady," he said.

"Then you need wonder no longer!" I said dryly. "I give my word for it that she is ignorant altogether of this scheme. She believed that her uncle was honestly attempting to carry out the plans for which his brother came to Europe, and as for searching for the money amongst her belongings, you might as well fly!"

"Where, then," Vanhallon demanded, "has it gone to? He has had so little time."

I opened my lips and closed them. After all, I had gained my end, and I had realized a little the folly of meddling with things which did not concern me. So I held my peace. I went and sat down by the side of my lady of the turquoises.

"Tell me," I said, "how did you find him? — and where? Has he been ill, or what is it that is the matter?"

I moved my head towards where Delora was sitting. The placid, child-like expression still remained with him. The tragedy which had happened only a few yards away had left him unmoved.

"I heard all about him from Henri," she said. "The scheme originally was his. Then they tried to hurry things through without us — without my man Henri, of whom they had made use. Henri came to London, and he died here! That much I know. How much more there is to be told, who can say? But I said to myself, 'I will be revenged!' I knew the hospital to which he had been taken — a private hospital from which few ever come out! But I went there, and I swore that I was his daughter. I frightened them all, for I knew that he had been drugged and poisoned till his brain had nearly given way. They thought him harmless, and they let him come with me. I brought him to England. I brought him here."

"And now?" I asked.

"Now I must go back," she answered, "but at least Henri is avenged!"

She leaned towards me.

"Tell whoever takes care of him," she whispered in my ear, "that he cannot live long. The doctors have assured me. It is a matter of weeks."

I walked with her to the door.

"It was an expensive journey for you," I remarked.

She laughed.

"Henri did leave me everything," she said. "I have no need of money. If monsieur —"

She sighed, and looked towards the door of Felicia's room. Then she fluttered away down the corridor, and I slowly retraced my steps. Felicia came out in a few minutes and sat by her uncle's side. The others had all departed, and we were left alone.

"Dear," I said, "this is no place for you any longer. You must come with me, and bring your uncle."

She held out both her hands.

"Wherever you say, Austen!" she murmured.

A year afterwards I persuaded Felicia to lunch at the Milan. She was no longer nervous, for we were intensely curious to know if Louis were still there.

"There is no doubt," I reminded her, "that your Uncle Maurice received the sum of forty thousand pounds in notes. When he was found shot, there was in his pocket-book a draft to the amount of one hundred and sixty thousand pounds. The notes had vanished. I wonder where!"

"I wonder!" she answered.

A waiter whom I knew came up to greet us. I asked him about Louis. He held out his hands.

"Monsieur Louis," he declared, "had the great good-fortune. A relative who died left him a great sum of money. The hotel of Benzoli in St. James' Street was for sale, and Louis he has bought it. He makes much money now."

"Lucky Louis!" I murmured. "How much was this legacy? Do you know?"

"I have heard, sir," the man said, bending down, "that it was as much as forty thousand pounds!"

"So do the wicked flourish!" I murmured to Felicia.

"Monsieur will doubtless pay a visit to the Café Benzoli?" the man continued. "The *cuisine* is excellent, and many of Louis' friends have followed him there."

Felicia and I exchanged smiling glances.

"Somehow or other —" she murmured.

"I think the Milan will be good enough for us!" I said decidedly.

THE END

Popular Copyright Books

AT MODERATE PRICES

Ask your dealer for a complete list of
A. L. Burt Company's Popular Copyright Fiction.

Popular Copyright Books

AT MODERATE PRICES

Ask your dealer for a complete list of
A. L. Burt Company's Popular Copyright Fiction.

Circle, The. By Katherine Cecil Thurston (author of "The Masquerader," "The Gambler.")
Colonial Free Lance, A. By Chauncey C. Hotchkiss.
Conquest of Canaan, The. By Booth Tarkington.
Conspirators, The. By Robert W. Chambers.
Cynthia of the Minute. By Louis Joseph Vance.
Dan Merrithew. By Lawrence Perry.
Day of the Dog, The. By George Barr McCutcheon.
Depot Master, The. By Joseph C. Lincoln.
Derelicts. By William J. Locke.
Diamond Master, The. By Jacques Futrelle.
Diamonds Cut Paste. By Agnes and Egerton Castle.
Divine Fire, The. By May Sinclair.
Dixie Hart. By Will N. Harben.
Dr. David. By Marjorie Benton Cooke.
Early Bird, The. By George Randolph Chester.
Eleventh Hour, The. By David Potter.
Elizabeth in Rugen. (By the author of "Elizabeth and Her German Garden.")
Elusive Isabel. By Jacques Futrelle.
Elusive Pimpernel, The. By Baroness Orczy.
Enchanted Hat, The. By Harold McGrath.
Excuse Me. By Rupert Hughes.
54-40 or Fight. By Emerson Hough.
Fighting Chance, The. By Robert W. Chambers.
Flamsted Quarries. By Mary E. Waller.
Flying Mercury, The. By Eleanor M. Ingram.
For a Maiden Brave. By Chauncey C. Hotchkiss.
Four Million, The. By O. Henry.
Four Pool's Mystery, The. By Jean Webster.
Fruitful Vine, The. By Robert Hichens.
Ganton & Co. By Arthur J. Eddy.
Gentleman of France, A. By Stanley Weyman.
Gentleman, The. By Alfred Ollivant.
Get-Rick-Quick-Wallingford. By George Randolph Chester.
Gilbert Neal. By Will N. Harben.
Girl and the Bill, The. By Bannister Merwin.
Girl from His Town, The. By Marie Van Vorst.
Girl Who Won, The. By Beth Ellis.
Glory of Clementina, The. By William J. Locke.
Glory of the Conquered, The. By Susan Glaspell.
God's Good Man. By Marie Corelli.
Going Some. By Rex Beach.
Golden Web, The. By Anthony Partridge.
Green Patch, The. By Bettina von Hutten.
Happy Island (sequel to "Uncle William"). By Jennette Lee.
Hearts and the Highway. By Cyrus Townsend Brady.
Held for Orders. By Frank H. Spearman.
Hidden Water. By Dane Coolidge.
Highway of Fate, The. By Rosa N. Carey.
Homesteaders, The. By Kate and Virgil D. Boyles.
Honor of the Big Snows, The. By James Oliver Curwood.
Hopalong Cassidy. By Clarence E. Mulford.
Household of Peter, The. By Rosa N. Carey.
House of Mystery, The. By Will Irwin.
House of the Lost Court, The. By C. N. Williamson.
House of the Whispering Pines, The. By Anna Katherine Green.

Popular Copyright Books

AT MODERATE PRICES

Ask your dealer for a complete list of
A. L. Burt Company's Popular Copyright Fiction.

House on Cherry Street, The. By Amelia E. Barr.
How Leslie Loved. By Anne Warner.
Husbands of Edith, The. By George Barr McCutcheon.
Idols. By William J. Locke.
Illustrious Prince, The. By E. Phillips Oppenheim.
Imprudence of Prue, The. By Sophie Fisher.
Inez. (Illustrated Edition.) By Augusta J. Evans.
Infelice. By Augusta Evans Wilson.
Initials Only. By Anna Katharine Green.
In Defiance of the King. By Chauncey C. Hotchkiss.
Indifference of Juliet, The. By Grace S. Richmond.
In the Service of the Princess. By Henry C. Rowland.
Iron Woman, The. By Margaret Deland.
Ishmael. (Illustrated.) By Mrs. Southworth.
Island of Regeneration, The. By Cyrus Townsend Brady.
Jack Spurlock, Prodigal. By Horace Lorimer.
Jane Cable. By George Barr McCutcheon.
Jeanne of the Marshes. By E. Phillips Oppenheim.
Jude the Obscure. By Thomas Hardy.
Keith of the Border. By Randall Parrish.
Key to the Unknown, The. By Rosa N. Carey.
Kingdom of Earth, The. By Anthony Partridge.
King Spruce. By Holman Day.
Ladder of Swords, A. By Gilbert Parker.
Lady Betty Across the Water. By C. N. and A. M. Williamson.
Lady Merton, Colonist. By Mrs. Humphrey Ward.
Lady of Big Shanty, The. By Berkeley F. Smith.
Langford of the Three Bars. By Kate and Virgil D. Boyles.
Land of Long Ago, The. By Eliza Calvert Hall.
Lane That Had No Turning, The. By Gilbert Parker.
Last Trail, The. By Zane Grey.
Last Voyage of the Donna Isabel, The. By Randall Parrish.
Leavenworth Case, The. By Anna Katharine Green.
Lin McLean. By Owen Wister.
Little Brown Jug at Kildare, The. By Meredith Nicholson.
Loaded Dice. By Ellery H. Clarke.
Lord Loveland Discovers America. By C. N. and A. M. Williamson.
Lorimer of the Northwest. By Harold Bindloss.
Lorraine. By Robert W. Chambers.
Lost Ambassador, The. By E. Phillips Oppenheim.
Love Under Fire. By Randall Parrish.
Loves of Miss Anne, The. By S. R. Crockett.
Macaria. (Illustrated Edition.) By Augusta J. Evans.
Mademoiselle Celeste. By Adele Ferguson Knight.
Maid at Arms, The. By Robert W. Chambers.
Maid of Old New York, A. By Amelia E. Barr.
Maid of the Whispering Hills, The. By Vingie Roe.
Maids of Paradise, The. By Robert W. Chambers.
Making of Bobby Burnit, The. By George Randolph Chester.
Mam' Linda. By Will N. Harben.
Man Outside, The. By Wyndham Martyn.
Man in the Brown Derby, The. By Wells Hastings.
Marriage a la Mode. By Mrs. Humphrey Ward.
Marriage of Theodora, The. By Molly Elliott Seawell.
Marriage Under the Terror, A. By Patricia Wentworth.
Master Mummer, The. By E. Phillips Oppenheim.
Masters of the Wheatlands. By Harold Bindloss.

Popular Copyright Books

AT MODERATE PRICES

Ask your dealer for a complete list of
A. L. Burt Company's Popular Copyright Fiction.

Max. By Katherine Cecil Thurston.
Memoirs of Sherlock Holmes. By A. Conan Doyle.
Millionaire Baby, The. By Anna Katharine Green.
Missioner, The. By E. Phillips Oppenheim.
Miss Selina Lue. By Maria Thompson Daviess.
Mistress of Brae Farm, The. By Rosa N. Carey.
Money Moon, The. By Jeffery Farnol.
Motor Maid, The. By C. N. and A. M. Williamson.
Much Ado About Peter. By Jean Webster.
Mr. Pratt. By Joseph C. Lincoln.
My Brother's Keeper. By Charles Tenny Jackson.
My Friend the Chauffeur. By C. N. and A. M. Williamson.
My Lady Caprice (author of the "Broad Highway"). Jeffery Farnol.
My Lady of Doubt. By Randall Parrish.
My Lady of the North. By Randall Parrish.
My Lady of the South. By Randall Parrish.
Mystery Tales. By Edgar Allen Poe.
Nancy Stair. By Elinor Macartney Lane.
Ne'er-Do-Well, The. By Rex Beach.
No Friend Like a Sister. By Rosa N. Carey.
Officer 666. By Barton W. Currie and Augustin McHugh.
One Braver Thing. By Richard Dehan.
Order No. 11. By Caroline Abbot Stanley.
Orphan, The. By Clarence E. Mulford.
Out of the Primitive. By Robert Ames Bennett.
Pam. By Bettina von Hutten.
Pam Decides. By Bettina von Hutten.
Pardners. By Rex Beach.
Partners of the Tide. By Joseph C. Lincoln.
Passage Perilous, The. By Rosa N. Carey.
Passers By. By Anthony Partridge.
Paternoster Ruby, The. By Charles Edmonds Walk.
Patience of John Moreland, The. By Mary Dillon.
Paul Anthony, Christian. By Hiram W. Hays.
Phillip Steele. By James Oliver Curwood.
Phra the Phoenician. By Edwin Lester Arnold.
Plunderer, The. By Roy Norton.
Pole Baker. By Will N. Harben.
Politician, The. By Edith Huntington Mason.
Polly of the Circus. By Margaret Mayo.
Pool of Flame, The. By Louis Joseh Vance.
Poppy.. By Cynthia Stockley.
Power and the Glory, The. By Grace McGowan Cooke.
Price of the Prairie, The. By Margaret Hill McCarter.
Prince of Sinners, A. By E. Phillis Oppenheim.
Prince or Chauffeur. By Lawrence Perry.
Princess Dehra, The. By John Reed Scott.
Princess Passes, The. By C. N. and A. M. Williamson.
Princess Virginia, The. By C. N. and A. M. Williamson.
Prisoners of Chance. By Randall Parrish.
Prodigal Son, The. By Hall Caine.
Purple Parasol, The. By George Barr McCutcheon.

Popular Copyright Books

AT MODERATE PRICES

Ask your dealer for a complete list of
A. L. Burt Company's Popular Copyright Fiction.

Reconstructed Marriage, A. By Amelia Barr.
Redemption of Kenneth Galt, The. By Will N. Harben.
Red House on Rowan Street. By Roman Doubleday.
Red Mouse, The. By William Hamilton Osborne.
Red Pepper Burns. By Grace S. Richmond.
Refugees, The. By A. Conan Doyle.
Rejuvenation of Aunt Mary, The. By Anne Warner.
Road to Providence, The. By Maria Thompson Daviess.
Romance of a Plain Man, The. By Ellen Glasgow.
Rose in the Ring, The. By George Barr McCutcheon.
Rose of Old Harpeth, The. By Maria Thompson Daviess.
Rose of the World. By Agnes and Egerton Castle.
Round the Corner in Gay Street. By Grace S. Richmond.
Routledge Rides Alone. By Will Livingston Comfort.
Running Fight, The. By Wm. Hamilton Osborne.
Seats of the Mighty, The. By Gilbert Parker.
Septimus. By William J. Locke.
Set in Silver. By C. N. and A. M. Williamson.
Self-Raised. (Illustrated.) By Mrs. Southworth.
Shepherd of the Hills, The. By Harold Bell Wright.
Sheriff of Dyke Hole, The. By Ridgwell Cullum.
Sidney Carteret, Rancher. By Harold Bindloss.
Simon the Jester. By William J. Locke.
Silver Blade, The. By Charles E. Walk.
Silver Horde, The. By Rex Beach.
Sir Nigel. By A. Conan Doyle.
Sir Richard Calmady. By Lucas Malet.
Skyman, The. By Henry Ketchell Webster.
Slim Princess, The. By George Ade.
Speckled Bird, A. By Augusta Evans Wilson.
Spirit in Prison, A. By Robert Hichens.
Spirit of the Border, The. By Zane Grey.
Spirit Trail, The. By Kate and Virgil D. Boyles.
Spoilers, The. By Rex Beach.
Stanton Wins. By Eleanor M. Ingram.
St. Elmo. (Illustrated Edition.) By Augusta J. Evans.
Stolen Singer, The. By Martha Bellinger.
Stooping Lady, The. By Maurice Hewlett.
Story of the Outlaw, The. By Emerson Hough.
Strawberry Acres. By Grace S. Richmond.
Strawberry Handkerchief, The. By Amelia E. Barr.
Sunnyside of the Hill, The. By Rosa N. Carey.
Sunset Trail, The. By Alfred Henry Lewis.

Popular Copyright Books

AT MODERATE PRICES

Ask your dealer for a complete list of
A. L. Burt Company's Popular Copyright Fiction.

Susan Clegg and Her Friend Mrs. Lathrop. By Anne Warner.
Sword of the Old Frontier, A. By Randall Parrish.
Tales of Sherlock Holmes. By A. Conan Doyle.
Tennessee Shad, The. By Owen Johnson.
Tess of the D'Urbervilles. By Thomas Hardy.
Texican, The. By Dane Coolidge.
That Printer of Udell's. By Harold Bell Wright.
Three Brothers, The. By Eden Phillpotts.
Throwback, The. By Alfred Henry Lewis.
Thurston of Orchard Valley. By Harold Bindloss.
Title Market, The. By Emily Post.
Torn Sails. A Tale of a Welsh Village. By Allen Raine.
Trail of the Axe, The. By Ridgwell Cullum.
Treasure of Heaven, The. By Marie Corelli.
Two-Gun Man, The. By Charles Alden Seltzer.
Two Vanrevels, The. By Booth Tarkington.
Uncle William. By Jennette Lee.
Up from Slavery. By Booker T. Washington.
Vanity Box, The. By C. N. Williamson.
Vashti. By Augusta Evans Wilson.
Varmint, The. By Owen Johnson.
Vigilante Girl, A. By Jerome Hart.
Village of Vagabonds, A. By F. Berkeley Smith.
Visioning, The. By Susan Glaspell.
Voice of the People, The. By Ellen Glasgow.
Wanted—A Chaperon. By Paul Leicester Ford.
Wanted: A Matchmaker. By Paul Leicester Ford.
Watchers of the Plains, The. Ridgwell Cullum.
Wayfarers, The. By Mary Stewart Cutting.
Way of a Man, The. By Emerson Hough.
Weavers, The. By Gilbert Parker.
When Wilderness Was King. By Randall Parrish.
Where the Trail Divides. By Will Lillibridge.
White Sister, The. By Marion Crawford.
Window at the White Cat, The. By Mary Roberts Rhinehart.
Winning of Barbara Worth, The. By Harold Bell Wright.
With Juliet in England. By Grace S. Richmond.
Woman Haters, The. By Joseph C. Lincoln.
Woman in Question, The. By John Reed Scott.
Woman in the Alcove, The. By Anna Katharine Green.
Yellow Circle, The. By Charles E. Walk.
Yellow Letter, The. By William Johnston.
Younger Set, The. By Robert W. Chambers.